A SHAMEFUL MURDER

A SHAMEFUL MURDER

Cora Harrison

This first world edition published 2015
in Great Britain and the USA by
SEVERN HOUSE PUBLISHERS LTD of
19 Cedar Road, Sutton, Surrey, England, SM2 5DA.
Trade paperback edition first published 2015
in Great Britain and the USA by
SEVERN HOUSE PUBLISHERS LTD.

British Library Cataloguing in Publication Data

Harrison, Cora author.
  A shameful murder. – (A Reverend Mother mystery)
  1. Nuns–Ireland–Cork–Fiction. 2. Murder–
  Investigation–Fiction. 3. Ireland–History–Civil War,
  1922-1923–Fiction. 4. Detective and mystery stories.
  I. Title II. Series
  823.9'2-dc23

ISBN-13: 978-0-7278-8511-1 (cased)
ISBN-13: 978-1-84751-614-5 (trade paper)
ISBN-13: 978-1-78010-665-6 (e-book)

All Severn House titles are printed on acid-free paper.

Severn House Publishers support the Forest Stewardship Council™ [FSC™],
the leading international forest certification organisation. All our titles that
are printed on FSC certified paper carry the FSC logo.

Typeset by Palimpsest Book Production Ltd.,
Falkirk, Stirlingshire, Scotland.
Printed and bound in Great Britain by
TJ International, Padstow, Cornwall.

ONE

St Thomas Aquinas:
Videtur quod voluntas Dei non sit causa rerum.
(It can be seen that the will of God is not the cause of things.)

It was Reverend Mother Aquinas who found the body of the dead girl. It lay wedged within the gateway to the convent chapel at St Mary's of the Isle, jettisoned by the flood waters. For a fanciful moment she had almost imagined that it was a mermaid swept up from the sea. The long silver gown gleamed beneath the gas lamp, wet as the skin of a salmon, and the streams of soaked curls were red-brown just like the crinkled carrageen seaweed she had gathered from the windswept beaches of Ballycotton when she was a child. Her heart beating fast, the Reverend Mother unlocked the gate and looked down at the sightless blue eyes that stared up from beneath a wide high brow at the blanched, soaked flesh of the cheeks and knew that there was nothing that she could do for the girl. She bent over, touched the stone-cold face and then with a hand that trembled slightly she signed the forehead with a small cross. The Reverend Mother had seen death many times in her long life, but in the young she still found it was almost unbearable.

She straightened up and looked around. There was no one near. She had left the convent hurriedly, gone out into the fog, unable to bear with patience the sanctimonious comments of Sister Mary Immaculate about the floods being the will of God. Reverend Mother Aquinas, like her namesake, the great philosopher Thomas Aquinas, had no belief in the doctrine of the will of God – it was, for her, just an easy way out, of excusing man's inhumanity, inefficiency and lack of social responsibility. These terrible floods would not happen season after season if some of the wealth of the city was spent on preventing them. Sister Mary Immaculate, she thought with irritation, would not have been so quick to trot out the customary platitude about God's will if she, like the families of the children who attended the school of St Mary's of the Isle, lived in one of those crowded crumbling buildings flooded with sewage by the overflowing drains. As always it was the poor who had suffered. The rich moved to the hills outside the city.

Floods were nothing new in Cork. The city had been built on a marsh, criss-crossed by streams, beginning with a small monastic settlement, named St Mary's of the Isle, progressing, with the advent of the Vikings, to a second island and then, with the Normans, to a third. Later the inhabitants linked the Viking and Norman islands with a bridge and enclosed them with a high wall, forming the medieval city of Cork, perched just above the swamp, edged with a sheltered harbour and joined to the ocean by the River Lee. The city had become rich, trading its butter, its meat and its hides from the hinterland with nearby England and not-too-distant France and Spain. In the eighteenth century the wealthy merchants had tamed the channels of the river with limestone quays and had built stately homes above basement warehouses, their entrances, like those to medieval castles, placed high above the water with steps leading up from the mooring places. Like a Venice under a grey northern sky, the city grew prosperous and ambitious; but unlike in Venice the merchants were not content with their waterways. They confined the marsh streams into culverts and built wide streets on top of all but two of the river channels. And these two arms of the River Lee, the north and south, still encircled the town and the water beneath the streets remained part of it. From time to time it escaped and the city flooded.

Dead bodies washed up by the flood waters were nothing new, either. The Reverend Mother sighed as she rang the bell on the gate for the gardener, sent him to fetch Sergeant Patrick Cashman from the barracks and waited resignedly for Sister Mary Immaculate to pop out to find the reason for the summons.

'I was just coming to see you, Sister,' said the Reverend Mother as soon as her assistant appeared. 'Could you go into the kitchen and ask Sister Rosario to serve some hot porridge to any of the children who manage to get here this morning. Oh, and get some of those socks out of the cupboard so that they each can have a dry pair.' That, she thought with some satisfaction, should keep Sister Mary Immaculate busy until the bell rang for the beginning of morning school. Then she excused her lack of charity to her fellow nun by reflecting with pleasure on the comfort that hot porridge and thick warm socks, knitted in such profusion by some of the very elderly nuns, would give to the children. She fished out from her capacious pocket the watch that hung on a silver chain from her belt and looked at the time. Still only quarter to nine – Patrick would probably not arrive at the barracks before nine o'clock and already she could hear the voices of the children coming down the street, excitedly capping each other's stories about the overnight flooding and the size of the rats that scampered around the hallways and crumbling stairs of those four-storey Georgian buildings in Cove Street and Sawmill Lane. Smiling to herself at their animation, and their high spirits, she went back to keep watch over the body, glancing at her watch from time to time as the slow minutes ticked away.

And then she tightened her lips with a grimace of annoyance as she heard the back door to the convent open and the high-pitched voice of Sister Mary Immaculate shouting orders. Of course, she should have remembered that the nun had the habit of marching the older girls into the chapel before the start of morning school.

She was only just in time. Sister Mary Immaculate had already lined up the senior girls, each with a prayer book in hand, for their daily trip to proffer up prayers to God. She'd be better off teaching these thirteen- and fourteen-year-olds extra arithmetic so that a few of them might have some remote hope of getting a job in shop or as a clerk, thought the Reverend Mother tartly as she ordered them to return to their classroom. And then her eyes widened. The last girl in the line was wearing a six-inch-wide flounce of yellow flannel pinned with enormous safety pins to the bottom of her navy-blue gymslip.

'What on earth is Nellie O'Sullivan wearing?' she asked. Nellie, with her mass of curls, was a pretty girl who from the age of five had always come to school looking fairly clean, tidy and well dressed – in cast-off clothes distributed by the St Vincent de Paul Society. Since Nellie's taste ran to pink frilly party dresses, eventually Sister Mary Immaculate bestowed an ancient navy blue gymslip on her and added a lecture about suitable clothes to wear in school.

The Reverend Mother rather liked Nellie. She was not particularly academic, but was a well-motivated, cheerful girl who had not escaped from school at the first possible moment – like her eldest sister, Mary – but had stayed on and worked hard. A confident girl, with a strong streak of common sense; the Reverend Mother was annoyed to see her victimized.

Sister Mary Immaculate smiled with pious satisfaction at her question. 'Some of those girls have been shortening their gymslips to a ridiculous degree – so every morning, first thing, I make them kneel on the floor and if their skirt does not touch the boards then they wear the frill until they let the hem down again,' she said smugly.

For heaven's sake! Reverend Mother choked back the words. These girls, she thought, did not have much fun. They were poor in a prosperous city. Their youth was being spent in a country at war. The War of Independence had started in early 1919 and had petered out in July 1922 with a treaty that agreed to the partition of Ireland and less than a year later the bitter civil war had begun when brothers and cousins had lined up against each other, and where Michael Collins, hero and leader in the struggle against British troops, had been shot by his former companions. *A plague on both your houses*, the Reverend Mother had often thought, but her pupils were caught in the centre of the hostilities. Day after day, for the last few years, they had been sent home early from school because there had been shooting on the streets; first between the Republicans and the Black and Tan auxiliaries to the Royal Irish Constabulary and later between the Free State Army and the Republicans; between those who were for the treaty and those who were against it – the bitter civil war was almost over in theory, but in practice the guns still spluttered. The children had witnessed the burning down of Patrick Street by the Black and Tans, had dodged the grenades, and the armed battles that had followed each outrage, had endured raids, poverty, disease, poor feeding and bad housing. She was pleased to think that they had life and spirit enough left in them to turn up the hems of their ugly, shapeless gymslips to a 1920s fashionable length. She would have to have a quiet and tactful talk with Sister Mary Immaculate, who was in charge of the school – perhaps get the children to agree on a sensible length for a gymslip – no more yellow flannel, though, she decided – there was something about that image which revolted her.

However, this poor dead girl on her doorstep had to be cared for now. She sent a messenger around to the other classes ordering that the children be kept within doors for the next couple of hours and then went back to her vigil over the quiet body until she heard the sound of the convent doorbell.

'Sergeant Cashman to see you, Reverend Mother.' Sister Bernadette, keys clanking, came in through the garden door. He's been quick, thought the Reverend Mother; well, this is the age of the car and the bicycle. She moved up the path to greet him, nodding pleasantly at Sister Bernadette. A nice woman, but a terrible gossip, so she waited until the lay sister had disappeared in the direction of the kitchen, before addressing the civic guard.

'Well, Patrick, how are you and how is your mother?' she queried. Even a dead body would not be considered a reason to omit the customary enquiries, although his widowed mother lived next door to the convent and probably Mother Aquinas knew as much about her health as did her busy son.

Patrick Cashman, like all the small boys of the neighbourhood, had attended the convent school until the age of seven, when they had sent him on to the Christian Brothers' elementary school. She remembered all of her pupils, but he had a special place in her heart. He had first come to her notice about fourteen years ago, because he had refused to return from the playground to the classroom until he had finished counting the ants that were coming out of a hole at the bottom of the wall. He had ignored a couple of sharp smacks on his bare and rather dirty leg from his teacher and had persisted. Mother Aquinas, usually appealed to as the last sanction, had come out from her study to save him from further punishment. Sister Philomena, red with anger, had marched the other children inside, leaving the playground empty except for one small boy and one middle-aged nun who was wrestling with a problem. How long would he keep it up for, she had wondered and then had allowed her thoughts to drift back. Should she leave this place and accept the suggestion made by the Bishop that she should go to Rome as Mother-General of the Order? Had she done all that she could do in making this school somewhere to give hope to the poor? Would she stagnate if she stayed? Would the new position offer a challenge to her brains, to her organizing ability? Should she go, or should stay? She had looked down at the small boy still muttering numbers under his breath and waited peacefully, allowing her mind to take a rest from the problem.

The answer to both of their questions came minutes later when the seven-year-old had looked up at her with a beaming smile, made rather endearing by a couple of missing teeth.

'You'll never guess, Reverend Mother,' he'd said confidently. 'Not even Holy God himself would have guessed. There's nine hundred and fifty-seven of them little ants all living in the one little house under that brick.'

Worse even than the slums of Cork, had thought Mother Aquinas: overcrowding in Cork was officially set at a figure of over nine people living and sleeping in the one room and even so the statistics were frightening. Aloud, she suggested that they go and tell the rest of the class about this. She had been amused at the time, but in the years to come she had thought it had been a good indication of his character. He was not outstandingly clever, but was tenacious and hard-working and once he had something to do he could not be deflected until it was finished. And that day she had taken his concentration, and the intense interest shown by the other seven-year-olds in the life of ants, as a sign that she should stay where she was and try to offer a worthy education to the sharp-witted slum-dwellers of Cork city. She had not regretted her decision. And, partly because he had been connected with her deciding moment, she had always kept an interest in Patrick Cashman. Through sheer hard work and perseverance he had got one of the coveted scholarships to the Christian Brothers' Secondary School at the age of fourteen and so, on leaving school, had the education to get into the newly formed civic guards which had replaced the Royal Irish Constabulary after the War of Independence.

And now there he was, a fortunate young man, earning three pounds a week, in a city that despite independence from England was still full of unemployment and terrible poverty.

He replied politely to her queries and then waited to see what she wanted, glancing in a puzzled way at her as she led the way down towards the chapel.

'There's a body washed up in the lane; it came from the river, I suppose,' she said abruptly once they were alone. 'Come and see, Patrick.'

He was as methodical and sensible as ever, she thought. No loud exclamations; just followed her down through the fog-enveloped gardens. And then there was a quick appraisal of the situation. He checked the body, as she had done, for signs of life. He produced a notebook and pencil and began to write in a fluent and rapid hand that did credit to the teaching of the Christian Brothers. Then he made a few measurements with the tape measure that he took from his pocket, drew a neat map in his notebook. She watched him with an indulgence which reflected their past relationship, but with the impatience of a quick mind confronted with a slower and more methodical one.

'What do you think?' she asked; her eyes were on the dead girl. She could barely contain her impatience to get to the heart of the puzzle.

'Bit different to the usual bodies that we get from the river; normally it's the girls of the street and that like; I've seen plenty of them,' he said slowly and she glimpsed, behind the simple words, a world of experience that was even deeper than hers.

'I suppose,' she said hesitantly, 'this sort of thing often happens; is that right, Patrick?'

'They don't usually look so dressed up,' he said. 'But yes, we do get plenty of bodies.'

'Seems a shame,' she said, thinking of the guns, the killing, the plotting, the great speeches, the treaties and the promises. Her emotions told her that it was sad that nothing had changed, nothing had improved for people, but her experience of life told her that it was unlikely that anything else would have happened.

He shrugged his shoulders. He would not, she thought, be one to bemoan what could not be achieved by him personally.

'There's a lot of trouble around here,' he said, almost apologetically, almost as though he were responsible for the unrest that happened in the streets around where he had spent his childhood. 'Not very good housing, in this place,' he added and both he and she could visualize the street where he had been brought up, the stately Georgian terraced house which was now a crumbling home for twenty or thirty families with no work, little food and no hope. 'Lots of fights, people get frustrated, they'll fight over a handful of coins, and then there are the suicides – some of them can't stand things any longer. But,' he said, reverting to the body in front of him, 'this looks like something different.'

She knew what he meant, when he said that the body before them looked different. This girl was no prostitute from Sawmill Lane or beggar from North Main Street. Even the soaking from the river water couldn't disguise the quality of the gown that she wore – satin, she thought – expertly tailored – elbow-length gloves of fine soft leather clung to her arms, a lustrous pearl necklace was around her neck and a pair of expensive-looking, brand-new – by the soles of them – high-heeled satin shoes were strapped around her ankles. Oddly enough there was something familiar about the hair and the eyes, but she could not think of any young lady of her acquaintance – her life, for the last fifty years, had been spent among the poor of the city.

He was methodical as ever now that he had returned his attention to the dead girl. He took out the notebook again and she could see how his eyes travelled up and down the body, checking that he had noted all the details of the girl's clothing.

'She's got something around her wrist,' he said.

'An evening bag,' said the Reverend Mother sadly. 'It

matches her dress.' Her mind went back to the dances of over fifty years ago. The gallant officers who had written their names on her dance programme; did they still do this, nowadays? she wondered. It had been a long time since she had indulged herself enough to think back to the days when she too dressed in silks and satins, wore an evening bag around her wrist.

'I'll see if I can get it off.' The string was wound around the narrow wrist twice, but eventually he managed to disentangle it.

She admired the care with which he opened the soaking wet bag – it was closed only with a drawstring. He put his hand inside it carefully once he had teased the layers apart, drew out something and held it up.

'Ten-pound note,' he said reverently. It was, she thought, despite his dazzling new salary as a civic guard, still a big sum of money to him. He replaced the bag on the dead girl's body and put the banknote carefully inside an envelope that he produced from a pocket. He took his indelible pencil from another pocket, licked its tip and then signed his name over the flap.

'Would you mind, Reverend Mother?' He handed her the envelope and the pencil and she signed below his signature.

'You're very careful, Patrick,' she said approvingly.

'I'll hand it in as soon as I get back to the station,' he said as he stowed it away. Then he went back to the bag again. Patrick, thought the Reverend Mother, would always go back and double-check.

He did not comment on the next item, just held it up so that she could see a small dance booklet with tiny pencil still attached. *The Merchants' Annual Ball*, it said, printed in a fancy, gold-lettered script, and she nodded. Of course, it was March, the first week in March, and then she frowned.

'The Imperial Hotel?' she queried. The Merchants' Balls had been held there in her youth, and were, she thought, still held there. But the Imperial Hotel was not by the river and it was more than half a mile away from St Mary's of the Isle. How had the body got here? She looked out at the lane where murky water still burst out from what was once a covered drain. The morning tide had receded a little, but the narrow lane that ran beside the convent grounds still bubbled like a mountain stream with water from the drains and from the nearby river. It had been the usual result of days and nights of rain allied to a south-easterly gale that had blown the spring high-tide seawater straight up the River Lee.

His eyes followed hers, but he did not comment. She felt the sharp, acrid smell of the fog rise up inside of her and swallowed hard.

'There's something else,' he said. 'It's stuck to the lining.' Slowly and carefully he separated the object from the silk. It was small and oblong in shape, soaking wet but not yet pulp. A ticket, she realized; the print was still black and quite visible. It bore the name of the Cork Steam-Packet Shipping Company and was a first-class ticket for the ferry that left Albert Quay and went across to Liverpool three times a week. The date was printed, also: 5 March, 1923 – the midnight ferry, she thought. Patrick looked at it for a long minute before placing it into another envelope and then into one of his wide pockets.

'What do you think that means?' she asked eagerly and then was slightly ashamed when he didn't reply. It was nothing to do with her, this ticket for a journey from Cork to England in a first-class cabin. Her role in this affair should now be at an end. She had reported the finding of a body to the civic guard and they would now take over. He had stood up and straightened himself decisively and she knew that he would not answer: Patrick Cashman did not deal in speculation, but in facts.

'What will you do next?' she asked then, as a substitute question.

'Send to the barracks for a conveyance for the body to be taken to the vault, check the missing persons' list, make a report to the superintendent, contact the coroner, send for the doctor to perform the post-mortem . . .'

He thought for a moment as though mentally scanning his rulebook and then nodded, 'And take it from there,' he finished.

'You go and report and I will stay and keep guard over the body,' she said. 'That will get everything moving more quickly and the less said about this the better, in case there are any political links,' she finished. It was possible that the death was accidental, or self-inflicted, but murder could not be ruled out. Cork, in its first year of independence, simmered in the heat of a deadly civil war and the resolution of political differences was often murder.

Not *the will of God*, she thought with a sudden anger. No God could wish evil on this child, whoever she was. Her eyes rested on Patrick. He lingered for a while, gently moved aside a strand of wet hair and then stayed very still for a moment, his eyes on a black bruise on the centre of the girl's throat. He made another note and the Reverend Mother bowed her head. She had noticed the bruise when she examined the pearl necklace. This girl, she thought compassionately, had known the fear and intense pain of strangulation before death took her.

TWO

St Thomas Aquinas:
Ignis est essentia Dei.
(Fire is the essence of God.)

Alone with the girl, the Reverend Mother's eyes lingered over the water-logged body at her feet and then went to the throat. The flood had delivered the body to her gate – she would take that as a sign that she should involve herself in this murder – nothing to do with the will of God, she thought irritably, remembering Sister Mary Immaculate, as she bent her mind to the problem with a combination of compassion and of intellectual curiosity. This was a girl from a privileged background like her own – she would be a daughter of one of the rich merchant families of Cork; even without the dance programme the dress, the gloves, the necklace of pearls, all of these proclaimed her origins.

And why did this fortunate girl have a ticket for the night boat to Liverpool tucked into her satin evening bag? Was she going alone? It looked like it. A male companion would surely keep both tickets in a more substantial wallet.

Reverend Mother shifted uneasily. Her feet were growing cold and the fog that had settled over the flooded city was getting into her lungs and making her cough. She was tempted to go back for her warmer cloak – no one was likely to come – the lane was only an entrance for the local people to visit the small chapel without going into through the convent grounds – after it passed the narrow iron gate, it ended at the river's edge. The original red sandstone to build the chapel, convent and school had been floated up the south arm of the river and then taken by cart, along this lane, on to the higher ground of St Mary's of the Isle. Nonetheless, she thought, looking down at the still figure by her feet, to watch by the body was the only thing left to do for her now; the last service that she could pay to this unfortunate girl. She rubbed her hands together and then tucked them into her large sleeves and stood immobile, as though listening to the gospel readings at the Mass, gazing at the flood waters that had delivered the body to her gate. Odd, she reflected, that the philosopher Thomas Aquinas used the analogy of fire for the essence of God. Surely water came first. Water was the source of all life, the source of all good but also the source of all evil, depending on how man used it.

But her mind, always the most active part of her, was busy. It was over fifty years since she had danced at the Merchants' Ball in the Imperial Hotel, but she remembered the place well – its cosy, intimate supper rooms upstairs, its magnificent ballroom on the ground floor, the broad stairs of shining wood, the marble-floored hallways with shadowy alcoves. Her mind ranged over it, imagining a quarrel, a struggle. But surely not within the Imperial Hotel! Her memories supplied it with a huge staff, discreetly present in all parts, ready for every eventuality. The Merchants' Ball was the biggest event of the year. What had happened there last night? And how had the body been taken from the hotel and launched into the river?

She was deep in thought when a slight noise took her attention and then she realized that she was not alone. A head had appeared above the wall that surrounded the convent gardens; a head wearing a beret, suddenly silhouetted in the hazy light from the gas lamp. The Reverend Mother stood very still, hands tucked into large sleeves, body half-turned towards the gate. Her cloak, she knew, would cover her white breastplate and she lowered her head so that the black veil threw a shadow over the snowy linen wimple that enclosed her forehead. A long leg with a shining boot swung over the wall, and a shining gold ring appeared, held steady in a gloved hand, as the figure lowered itself down with a slight splash into the flooded lane.

A pistol; thought the Reverend Mother and stayed very still. There was a certain amount of respect still for the clergy, but nerves were at trigger point during these fearful days where brother fought against brother. She had no wish to alarm this young man – a Republican, she thought – and was glad that

Patrick had left. He would have felt it his duty to arrest the stealthy figure and the civic guards were unarmed.

She had been seen, though. A torch was suddenly produced and it flared its light upon her.

The muzzle of the pistol pointed towards her for a second and then was hastily lowered. And so was the torch.

But by then Reverend Mother had seen enough.

'Good morning, Eileen,' she said in icy tones and by the light of the torch saw the long legs shuffle uneasily.

Eileen O'Donovan had been one of the most gifted and most advanced pupils that the school on St Mary's of the Isle had ever produced. When the Reverend Mother had seen her last she had been dressed in a navy-blue gymslip with a blouse that was supposedly white, but had turned to pale grey from the smuts and smoky emissions of the foggy city, and a much-darned navy cardigan. Her black hair had been demurely confined to twin plaits, but now it streamed down her back from her beret and instead of a gymslip she wore a tailored tweed jacket, well-fitting breeches and below them a highly polished pair of knee-high leather boots. For a moment the girl said nothing and then, in a voice that she strove to make sound casual, she said politely: 'Good morning, Reverend Mother. It's a terrible morning, isn't it?'

Reverend Mother ignored this. 'Are you a member of the Republican Party, Eileen?' she asked, trying to keep the note of censure from her voice. It was, after all, none of her business what her past pupils did with their lives.

'Yes, I am.' By the gas lamp Eileen's face was defiant. She added a perfunctory, 'Reverend Mother,' but closed her lips firmly after that. She was not going to make any excuses or explanations.

'Your mother told me that you had a good office job.'

'And so I do; I'm press officer for the Republicans. I've had pieces published in all the newspapers – telling our side of the story.' There was a note of pride in the girl's voice. She looked in blooming health. She was well and warmly dressed in that good quality cloth and the hollow cheeks had filled out. It was well known that the Republicans paid well – the Reverend Mother had heard that even respectable young solicitors were not averse to taking part in Republican Courts as the fee was double their usual one from the newly formed Free State. What the Republicans needed, they did not hesitate to take from the prosperous shops in Patrick Street, cheerfully assuring the owners that it was all in a good cause.

'You always did write . . . did write well,' murmured the Reverend Mother. She had hastily suppressed the words '*very imaginative stories*' as perhaps an inappropriate phrase in the circumstances. She shouldn't have been surprised, though; Eileen had always been a rebel. She remembered a lively lesson with the most advanced girls in the school when the struggle through Milton's poem *Paradise Lost* had been enlivened by Eileen's sudden adoption of Satan as a revolutionary hero rising up under oppression. However, words were one thing, guns and the taking of life was another. Her eyes went to the pistol which Eileen had hastily shoved back into her pocket and then to the dead girl at her feet.

Eileen's eyes followed those of her former teacher and she shook her head firmly.

'This is nothing to do with us, Reverend Mother, nothing to do with the Republican Party,' she said with emphasis. 'We were notified and I was sent up to see what had happened.'

'Notified . . . I see – Jimmy Logan, I suppose.' Mother Aquinas had wondered why the gas lamp had not been extinguished, but now the matter was explained. Jimmy, the lamplighter, would be a good source of intelligence for the Republicans as, legitimately, curfew or no curfew, he was on the streets every morning and every evening, carrying his ladder with him, and stopping to talk to everyone in the neighbourhood. An unreliable man, she thought dispassionately, a man who had no aversion to manufacturing news when there was none available. He was, of course, in his element in these troubled times.

'And what have you been sent to do, Eileen?' She reminded herself that she was no longer Eileen's teacher.

'First of all to make sure that no one left any false information – you'd be surprised at the number of dead bodies that have a placard around their neck and the words *Informer*

Executed by Order of the Irish Republican Party written on it
– mostly misspelt,' she added with the disdain of one who
had mastered spelling of words like 'committee' by the time
she was eight years old.

'No, there was nothing left like that; I was the one who
found the body,' said the Reverend Mother and her eyes went
to the quiet figure at their feet. Young lives wasted, she thought
sadly. This girl here, this child of a wealthy family, with
everything to live for – she was dead and Eileen, her past
pupil, one of her girls, with all her brains – what would be
her future? Long years in prison, death at the end of a rope,
death at the back of an alley with a bullet through her heart?
Through tears that welled into her eyes, she saw Eileen take
out a notebook, rather like the one that Patrick had produced,
and make a few notes, looking all around her and then focusing
on the body again.

'She's posh, isn't she? Is that velvet, Reverend Mother – that
dress of hers?'

'No, it's satin.' The Reverend Mother heard the note of
sadness in her own voice, as she blinked back her tears, and
knew that this time the sadness was for Eileen as much as
for the poor dead girl. Eileen had devoured stories about
well-off young ladies going to balls and parties in the works
of Jane Austen, Dickens and Thackeray, but her practical
knowledge of silks, satins and velvets was as imprecise and
vague as the convent's teaching about the angels of heaven
and the devils of hell.

'We'll be blamed for it; you know that, don't you?' Eileen
was still writing busily. 'Or at least we will if I don't get in
quickly. Today is Tuesday so there won't be much in the paper
tomorrow – no markets today. I was going to try and do an
article on the lunatic asylum and what a disgrace it is that no
money is spent on it and they are talking about spending
£100,000 on a new city hall – a few of the boys were going
to come up with me so that I could have a look without being
thrown out. But now, I think I'll do one about her instead.
The other will keep – this is topical.' She looked thoughtfully
at the figure on the ground. 'Wonder who did it?' she asked,
speaking more to herself than to her past teacher.

Eileen would have been used to dead bodies over the last few years, thought the Reverend Mother and then was surprised to see her touch one knuckle to the corners of her eyes in a childlike gesture that brought back affectionate memories.

'Poor lasher,' she said compassionately, the Cork slang word coming easily to her lips. 'There she was all dressed up – wonder whether she was at the Merchants' Ball last night. The place was stiff with civic guards in front of the Imperial Hotel when I passed down the South Mall last night. Do you know what, Reverend Mother? I'd love to put a bullet in the mullacker that did that to the poor girl – strangled her, didn't he? You can see the marks of it on her throat.'

The Reverend Mother allowed this to pass. A sudden thought had struck and she grimaced, uncomfortable at her lapse.

'I should have sent for the priest,' she said aloud.

Eileen grinned. 'Well, you'll excuse me if I don't go to fetch him, Reverend Mother,' she said airily. 'We're not in great favour with the priests. The Bishop has excommunicated all Republicans – called off the altar we all were. My mam nearly died at the idea of me going to hell. She's a great one for borrowing trouble, is my mam.'

The Reverend Dr Cohalan, Bishop of Cork, had been most unwise in this blanket condemnation, thought the Reverend Mother; there had been acts of violence on both sides – some acts by the official authorities had out-done, in brutality and loss of life, any action by an illegal organization like the Republicans. The people of Cork would never forget how the Bishop had refused to condemn the burning down of the city streets by the Black and Tans, the so-called auxiliary police, which had left thousands without housing or jobs, but had excommunicated the Republicans for their assault on an army barracks. However, in front of Eileen, she maintained a discreet silence and only said aloud, 'Well, the civic guards will be back in a few minutes with something to take the body to the barracks. Perhaps it would be best if the priest near there will see to the matter; our Father Murphy is rather elderly to be brought out in this flood and rain.'

'The civic guards.' Eileen had picked this up and she stowed her notebook and pencil away in a businesslike manner. 'I'd better be off. You don't mind if I go through the convent gardens again, Reverend Mother, do you? Everywhere is flooded except for around St Mary's of the Isle.'

'Go through the gate this time.' The Reverend Mother hesitated for a moment and then added, 'Take care of yourself, Eileen, body and soul.'

A just war, according to St Thomas Aquinas, *must take place for a good and just purpose rather than for self-gain – and peace must be its object*, she remembered, as she watched the trim, long-legged figure springing lightly up the steep steps. What would he have thought of the aims of the Irish Republican Party?

And then the sound of a wagon trundling down the lane, the horse splashing noisily through the flood and from time to time snorting irritably at the water that washed around its knees; the civic guards had arrived, using horse power rather than an engine which could be wrecked in the flood, and the Reverend Mother composed her face to receive them with dignity and to make sure that the body was handled carefully as it was taken under the jurisdiction of the present authority. There were a number of people there – two civic guards who were not introduced to her; Patrick's assistant, a silent young man called Joe; and the doctor.

The Reverend Mother knew Dr Scher, as he had been the convent's doctor for decades. Younger than herself by a good ten years, he had mostly retired from general practice, though he retained his lectureship in dissection at the university – Queen's, she still called it, though now it had been renamed University College, Cork, and he did occasional work for the civic guards. A kind man, though, like Sister Bernadette, a terrible gossip, always on the lookout to increase his knowledge of the latest rumours and scandals in this city of talkers. He shouldn't have retired, she thought. He had been bored ever since, though he still found room in his generous heart to lavish his skill on some of the poor who could not afford a doctor. The children in her school often talked of Dr Scher and of the small presents that he gave to them and of how nice his medicine tasted. She guessed that the pharmacist was ordered to lace each bottle with plenty of sugar.

'Morning, Reverend Mother,' he said heartily, climbing down

from the heavily built brewery wagon and politely removing his glove to shake her by the hand, while his eyes slid across to the girl.

'Strangulation, is it?' said Dr Scher and Patrick made no reply, just stood looking down into the dead girl's face. A tiny crease had appeared between his eyebrows and his hazel eyes were alert and attentive – not, thought the Reverend Mother, looking at the girl's throat, but at the widely opened eyes that stared sightlessly up into the mist. There was a moment's silence. Dr Scher had expected agreement – that was obvious by the sharp glance that he gave into the young civic guard's face – but when he received none, he looked again at the corpse and then cleared his throat.

'Hm,' he said, and then, after a few more seconds, 'well, we'll see. Do you know her at all? Could she be an informer? The Republicans have taken to murdering these just to deter the others.'

Improbable, thought the Reverend Mother. She was surprised at Dr Scher. She would have thought that he had more sense, more knowledge of what went on in the city around him. Girls dressed like that, in an expensive satin gown, were unlikely to be seen going to a civic guards barracks to inform on a member of the Republican Party. They might murmur something in the ear of a father or a brother, but they would not get involved. She looked across at Patrick wondering whether he would tell Dr Scher about the dance programme in the girl's bag, but the face of the young guard was wooden and unresponsive.

'Would you like to have her brought back to the barracks now, Doctor?' he asked, his voice even and without inflection.

Interesting, she thought, looking from the taciturn young man to the gregarious old one. The Irish were the ones that had the reputation of being garrulous and free with information and the English were supposed to be reserved and cautious in their dealings with their fellow men. Still, Dr Scher was Russian in origin, though he himself had been born and had spent his boyhood in Manchester. Perhaps that made a difference.

'Yes, yes.' The doctor did not look at him; he was busy studying the body, looking now at the clothes. 'Any missing persons?' he asked.

'Not so far.' This was answered by Joe. 'Probably one of the girls of the quays – their night lasts until the lights are put out,' he added with a quick glance at the lamp still burning in the yellow fog. And then he looked at Patrick's still face and became very stiff and still himself. Joe, thought the Reverend Mother, was very young. Not long out of school, she reckoned. He would have even less knowledge of silks and satins than Eileen and would not know that it was most unlikely that a girl of the street would be dressed in a gown like this.

Dr Scher looked at him impatiently and scornfully, but seemed to decide that his remark was not worthy of an answer and he bent over the girl again, a frown on his lined face. A hot-tempered man, Dr Scher – she had heard tales of his outbursts when he did not hesitate to roar at any of the medical students who treated a dead body with jokes or disrespect. Joe shifted uneasily and looked at his superior. Patrick remained aloof, just signalling to the two guards to lift the body into the back of the vehicle. Reverend Mother thought once again about her failure to summon a priest, but said nothing. The matter was now out of her hands.

THREE

Cork Examiner, 22 January, 1923:
'Ten or twelve armed men robbed the Bank of Ireland at
Kilbeggan of £2,000 after previously proceeding to the barracks
and threatening to shoot the civic guards if they intervened.
They also robbed other business premises before
making good their escape.'

Patrick wasn't sure whether he wanted to see this post-
mortem. Normally he forced himself to attend, but today
he did not feel as though he could bear to. There was a
lot to do, he told himself. He had to identify this girl quickly.
One glance at her gown, her necklace and her gloves and he
had known that there would be a fuss about her. The newly
formed civic guards were apt to be criticized by the well-off
merchant class of the city, used to the old order of the Royal
Irish Constabulary. He, as part of this new police force, could
not afford to be found lacking.

Tommy O'Mahoney was the duty constable; he would go
and see him. He glanced at the clock on the corridor. Ten
o'clock. By now, surely a girl like this would have been missed;
unless, of course, someone in England was expecting her off
the Liverpool boat.

'Any missing persons, Constable?' he asked as he came up
to the glass-fronted booth that Tommy O'Mahoney had occupied, so it was said, for the last fifty years.

'Nobody, Sergeant.' Tommy stood up. He was older than
Patrick's father would have been, but he was always very correct.

'Dr Scher is in with the superintendent,' he added.

And it was at that moment that the door swung open, pushed
open and held open by a cab driver. Another man came
through. Three-piece pin-stripe suit, well-cut overcoat, silk tie,
bowler hat. 'My name is Fitzsimon – my daughter is missing.
There might have been an accident . . .'

Patrick felt sorry for him. He always felt sorry for people coming in with this sort of query. Most of them had a mixture of hope and fear in their voices, and many, like this man, tried to sound as though they were convinced of their silliness in making a fuss.

'I'm afraid I might have bad news for you, Mr Fitzsimon,' he said quietly. 'A young woman was found dead and brought in just ten minutes ago. Perhaps we should eliminate that possibility first before you take details,' he said over the counter to Tommy and Tommy gave a quick nod.

'Come with me, Mr Fitzsimon.' Fitzsimon, he thought as he led the way down the long corridor, Fitzsimon the retail merchant, one of the so-called merchant princes of Cork. There was little doubt now in his mind that they had found a name for the dead girl. The daughter of Joseph Fitzsimon would undoubtedly have attended the Merchants' Ball. He knew all about these affairs – members of the constabulary were usually called upon to stand by the red carpet and make sure that the poor, the starving, the homeless did not get within shouting distance of the rich of the city. When he was a new recruit to the civic guards he had got landed with that duty.

'You were present at the Merchants' Ball, sir?' he asked.

'Yes, of course.'

Patrick forgave the impatient tone of the answer. After all, this man was in a fever of anxiety about his daughter. Strange not to miss her until this hour of the morning, though – surely he would have taken her home, or seen that someone else did . . . And why had she a ticket for the midnight ferry to Liverpool in her bag?

'I didn't see her – I was upstairs for the whole evening,' he ended.

And, of course, that was the way that it would have been. Patrick had been 'back-stage' at this event last year, allowed to roam around the Imperial Hotel and make sure that no sneak thieves got in through some window. The merchants and their wives dined aloft and their sons and daughters danced in the big hall beneath, with the finest orchestra in Cork engaged to play for them. Supper for these younger ones, remembered Patrick, was a buffet, laid out on long tables covered by starched linen tablecloths between the pillars at each side of the majestic hall. Their fathers and mothers were safely aloft and there seemed to be many covert flirtations going on under the arcades and in dark corners around the corridors – though not even the daring ones slipped out through a side door and into the dangerous back lanes behind the Imperial Hotel.

'This way, sir,' he said. He wondered whether he should take the man's arm as he led him in through the door, but then decided that this might be a liberty. Whatever lay before Joseph Fitzsimon, one of the richest men in the city of Cork, it was not for a humble man from the marsh of the city, schooled only by the Christian Brothers at the North Monastery, to try to console him.

'The face will look a little different,' he warned; his hand still on the knob of the door. 'She was in the river for several hours, we think. Still you will recognize the hair, and the dress . . .' He walked in front of the man. Only one gas lamp was lit – just over the body – and most of the room was filled with shadows. He led the way in silence and went to the far side of the table leaving the way clear for the father.

He was prepared for a sigh of relief, or a violent onslaught of weeping, but Joseph Fitzsimon just stood like a man turned to stone. And then, quite unexpectedly, his face flushed to a deep dark red shade – almost an angry red. He said nothing but stared down at the girl for an instant and then averted his eyes.

'Yes,' he said in choked and muffled tones. 'Yes, that is Angelina.'

'You're sure?' Patrick asked the question in a gentle voice.

'Got that dress from Dowden's only last week. Cost me a fine sum.' Joseph Fitzsimon had control over himself now. Odd thing to say, though, thought Patrick, almost as though the dress was of more importance than the girl. Of course, Dowden's was the most expensive shop in Cork. He had wanted to buy his mother a new hat there when he had been promoted to sergeant and she had screamed at the very idea.

'The gloves, too. Kid gloves – you wouldn't believe . . .' Suddenly he stopped and produced a snowy white mono-grammed handkerchief and held it to his eyes. Patrick preserved a respectful silence for a moment. He should cover the body, he thought. There should be a sheet in one of the drawers at the side of the room. Still, best to get the father out of there first. Old Tommy would make him a cup of tea and the superintendent, when he heard that the tea merchant was on the premises, would probably offer him a drink. After a minute he touched the super-fine broadcloth of the sleeve.

'Do you feel able to come with me and give me a few details now, sir?' he asked in respectfully hushed tones.

A nod was the only answer so Patrick turned and went towards the door. Let the man have a moment alone with his child, he thought, kiss her goodbye, perhaps. But then he realized that Joseph Fitzsimon was at his heels as he fumbled in the shadows for the wooden knob. Smooth with the hands of the constabulary over the centuries, he thought as he opened the door and stood back to allow the merchant to pass through ahead of him. Suddenly all of his instincts, the instincts of a good policeman, had been awakened. The light from the corridor shone on the man's face. The sudden flush had died away and the face was pale with the aquiline nose jutting out from the smooth cheeks, above the well-trimmed beard and moustache. There were no traces of tears on those cheeks, though, no reddening of the blue eyes and the handkerchief had not lost the crispness of its starch when he had replaced it in his pocket. Not a backward glance at the poor child, either. No, he walked firmly out, and waited as Patrick closed the door gently and locked it again.

Patrick made a quick decision. He would see Dr Scher later on.

The taxi driver did not hesitate when they got in. It was a small city. Joseph Fitzsimon would be known to them all.

'South Mall, sir?' he enquired. Ignoring Patrick and Joe, he addressed himself to Mr Fitzsimon and did not falter when the man shook his head and said briefly, 'No, home.' Without further query he turned the car around and they were off descending down into the flat of the city.

Home, thought Patrick – well, not Montenotte, that colony of expensive houses on the hillside north of the River Lee –

the taxi was going east, the wheels sloshing through the flood water along the quays that bordered the side of the south branch of the River Lee. Probably Blackrock, he thought. There were some very fine houses built down there, high on a bank above the river and a good mile or so away from the smells and diseases of the crowded city – and away from desperate men who prowled the badly lit streets at night and would kill for a fine suit of clothing and a well-filled wallet. The Fitzsimons were among the rich of the city – old money, his mother used to say, shaking her head wisely. Of course they were tea merchants and had begun shipping it into Cork nearly two hundred years ago when tea was a rare and expensive luxury.

'Very bad, the South Mall today,' said the taxi driver chattily. 'I dropped off a fare from the station to there earlier this morning and I wished I had horses again – they could swim! The water was halfway up the wheels. We had to crawl along. Never so glad to get out of the place and get into Tuckey Street and along South Main Street. Never floods much there, do it? Funny, that?'

Some barefoot, ragged children in Cove Street were flat on their stomachs, thrusting their hands down sewerage drains – trying to grab eels, he thought, and felt sick for a moment. The mothers, though, would not care where a dinner came from. These poor children might live down Sawmill Lane or Rutland Street. Families were big and work for the fathers – if they had not skipped off to England – would be fairly unknown. Food would often just be charity donations from the St Vincent de Paul Society, or stolen from barrows at the Coal Quay Market.

As they came along Albert Quay, Patrick noticed that Joseph Fitzsimon didn't even glance towards where the roof of the Imperial Hotel rose high above the surrounding buildings. How strange, thought Patrick – considering that, according to him, his last sight of Angelina was at that place. And why didn't he notice his daughter disappearing from there? Surely one of those young ladies would never go home on their own. He had to admit that someone of his background knew little about the young ladies from Blackrock or from Montenotte. Perhaps in those big houses parents hardly saw their children from one end of the week to the other and they didn't have the same feeling for each other.

The Fitzsimon house at Blackrock had the dignity of a paved archway at the side where the fortunate owners could shelter from the weather while they paid off the taxi. Patrick fumbled in his pocket, but Joseph Fitzsimon had already taken out a coin and handed it to the taxi driver.

'This way,' he said and led the way along a covered passageway towards a small door at the side of the house, but then clicked his tongue with annoyance. 'Locked,' he said and went swiftly to the front.

It was a splendid house, thought Patrick, standing back and looking up. It was built high above the river but would, if it were not so foggy, have a fine view of the water as it broadened out on its way into the fifteen square miles of Cork Harbour. It was three storeys high, about hundred years old, probably built in the reign of one of the Georges. A typical house of its time, like a child's drawing, front door, porch with marble pillars, two windows on either side of it with all of the rest of the windows carefully arranged in neat rows as it rose to the roof.

The door was opened by a maid, but she was thrust aside by a young man.

'Did you find . . .?' he began and then stopped at the sight of the uniforms.

'Come in,' said Joseph Fitzsimon to Patrick. He had ignored Joe from the start but did not object to him crossing the threshold also. The fire in the stove at the back of the hallway had just been lit and smelled strongly of coal smoke and tarred sticks. Patrick looked from it to the face of the young man. Apprehension, he thought. That was what the face showed.

'Any sign?' he said now to his father, glancing uneasily at the policemen.

'Come into the library,' said the tea merchant and added in a rather perfunctory way. 'This is my son, Mr Gerald.'

I'll be damned if I call him 'Mr Gerald' as if I were one of his servants, thought Patrick but he followed the two men into the library and said nothing until Joe had closed the door behind them.

'Sergeant Patrick Cashman and Guard Joe Dugan, sir,' he said briskly to the younger Fitzsimon. He was very like the sister, he thought. Red-brown hair and very bright blue eyes – inherited from the father, he thought. Gerald gave a nod. No greeting, but perhaps that was natural. His eyes went to his father.

'She's been found,' said the tea merchant – not *Angelina has been found*, noted Patrick. 'She was washed up on St Mary's of the Isle.'

Gerald said nothing for a moment, just waited, but then when his father said no more, he breathed one word. 'Drowned.'

And then after a minute, seeming to notice his father's eyes on him, he said in a harsh, cracked voice. 'I have no idea of how she could have got into the river.'

There was a moment's silence while father and son looked at each other and then the son shrugged his shoulders and looked away.

Patrick intervened. 'Perhaps we could all sit down.' Whenever he felt slightly ill at ease he recited part of the rule book to himself. Now mentally he went through the section on preliminary interrogation and the curt sentences that he could see before his eyes steadied him and gave him confidence. There was a highly polished table in the centre of the room with eight chairs around it. He took a chair with his back to the window. Joe pulled out two of the chairs opposite so that the two men were seated facing Patrick and then took himself and his notebook to the very end of the table.

'We'll just take down a few details first, sir, if you please,' said Patrick. 'How old was your daughter Angelina?' That was, he thought, a nice, easy, innocuous question to start off with. It was important to get their cooperation. He had noted, though, the interchange of glances between the two. Almost as though each were suspicious of the other – it certainly was odd that neither had missed her from the ball. And what was the significance of the son's declaration that he had no idea how his sister got into the river?

'She was twenty – her twenty-first birthday would have been on the eleventh of June.'

Slipped into the past tense very quickly, thought Patrick as he nodded to Joe to take down the details. That was unusual for a parent – even the poor, with more children than they could feed, for days afterwards still spoke of their child as though it were alive.

'And just a few details about you, sir; and your son, while he is here; we need full name, age, occupation.'

No surprises with Joseph Fitzsimon – he was fifty-three and looked every day of it. Young Gerald was twenty-three and was a medical student. That accounted for the fact that he was still around the house at that hour.

'And Mrs Fitzsimon – would you like to be the one to break the news to her?' Patrick found Joe's eyes fixed on him, trying to convey some sort of message.

'Mrs Fitzsimon is not . . . is not well, she is not present in this house. She does not live here.'

'May I ask her address, sir?'

There was a long pause after that. Patrick looked down to the end of the table and saw Joe's eyes fixed on him as though trying to convey a message. Joe had been to Cork Grammar School and knew lots of things about the wealthy of the city. He certainly didn't look surprised when Joseph Fitzsimon said eventually, 'Mrs Fitzsimon is in Sunday's Well, at the Eglinton Asylum.'

The lunatic asylum! Mad! Oh my God, I wonder is there insanity in the family, thought Patrick? Was the girl mad? Perhaps this would be a suicide case after all. The girl was mad and she left the Merchants' Ball and threw herself into the river. That would be an easy solution. Old Fitzsimon was probably best friends with the proprietor of the *Cork Examiner*, and the affair would be hushed up. The priests would be under his control, too. *Suicide, while the balance of the mind was disturbed* – that would be the verdict of the inquest. *Deepest sympathy to the family*. A good solution. But was it the right one? There was an instinct deep within Patrick which did not allow him to accept an easy answer to everything. Police work suited him. He would gather all the evidence, make notes, put his ideas into columns, sort out possibilities. His mind looked forward to the prospect while he turned a bland and polite face towards the father of the dead girl.

'I see, sir,' he said. 'And have you any more children?'

'No, just Miss Angelina and Mr Gerald.'

'And did you also attend the Merchants' Ball, sir?' he asked directing his question at Gerald.

'Yes, I did, of course. Everyone attends the Merchants' Ball.'

Everyone, who is anyone, thought Patrick.

'And you danced with your sister?'

Gerald laughed in an amused fashion – not quite the demeanour that might have been expected from a young man who had just learned that his only sister, his only sibling, was dead.

'No, Sergeant, I certainly did not. I was in the bar most of the evening with my friends.'

'And the bar is upstairs, is that right, sir,' said Patrick, casting his mind back.

'That's right.' Gerald sounded bored. Perhaps now was the moment for the bombshell.

'I understand that your daughter was on her way to England, sir,' said Patrick purposefully keeping his voice flat. He looked from one to the other. He could have sworn that they would both be genuinely shocked. But that was not true. They seemed to look at each other, to look as though suddenly they understood things.

'So that was it. That was the reason for it,' said Gerald slowly and his father nodded.

'The young scoundrel – he persuaded her to run away with him.' Joseph's eyes shone very blue. Unusual to see such a deep colour in a grey-haired man, thought Patrick. He looked down at Joe, who had just written something. He was good at shorthand, Joe. He had thoughts of being a solicitor's clerk when he left school, but had decided that the police would suit him better.

'That money!' The words seemed to explode from Gerald.

'There was a ten-pound note – that was all – found on the body,' said Patrick quietly. 'I will make sure that you have a receipt for that as well as everything else.' He purposely left the last sentence a little vague and saw them look at each other.

'And, you suspect that your daughter had planned to run away, to elope . . .' He allowed the sentence to tail off. 'And the name of the young man, sir?' He stole a glance to the bottom of the table. Joe was looking interested rather than knowing, so this was not common knowledge in this city of gossips.

'Eugene Roche,' said Gerald promptly. 'He's a lecturer in English Literature at the university.'

Joe had finished writing, but Patrick allowed the pause to lengthen. He saw the tea merchant make a visible effort to gather himself together, to raise his chin.

'My daughter, Sergeant, got the notion of studying at the university – nonsense, of course, I don't know what she wanted to bother doing a thing like that for, but unmarried girls get these strange ideas from time to time. My son spoke out of turn – there was, in fact, no real relationship between this young man and my daughter – she met him purely in pursuance of this ridiculous idea. I forbade her to see him again. For a moment, I wondered, but now on thinking it over, I am sure that there was nothing in this. In fact, I hoped that soon I would be able to announce an engagement between Miss Angelina and a business associate of mine, a Mr Thomas McCarthy, here on a holiday from his tea plantation in India. The marriage was planned to take place in May before he returned to India.'

'Was this gentleman at the Merchants' Ball last night, sir?'

'Yes.' He hesitated and then continued. 'I believe that he danced with my daughter early in the evening, but then he came upstairs and joined my table. He said that Miss Angelina wanted to talk with a friend.'

Strange behaviour in a man who was about to get engaged to a girl, thought Patrick; but he decided not to pursue the matter. This death might well be suicide – the fact that there was madness in the family might seem to point in that direction – it would be hushed up, of course. Old Fitzsimon was a Roman Catholic and suicide was a mortal sin. Cynically, he thought that it would probably be a verdict of death by misadventure, rather than suicide while the balance of the mind was disturbed.

'And is Mr McCarthy staying here with you, sir?' he asked.

'No, in town, at the Imperial.'

You needed plenty of money to stay at the Imperial – the most expensive hotel in Cork. This McCarthy from India must be pretty rich if he were going to reside for a couple of months there.

'You mentioned money, sir,' he continued, looking across at Gerald. Let them do the talking.

'My son is referring to the fact that my daughter demanded money from me a few days ago.' Fitzsimon stopped after that. There was silence in the room, but from outside, in the hallway, he heard someone call: 'Ellen! Have you those fires done yet?'

The sound of the servants' voices seemed to galvanize Joseph Fitzsimon. Patrick could see the thought cross his mind that his servants might be questioned. He gave a short laugh.

'My daughter became a little hysterical. Demanded money. Wanted fifty pounds. Made quite a racket. I suppose that you wouldn't know much about girls of that age, Sergeant, but they do have those fits of hysteria, from time to time.'

Fifty pounds – that was quite a sum, thought Patrick. Aloud he said: 'You used the word "demanded", sir.' It wasn't quite a question and Joseph Fitzsimon didn't take it as one. He stared stonily ahead, perhaps reliving that interview with his daughter.

He said no more, though, so Patrick continued: 'Had Miss Fitzsimon an income of her own?'

It was a long shot, but he knew from Joe's quick glance that he might have hit the nail.

Once again they looked at each other. Joseph Fitzsimon tightened his lips.

'Or perhaps it would be easier for you if I asked that question of your solicitor,' said Patrick. He had to force himself into saying that. A boy from Cove Street didn't interrogate one of the merchant princes from Blackrock.

'She was under twenty-one,' said Joseph Fitzsimon after a minute.

'But once she became twenty-one . . . in three months'

time . . .' Patrick was conscious that Joe's pencil was lifted and remained poised in the air.

Again there was an exchange of glances.

'Once she was twenty-one my daughter was to inherit her grandmother's fortune – her grandmother left the money in trust for her.'

'And what was her grandmother's name?' Once again Patrick was conscious that glances were exchanged.

'Woodford,' said Joseph Fitzsimon briefly. Patrick saw Joe's busy pencil hesitate before he wrote the two syllables. Poor Joe. He would be bursting to enlighten his boss about all the ins and outs of family connections in this case. Joe's father had risen in the world and now had a good position in the menswear department of the Munster Arcade and brought home all the gossip about the well-off and the wealthy of Cork. But even Patrick knew that Woodford, in Cork, meant money; they were hugely rich. The tea merchant's fortune would pale beside what his daughter was due to inherit. How did Mr Fitzsimon like the thought of that money going out of his family, or would he have preferred it to be left to his son?

'And if Miss Fitzsimon died before the age of twenty-one?' Patrick heard the interrogative note in his statement and paused for a reply, deciding to say no more.

The answer was a long time coming and then it was the brother, not the father, who answered.

'The money would come to me,' said young Gerald defiantly.

He was going to be a very rich young man, now, thought Patrick. He could give up the medical studies – probably not that interested in them – otherwise what was he doing hanging around the house at eleven in the morning – been drinking most of the night, of course, but that was no excuse. For a moment Patrick thought of the midnight hours that he had spent studying, of the times when, at two o'clock in the morning he had gone out and walked up to the top of Barrack Street, gazing down at the sleeping city, feeling as though his head were going to explode. And, of course, not just Gerald would benefit. He must be costing his father a lot of money at the moment, and perhaps the father might think that there would be no end to it – that Gerald would never qualify as a doctor – and presumably he had no interest in his father's business. So he would be on his father's hands for the rest of Joseph's life.

It must have been very tempting to divert the Woodford fortune from a girl, who sooner or later would marry and bestow her money on a husband, and have it safely in the hands of the son who was possibly costing his father a lot of money, and seemed certain to cost him more.

FOUR

St Thomas Aquinas:

. . . quia Deus bonus est, sumus, inquantum sua bonitas est
ei ratio volendi omnia alia . . .

(. . . because God is good, then so, also, are we; since
his goodness is the reason for all else . . .)

The Reverend Mother thought about the dead girl from time to time throughout the day. None of my business, she told herself as the children went home from school at three o'clock. I don't suppose I will hear any more about it. Nevertheless, she was not entirely surprised when a few hours later Sister Bernadette ushered Dr Scher into her study.

'Just thought I'd pop in,' he said with a casual air as he was seating himself on the leather armchair. 'I've had a look at Sister Assumpta – she's doing as well as can be expected.

Sister Assumpta was as ancient as the old red sandstone hills around the city. She had been gently fading away for the past twenty years and would probably have another year or two in the same state. She was of great use as a perpetual excuse to Dr Scher to visit the convent whenever he wanted to have a gossip – either to impart some, or try to pick some up. Nevertheless, the Reverend Mother had to admit to herself that she was glad to see him.

'You'll join me in a cup of tea,' she said, not bothering to introduce a query into her voice. Dr Scher was never known to refuse and Sister Bernadette could be relied upon to bring it just the way that he liked it – strong enough for the spoon to stand upright, as they said in Cork, and to accompany it with some fruit cake. In the same mood of candour, she didn't bother making any further queries about the welfare of Sister Assumpta. There was something that he was on edge to communicate to her and she was willing to facilitate him.

'Funny you should say *tea*,' he said with emphasis as soon as the door closed behind the lay sister.

'Funny?' Now she did allow a query to enter her voice.

'Tea!' He nodded portentously, his round face creasing with the movement. 'They've put a name to the girl.'

Not one of the Fitzsimons, she thought, her heart suddenly giving a painful lurch. There had been something about that girl, something about the bright blue eyes and the red-brown hair, that rare shade of a perfectly ripened horse chestnut . . .

Dr Scher smiled as though he had access to her inner thoughts.

'That's right. She's a Fitzsimon, all right, from Blackrock. You remember the house.'

She nodded slowly. She remembered the house. She remembered everything. The eyes, the hair; she remembered everything. She looked at him closely but there was nothing to be seen on his face but the inveterate pleasure of conveying sensational news.

'It was a shock to him, a shock to Joseph Fitzsimon,' he said with relish, 'he came along himself, identified the body, young Patrick told me. Well, I suppose he got a shock,' he amended and then said: 'Nothing to the shock that he's going to get, though,' He waited for a moment, eyeing her and she said nothing, knowing that he would not be able to resist unburdening himself.

'Of course, I can rely on you to say nothing,' he said after a minute and then, eagerly and without waiting for a reply, 'Anyway, it will all have to come out in the inquest, so young Patrick says. That girl was pregnant; would you believe it? One of the Fitzsimons!'

For a moment she had felt sick and dizzy, but then pulled herself together as he went on.

'What was the cause of death?' she asked briskly.

'Drowning,' he said briefly. 'She had a bit of a bruise on her throat – dare say you noticed that, but I knew straightaway, once I examined her properly, that was not the cause of death. The eyes would have been more popping out. Strangulation makes them do that, poor things.' It made sense to her now, as she remembered Patrick's hesitation. He had looked at the eyes and had noticed that they were wrong for a victim of strangulation. A clever young man – discreet, too; he had waited and allowed the medical examination to reveal the facts. She bowed her head and listened to Dr Scher's account. He fell silent as Sister Bernadette's step was heard in the corridor and she made an effort to overcome the slight dizziness that had attacked her. The news had been a terrible shock to her. She saw Dr Scher look at her and saw a shadow of concern pass over his face. He knew her well, better perhaps than any of the sisters with whom she lived in such close company. He sensed this had disturbed her greatly.

There was a looking-glass hanging opposite the window – an attempt to bring light into the dark parlour – and the Reverend Mother, under the cover of the noisy entrance of the tea trolley, crossed over to it. She fumbled in the top drawer of the chest below and surreptitiously studied her face in it while Sister Bernadette poured tea and cut cake and giggled at Dr Scher's jokes and teasing. After a minute, she looked much the same as usual, she thought. Once past seventy perhaps you didn't show feeling too much – the same pale, oval face beneath the encasing wimple that had looked back at her for over half a century, the same heavy-lidded green eyes, the straight nose of which she had been proud once, and the eyebrows, still dark, still arched with that slightly haughty expression.

She glanced at an envelope from the drawer, closed it and resumed her seat, taking a cautious sip from the orange-coloured tea. She waited until Sister Bernadette, with an apologetic glance at Dr Scher, faded rapidly from the room.

By now she knew that she could trust her voice so she asked casually: 'What was her name? How old was she?'

'Angelina Fitzsimons.' That came out very quickly, but the answer to the second part of her question only came after he had meditatively chewed and then swallowed his slice of cake. 'Apparently her father says that she is twenty, almost twenty-one,' he said.

She looked at him. It was an odd way to put something, she thought. She said nothing, though. Long experience with garrulous people like Dr Scher had taught her that words came quicker in answer to silences.

'And that was odd,' he said slowly. 'The age, I mean. I could have sworn that she was only about seventeen. Very thin girl. Only a few months gone in pregnancy; not enough for it to show. She would always have been thin, I think.'

The Reverend Mother bowed her head. He was right. She had thought at the time, when she had been standing guard over the dead body, looking from Eileen's glowing, plump cheeks and sturdy frame to the girl at her feet, that the child of the slums looked healthier and heavier than the girl dressed in expensive satin.

'She may not have been very happy,' she said quietly and wished that she had kept more of an eye on the family.

'True, true. You can put the food on a plate but if the girl doesn't want to eat, then you can't force it. Did you notice the teeth?'

'No,' said the Reverend Mother. She slightly scorned herself for indulging in gossip, but she needed to know about this Fitzsimon girl and she bowed her head when he said succinctly, 'Small and crooked.'

Like the majority of our girls, here, she thought – that was why she had noticed nothing. Teeth like that were familiar. The children that attended her school lacked the calcium for their bones, had consumed none of the thousands of tons of cheese and butter exported from the city – exports that had made the fortunes of many of the prosperous families of Blackrock and Montenotte.

'What killed her?'

Dr Scher cut himself another slice of fruit cake and took a quick bite before answering. He shrugged then.

'They'll wrap it up at the inquest, but it was suicide, I suppose.' He frowned and she waited until he had finished chewing. 'Young Patrick – the sergeant – well, he's not too sure – thinks it may be murder – he's young and ambitious, of course. To solve a murder would bring him a pat on the back, but a suicide is nothing but a sad, three-day wonder and people will say that the civic guards should keep their thoughts to themselves.'

'Why does Patrick think it may be murder; was it because of the bruise on the throat?' Patrick was no windbag. He thought before he spoke. She had faith in his integrity. He would not twist facts to fit his convenience.

'It's because I found something in the stomach that surprised him – surprised both of us,' said the doctor reluctantly. He took another bite of cake and chewed it with relish and then said indistinctly: 'It was ether – there was ether in the stomach.'

'The stuff they give to get a tooth out?' She was puzzled. Perhaps Patrick was right – perhaps the girl had been killed by this.

Dr Scher had read her thoughts and was shaking his head. 'Only enough to make her slightly woozy, slightly light-headed, a little sick perhaps. Medical students often steal this stuff, have parties with it, make cocktails with it, give it to girls – good as alcohol and cheaper. Someone gave it to her, perhaps, or she took it herself. Her brother is a medical student. He would have been able to get his hands on it. Well, I'd better be going.' He got to his feet, dusting the crumbs from his hands on to Sister Bernadette's elegant tray.

'You'll keep what I told you to yourself, won't you?' he said as she rang the bell for the lay sister to show him out. 'Yes, of course, you will.' He had answered his own question before she could say anything. 'I dare say that you have half the secrets of Cork city wrapped up in that head of yours. Nothing like a nun to keep a secret – that's what I always say.'

She waited until she heard the voices cease. The heavy door slammed and Sister Bernadette's slippers shuffled back to the kitchen. Only then did she rise from her chair, go out into the corridor, lift the phone and say into it: 'Montenotte two, three, please.' She would, of course, say nothing on the phone. The people at the telephone exchange had a reputation for eaves-dropping on conversations and there was a strong possibility that Lucy's opulent home would have one or two extensions to the telephone within it.

I hope that Lucy is at home, she thought. At least her cousin's husband, a prosperous lawyer, would be safely ensconced in his office on the South Mall at this time of the day. There would be no danger that she would have to exchange platitudes with him or wonder, all the time that she spoke, whether he was listening in the background.

Lucy was at home – she would be on a miserable day of fog and floods, thought the Reverend Mother with amusement as she waited for the maid to summon her. Lucy was rather like an expensive white Angora, a well-fed, pretty cat with large blue eyes. Yes, she would definitely be by the fire today. She would not be anxious to be summoned forth. Well, it could not be helped.

'Lucy, I want you to come over here this afternoon; I have something that I must talk to you about,' she said crisply when the sleepy voice said her name.

There was an enormous yawn, and then the objection. She had known that there would be one. 'Oh, my dear, but the weather, and Rupert says that the whole city is flooded.'

'Come around by College Road and then you should have no problems,' said the Reverend Mother crisply and rang off before Lucy could suggest that it would be much better if her cousin could come out to Montenotte. To give Lucy her due, she would have offered chauffeur, car and everything, but the Reverend Mother had decided that a conversation in the convent could have much more privacy than in Lucy's luxurious house with servants coming in and out and the possibility of an inquisitive ear pressed to a keyhole, or even of the master of the house returning early and joining in the conversation.

In deference to her cousin, she gave orders for Sister Bernadette to build up the fire in her parlour and with her own hands placed an embroidered cushion and a warm rug on the easy chair in front of it. Lucy, she thought ruefully, had always been used to people cushioning her from the harsh realities of life. The tea, she hoped, would be perfectly to the taste of one who had sampled good food in most of the major cities of Europe. Rupert Murphy was not just a very successful lawyer, but he had inherited wealth from the great Murphy distilleries. It had been a very good match for anyone, especially for the orphaned seventeen-year-old, living under the protection of their cousins in Bordeaux.

But then Lucy was pretty and men were attracted to her.

When Lucy arrived the Reverend Mother was in the chilly front parlour, engaging in a polite battle with Mr Russell from the bookshop in Oliver Plunkett Street. He looked prosperous, and the word in the city was that the profits of his shop were good. The Reverend Mother dealt with him skilfully – assuming that he would be interested to give her cut-rates, or even better, on some books for the advanced readers in her top class.

'Of course,' she said graciously, 'I know the very high standards that you, and your father before you, have maintained and what I was about to suggest was that your assistants might possibly find on the shelves some shop-soiled articles that you could sell to us at a low price, or . . .' She took a deep breath and at that moment heard the ring on the doorbell and Sister Bernadette's ecstatic welcome to Mrs Murphy and Lucy's light, lilting, still almost-childish tones. 'Ah,' she said, with a gracious smile, 'Mrs Rupert Murphy has arrived. You know Mrs Rupert Murphy, I'm sure. She and her husband are so good about donating to our charities. But to go back to our business, I wonder whether there might be any possibility of even persuading you to donate some books.' She put a query into her voice and moved towards the door.

'Yes, yes, indeed!' He was stammering with eagerness and she rewarded him by opening the door and saying aloud: 'Oh, Mrs Murphy, how lovely to see you. And here is Mr Russell, who has just made such a generous donation to our school of some of his lovely books.'

Lucy played her part as she had expected, offering a kid-gloved hand to Mr Russell, allowing him to inform her of the latest Galsworthy novel, just in and bound in red leather which she promised to tell her husband about, and then he allowed Sister Bernadette to usher him out once he had promised to send over a box of books that very afternoon.

'How you do flirt with these men and you a Reverend Mother,' said Lucy in an undertone. She peeped into the chilly parlour with dismay, but Sister Bernadette closed the door firmly on the bookseller and beaming with joy led the way into the Reverend Mother's warm room, drawing out the easy chair and wheeling the trolley filled with refreshments over beside their guest before she managed to get herself out of the room. Lucy held out her well-creamed hands to the heat of the fire and then turned around sharply.

'You're looking at yourself in the mirror,' she accused. 'I haven't seen you do that for a while.'

'Just wondering if anyone would ever imagine that we were almost the same age – you're looking well, Lucy.'

Lucy preened herself. She had quite a cat-like face with high cheekbones and a pointed chin. Her large blue eyes did not have the intensity of colour that they had when she was seventeen years old, but their lids had been touched with a dab of azure powder and her eyebrows were carefully pencilled. The Reverend Mother went across and turned the key in the door and then drew the heavy draught-excluding curtain over it. Lucy's well-marked eyebrows went up but she said nothing, just turned her attention to the tea trolley. Carefully she poured out two cups of tea and added cream and sugar to her own.

'Lucy,' said the Reverend Mother, coming back and sitting down opposite her cousin, 'a dead girl was found, washed up by the tide, outside the back gate here.' She did not wait for a reaction and Lucy uttered none. She would know that there was more to come. The pretty, cat-like appearance always cloaked a keen brain. People said that Rupert Murphy took no step in any matter without consulting his wife and that inside that carefully tinted head of ash-blonde hair were most of the secrets of the wealthy of Cork.

'Her name,' said the Reverend Mother evenly, 'was Angelina Fitzsimon. She was the daughter of Joseph Fitzsimon.'

And then there was a very long pause. It was impossible to know what was going on behind the well-powdered face in front of her. Lucy sipped her tea; bit a small piece of icing from one of the tiny cakes arranged on the china plate. What was she thinking of? The images were passing through the Reverend Mother's mind. Ballycotton, the road down to the harbour, Thomas's sailing boat, the cliff walk, the caves, the two islands, one flat and rabbit-filled and the other tall and conical with the lighthouse crowning it. There must have been days of rain and fog, she supposed, but in her memory it was always sunny, the sea was always a dazzling shade of turquoise, the cliffs were covered in sweet-scented gorse and large blue butterflies thronged above the yellow flowers. Oddly, right through her life, that combination of blue and yellow always seemed, in her

mind's eye, to be the epitome of beauty. She heard a heavy sigh
from her cousin and wondered whether Lucy's thoughts had
followed hers, or whether they had gone ahead to that time in
Bordeaux with their cousins.

'Do you see much of them – the Fitzsimons, of Joseph?'
she asked and for once she heard her voice, normally so decisive and calm, break in a timid fashion. She had often thought
of asking that question, but had not liked to be the one to
bring up the subject.

Lucy had regained her composure. Her eyes hardened. She
took another piece of cake and chewed it with what appeared
to be genuine pleasure.

'Nothing,' she said decisively in clipped tones. 'Nothing at
all. Rupert doesn't like him. There was a bit of a scandal about
the way he treated his wife, you know, and not even the
Woodford money could hush up that. Rupert thinks . . .' She
allowed her sentence to tail away and gave her cousin a sharp
glance.

'I see,' murmured the Reverend Mother. Rupert, she thought,
would do as his wife wished. If she did not wish for the
acquaintance, then he would avoid the man. 'Of course, you
are up in Montenotte and he is down in Blackrock, so your
paths wouldn't cross too often,' she finished.

She had done her duty, had told her cousin the news. The
Fitzsimons of Bordeaux, managing the wine part of the
merchant business, had been the connection between them –
just second cousins to them both. Edmund and Angela had
been gentle and nice people, warm-hearted and generous, but
they were both long since dead. She and Lucy had outlived
most of their friends and relations. She studied her cousin's
determined face and decided that a secret would always be
safe with her. But at least she had passed on the news.

'It's quite a mystery about this poor girl,' she said conver-
sationally. 'It appears that she was at the Merchants' Ball the
night before . . .'

FIVE

St Thomas Aquinas:
Suicidium est contra inclinationem naturalem,
et contra caritatem.
(Suicide is against the natural inclination, and against love.)

'Suicide?' queried the Reverend Mother looking across at the young civic guard. She allowed the word to remain alone. She had no right to be cross-questioning Patrick. It had been politeness on his part that had brought him to the convent this afternoon to thank her for her help and to express a courteous wish that she had not caught cold while standing out in the freezing March wind and rain, waiting beside the body of the dead girl. He had, he was careful to explain, been just passing the convent after a visit to his mother who now lived, supported by her son, in a small cottage in the lane next to the convent.

He gave a quick grin at her word. 'You've had Dr Scher here, I see!' And when she didn't reply he said with a slight frown, 'He's keen on the notion – and so is the superintendent. So many of the girls that we fish out of the river are pregnant – and I suppose that some of them could be suicides – poor things!'

It was the last two words that made the Reverend Mother take a step outside her normal caution. These words moved her. Patrick had not forgotten his origins and he had a look of someone who wanted an understanding ear. Like Thomas Aquinas, perhaps he thought that suicide was a reflection on those around the dead person, as each person ought to be able to love themselves – a sin against charity – but whose was the sin? A child had to be loved before they could feel love in return.

'But you don't agree with Dr Scher and the superintendent,' she stated.

'She was almost strangled,' he said curtly. 'Not enough to cause death, but even Dr Scher admits that it might have been enough to make her lose consciousness.' He looked apologetically at her, but then stated firmly. 'It would be a bit of a coincidence, Reverend Mother, if someone attempted to kill her and then she then went out and finished the job herself. Of course, the actual cause of death was drowning, but that doesn't stop it being murder. If a man takes an unconscious girl and throws her into the river, then he is guilty of murder.'

The Reverend Mother nodded her approval of his reasoning. Patrick, she thought, with a trace of pride, would never take the easy way out.

'Do you believe that the man thought he had killed her and then he threw her into the river?'

'That's very likely,' said Patrick. 'If we didn't have an address for her – a name and address, we might think that perhaps he was walking her home. But the only way to Blackrock would have been to take a cab and to go east. The bad flooding only began at about two o'clock in the night – long after the ball finished at midnight. If she were someone else, then they might have gone along the South Mall and then across Parliament Bridge – the pavements were still above water at that stage. He might have thrown her over there. But, you see, Reverend Mother, this was a special night – the night of the Merchants' Ball. We were prepared for a bit of trouble – that ball might be something that the Republicans would like to disrupt – anyway, we were ready for them. We had a few men patrolling Patrick Street, warning people of the flood that was expected, but at the same time keeping an eye open. And there was one of our men on duty outside the front door to the Imperial Hotel for most of night – until the ball was over – and he swears that no woman came out on her own – a few courting couples, he said, but that was all, until the main crowd left – and then there was a big swarm of them, all exclaiming about the floods. The girl must have been with someone who murdered her. I've got a couple of men questioning the taxis, but no one remembers her coming out. Her father and her brother were at the ball; the brother went off with friends from Blackrock who dropped him off at Bellamonte – that's the name of the Fitzsimons' place in Blackrock – and the father went home by his car – the chauffeur called for him.'

'And neither missed the girl?'

'The old story,' said Patrick with a grimace. 'Both drunk, I'd say. Each thought that she was with the other. But that's not all.'

He hesitated for a moment and then picked up the travelling bag that he had put beside his chair. Mother Aquinas's eye had gone to it when he came in. A slightly old-fashioned leather bag, she thought, not new, slightly scuffed, but expensive-looking.

'She left this in the cloakroom,' he said. 'Got a ticket for it. The girl in the Imperial Hotel remembered her leaving it there. Was sure that it belonged to Miss Fitzsimon.'

He gave her a glance and then turned his attention to the bag. She watched while he opened it and methodically took out the garments one by one – skirts, blouses, jackets, night-dress, underclothes, none of them new, some even mended neatly in places, but all of a good quality – expensive clothes, but from a few years back, she thought, looking at the skirt-lengths. Her merry young ladies who turned up the hems of their gymslips would think them dowdy and out-of-date.

'And what's that?' she asked, seeing a price tag on an oilskin toilet bag.

'That's brand new. Bought in the Munster Arcade – bought two days ago – everything brand new inside – soap, wash flannel, tooth powder, comb, hairbrush – never been used.'

'So she was running away – to Liverpool – that's what the ticket said, didn't it, Patrick?'

'That's right and she had reserved a first-class cabin. Why did she want to go to Liverpool?' He did not hesitate, but answered his own question. 'Fits with the pregnancy, I suppose – but who was the father of the baby? And why didn't they get married?'

'Perhaps he was married already,' said the Reverend Mother sadly, her mind on the past.

'All the more reason for the man to murder her – that would provide a motive – perhaps she threatened to wreck his marriage, or something like that,' said Patrick quickly.

'But no one saw her leave the hotel? With a man or without a man?'

'That's right. We've questioned everyone. The Imperial Hotel had a full staff that night. The assistant manager himself was on the desk by the door. This is the big event of the year for them. They had to make sure that anyone who went near the ballroom or the suite of rooms above had a ticket, otherwise they were ushered into the bar at the front of the hotel, and, just for that night, the guests at the hotel had to use the back stairs. The assistant manager knows the Fitzsimons well – is quite certain that Miss Fitzsimon did not leave, either by herself or with a gentleman. He's a bright fellow; remembered the old man, Mr Fitzsimon, going home, and noticed that he was pretty drunk. The brother left with a big party – men and women – and the assistant manager said that he couldn't swear as to whether the sister was with them or not, but he didn't think so. He was able to reel off a lot of names – lots of the Blackrock crowd.'

The Reverend Mother nodded. The merchant princes of Cork city lived on the hill named Montenotte, or on the pleasant banks of the River Lee around the village of Blackrock. Blackrock had been her birthplace. She knew all of the surnames – the Murphys, the Lamberts, the Crawfords, the Newenhams, the Hewits, the Roches, the Fitzsimons and the Dwyers – they had all been part of her once.

'Was there a fiancé? A boyfriend,' she amended. It was Eileen who had informed her once that the word 'fiancé' belonged to the Victorian era and that modern girls of the 1920s used the word 'boyfriend'.

'I enquired about that – delicately,' said Patrick with a grimace. 'Neither the brother nor the father was very forthcoming, but when I told them about the ten-pound note, well, they opened up a bit.'

He told the story well, she thought, observing him as though he were still one of the pupils. She could see father and son, condescending to this policeman, this member of the newly founded civic guards, whose accent would immediately classify him as one of the lower orders in a city full of uneasy snobbery, where the rich sent their children to school in

England – not because the education was superior, but purely in order that they would never, ever, pronounce 'tea' as 'tay' or 'quay' as 'kay' and that the difficult digraph *th* would always be safe in their mouths.

Patrick would have been impassive, she knew. She could hear his voice, undisturbed, asking the questions, probing.

'So they were astonished to hear about the ticket to Liverpool and the ten-pound note in her evening bag,' she commented.

'No.' Patrick thought about this for a moment. 'No, not astonished for long,' he said slowly. 'It was odd really, almost as though it suddenly made sense. It turned out that she had asked for money from her father a few days ago, had demanded it. Gerald, *Mr Gerald*, the father kept calling him . . .' Patrick's grin was slightly lopsided, but the Reverend Mother did not comment. He would have to learn to deal with this sort of snobbery. It would do him no kindness to sympathize or to express disapproval.

'So Gerald . . .' she prompted.

'He was very open about the fuss – hysterical fuss – that Angelina had made, of how she had screamed and shouted and demanded fifty pounds.'

'Fifty pounds,' said the Reverend Mother meditatively. It was a considerable sum of money. One could buy a small house for that.

'That's right – Joe checked at the bank. She did cash the cheque. We checked the shipping office, too. She bought her ticket herself. They remembered her well when I showed a photograph.'

'Just the one ticket?' queried the Reverend Mother. She would have liked to see the photograph, but it was probably back at the station and, really, it could be none of her business. What would Lucy say, she wondered? Would she be interested? It was hard to tell with Lucy.

'Just the one ticket,' confirmed Patrick. 'It cost her five pounds, cabin and all.'

'And she had ten pounds in her bag,' mused the Reverend Mother. 'That leaves thirty-five pounds unaccounted for.'

'That's right and that's not the only thing – the son came out with a name – the father tried to shut him up, but it

was too late. Apparently Angelina had wanted to go to
college, to study at the university, but her father had not
wanted her to, had refused permission but she had signed
on to start her studies in English Literature next autumn
and she had become friendly with this fellow Eugene Roche,
who was a lecturer at the university. I gathered that the
father didn't approve of the relationship.'

'I know the family,' commented the Reverend Mother. 'They
would have been well off – in my day, anyway,' she added
smiling to think how long distant her heyday was now from
this modern year of 1923.

'I wouldn't know about that, but we can look him up.'
Patrick's voice was suddenly impatient and she understood his
feelings. If a man was a lecturer at the university, then surely
he could marry and maintain a wife and a family, even if there
was little of the family's inherited wealth for him to share in.

'Was he there, this Eugene Roche, there at the Merchants'
Ball?' But of course he would have been. Everyone who was
part of that circle would have been there. She hardly listened
to his answer, her mind shifting through the facts. It was
unlikely that Angelina and Eugene Roche planned to run away
to England. Any father, faced with a pregnancy, would have
immediately capitulated and agreed to a marriage.

But what if Eugene Roche had not wanted to marry Angelina
Fitzsimon?

Could he have decided to make a quick end to her and to
the unborn child?

'Yes, but the father was adamant that there was no relationship between them.'

'Didn't like the idea?' Perhaps, thought the Reverend
Mother, the Roches had taken a step downwards in the Cork
hierarchy.

'He had bigger fish to fry,' said Patrick. 'In fact, he told me
that he had hoped that soon he would be able to announce an
engagement between *Miss Angelina* and a business associate
of his, a Mr Thomas McCarthy, here on a holiday from his
tea plantation in India. The marriage was to have taken place
in May before he returned to India.'

'And was this gentleman at the Merchants' Ball last night?'

Reverend Mother began to feel her brain clicking over, shifting facts, slotting in those figures whose faces she could only vaguely picture, slotting them in beside that dead and slightly swollen face of the girl with red-brown curls and blue eyes. McCarthy, she thought, he must be the son, or perhaps the grandson of Richard McCarthy. Her mind went back to Richard. He had been very dashing, she thought. I wonder what this McCarthy is like?

'Yes. When I asked Mr Fitzsimon about this, well, he hesitated a bit. It took him a minute before he said: "I believe that he danced with my daughter early in the evening, but then he came upstairs and joined my table." He said that this fellow told him that Miss Angelina wanted to talk with a friend. I thought that sounded a bit odd,' said Patrick. 'I didn't comment, of course, but just asked whether McCarthy was staying with him at Blackrock and he told me that no, he was staying in the Imperial Hotel. I think that he, this McCarthy from India, must be pretty rich if he was going to live for a couple of months there – still, I can look into that.'

There was obviously something else on his mind so the Reverend Mother waited without comment. He had got up from his chair and was walking restlessly up and down the room, his heavy boots marking out a measured tread on the shining wooden floor.

'But how did her body end up in the river?' Patrick seemed to be asking the question of himself so she did not reply. 'It must have gone into the river, but for the life of me, I can't think how. No one saw her leave the Imperial Hotel,' he finished.

'She was soaked through,' began the Reverend Mother.

'That's right.' He nodded. 'And it wasn't just rainwater – there were traces of sewage in her clothes – you know what the river is like whenever there is flooding – it gets into the sewers and the sewers get into it. She was definitely in the river at some stage.'

'Sewage,' said the Reverend Mother meditatively. It was true of course that sewage did get into the river, and out on to the streets, and through the crumbling doors of the old Georgian houses on Cove Street and Douglas Lane.

Nevertheless, the word stayed in her mind.

When she had been a child she had known the Imperial Hotel very well. Her father, an importer of wines from Bordeaux, had been a great friend of the man who had designed it – the man who had gone on to be City Sheriff and then High Sheriff of Cork and one of its foremost citizens. He was proud of his achievement, this architect – Mr Deane – with an effort she remembered his name. He and her father had often lunched there at the Imperial Hotel and as a petted and spoiled only child of a widowed father she had accompanied him, grown bored with the long conversation and wandered around the splendid rooms and down into the basement. In later years her memories were of the magnificent ballroom and the side parlour where the ladies left their cloaks in the hands of obsequious attendants, but looking back into her childhood recollections of the late 1850s it was the part below ground – the kitchen, the basement and the cellars which had fascinated her.

And now she remembered the large manhole in one of the cellars. The kitchen boy had tried to frighten her once when he had prised up the iron cover and scraped a pot full of fish innards down into the fast-flowing water beneath.

'Tide's going out,' he had said nonchalantly. 'If you slipped in there you'd end up in the sea in a couple of hours.' She had taken a step backwards, she remembered, picturing her ten-year-old self, dressed in a full-skirted, ankle-length, dark green gingham dress with elaborately puffed sleeves edged with white lace. She had been proud of that dress and suddenly nauseated at the thought of it being splashed by the water from the sewer. For ages afterwards she had avoided going down there when the kitchen boy was anywhere near. The idea of floating down a dark passage with all of the muck and filth frightened her more than the idea of ending up in the clean ocean.

But last night, before dawn, there had been an abnormally high tide which had been driven up through the harbour and along the two channels of the River Lee, by a gale-force south-easterly wind that had only dropped down at dawn. The South Mall, the quays, the Grand Parade, even Western Road, leading

out of the city, had been badly flooded, as had the rest of the
east side of the town.

'Patrick,' she said slowly. 'Do you remember your history
of the building of Cork?'

His gaze was puzzled. 'Cork?' he queried. 'I was never too
interested in history – never one of your nationalists – we did
a lot about Sarsfield and the Treaty of Limerick, I remember,
but I don't think he was from Cork.'

Reverend Mother felt a moment's impatience. There was
no doubt that the highly nationalistic version of Irish history,
the struggles against the English, the futile battles, the organized land wars, as taught by the Christian Brothers, had resulted
in a lot of clever boys giving up their studies at the university
and going off to join the Republicans and spending their nights
hiding out in remote derelict farmhouses and their days in
attacking those deemed hostile to their dream of a republic.
It was just as well that Patrick, with an elderly mother to
support, had not taken that route.

'No, I wasn't thinking of people,' she said carefully. 'I was
thinking about how Cork was built.'

He was attentive and polite as she sketched out for him the
beginnings of Cork but his interest quickened when she told
how the eighteenth-century merchants had built arched and
solid brick culverts over the water channels and on top of
them streets – streets, such as Patrick Street whose meandering
path still mirrored the original stream beneath, also the Grand
Parade and the South Mall, streets that even still, a hundred
years later, periodically disappeared and reverted to rivers. 'It
used to be like Venice,' she explained, though she was uncertain
whether he would know anything about that city. Shakespeare's
Merchant of Venice, which he would have studied for his
schools' certificate, gave very little sense of place, unlike the
London plays of the Richards and the Henrys.

'You'll have noticed,' she continued, 'that most of those
houses along the South Mall, including the Fitzsimons' warehouses, have their front door twenty feet above the pavement
– with those steps leading up to it – there used to be boats
tied at the bottom of the steps,' she said – the image had
always delighted her – but he was beginning to look restive

so she finished hurriedly, 'the Imperial Hotel was built after that, of course. Its front door is at street level, but it was built on top of the remains of an old warehouse and it has a huge manhole in the cellar – or it used to have – and the sewers will go under the street and into . . .'

'And into the river that was arched over; the river beneath the South Mall!' He was on his feet. He had grasped the point instantly. 'So she might never have left the hotel,' he said, almost to himself. 'She might have been killed there.'

SIX

The Bishop of Cork, Daniel Cohalan, 1922:
'Anyone who within the diocese of Cork shall organize or
take part in any ambush, or kidnapping or otherwise, shall be
deemed guilty of murder and shall occur by the very fact
the censure of excommunication.'

'Have you heard the news, Reverend Mother?' Sister Bernadette, fresh from her morning chat with her friend, the postman had a flush of excitement on her face. She didn't wait for an answer, but poured out the whole dramatic story of how the Bishop of Cork, the Right Reverend Daniel Cohalan, had been shot in the arm, probably by a Republican while opening an extension to the nearby Sharman Crawford Technical Institute.

When the children arrived they were shocked and pale-faced. Most had their houses savagely searched by armed soldiers on the evening before and some even again this morning. The Reverend Mother was pleased when a sharp peal came from the doorbell and a minute later a beaming Sister Bernadette ushered in Lucy, accompanied by her chauffeur carrying a large box packed to the top with books.

'Well, Reverend Mother, these are for your girls,' said Lucy, signalling to the chauffeur to empty the books on to a table. She was exquisitely dressed. The girls were impressed by the books, expensively bound and gilt-edged, but perhaps more, thought the Reverend Mother, by her outfit. They clustered around her, staring at her in admiration, inhaling the expensive perfume that enveloped her.

'Thank you very much,' said one and then, impulsively, but effectively, Nellie O'Sullivan said: 'I do like your costume!'

Nothing could have worked better. Lucy, still a showgirl at heart, did a twirl and showed off the lavender blue of her tweed two-piece and rested her chin on the warm brown of

the furs, peeping coquettishly over her shoulder at them. The
girls laughed and applauded and then eagerly began to pick
up the beautiful books.

'They might as well have them,' said Lucy. 'I caught Rupert
using one to kill flies. That's the only time I've seen him open
one for months, I told him. I think his father bought them by
the yard when he furnished the house for us after our marriage.
They will be appreciated here. You will tell them all sorts of
interesting things about the authors and how wonderful they
are.' She smiled benignly as the girls bent over the box and
added in a stage whisper: 'How singularly unbecoming that
wretched gymslip is, isn't it? I'll have a word with Susan. Her
three girls have more clothes than they know what to do with.
We'll pass them on to these pretty girls.'

The Reverend Mother smiled. Lucy's granddaughters'
clothes would be very appreciated by these girls, but she
knew that the gift of books was not the only reason why
Lucy had appeared on St Mary's of the Isle so early on the
morning.

'I'll leave you girls to look through the books and to note
the titles and authors for the library,' she said and then escorted
her cousin from the room. It was no wonder, she thought, that
Nellie had admired the costume of lavender blue – fashionably
short, though not, perhaps, short enough for Sister Mary
Immaculate to have pinned a frill to it – and the furs on her
cousin's shoulders were luxuriant and glossy.

'That was very kind of you, Lucy,' she said.

'Not at all,' returned Lucy. 'They're so pleased, aren't they?
It's amazing. I don't think that any one of my granddaughters
would thank me for a book.'

'These children haven't had much fun in their lives,' said
the Reverend Mother simply. 'They've had a shock. The whole
district is being searched for the gunman who shot the Bishop.
They're all frightened, though that's nothing new for them.
They haven't had an easy time over the past few years. I
suppose you could say that they've grown up with fear. A box
of books is a nice diversion.'

She said no more until they were safely ensconced in her
room. She did not bother to ring for Sister Bernadette. Lucy

had something to talk about and the sooner it was aired, the better.

'I was having a chat about Joseph Fitzsimon to Rupert, last night,' she began and the Reverend Mother wondered momentarily about that very detached tone.

'He was telling me about the wife,' continued Lucy. 'I thought you might be interested to hear.'

The Reverend Mother bowed her head and tucked her hands into her sleeves. She did not lower her eyes, though, but kept them fixed on her cousin's face.

'Joseph,' continued Lucy 'is, of course, the living image of his father.' Her voice hardened and her enormous blue eyes were stony and fixed. 'He's the same selfish bastard,' she declared and the Reverend Mother did not contradict or reprove.

'Somehow the wife did not suit him, so he managed to bribe Dr O'Connor to certify her and to place her in the lunatic asylum. Who would want to be the wife of a man like that? And, of course, now he has the use of her money – that's all that matters to him – he's just like his father.' Lucy's voice was venomous, though the placid appearance of her well-powdered face did not alter.

'And what about the children, Joseph's children,' said the Reverend Mother, keeping her voice even and detached while she watched her cousin's blue eyes. The marriage with Rupert Murphy had resulted in three girls and that, perhaps, had suited Lucy. She had been a good mother, and was now a good grandmother to a bevy of fashionable young ladies.

Lucy gave a shrug. 'He doesn't seem to have done well by them,' she said. 'Not if the girl committed suicide.'

'I think that, more likely, she was murdered,' said the Reverend Mother, looking at her cousin. Her gaze, she knew, was very straight and very direct and it gave Lucy no way out.

'And murder,' she added firmly, 'must not be allowed to succeed.'

'Murder,' said Lucy slowly. 'But who would have wanted to murder the girl? Unless . . . Yes, I remember now – something that Rupert told me a couple of months ago. It was that girl; it must have been.'

The Reverend Mother said nothing. It would be no good to

urge Lucy to tell what she knew. Under that sweet appearance she was as stubborn as ever.

'Well, I suppose I can trust you to keep Rupert's name out of this,' said Lucy after a moment. 'You seem to have the police eating out of your hand – like all nuns.'

'There is always a way of putting matters forward in a discreet fashion, and without mentioning names,' said the Reverend Mother, mildly, and Lucy gave a chuckle and leaned forward.

'Well, you know that Rupert's office is up on the first floor on the South Mall and Sarsfield, the solicitor, has his rooms on the floor beneath, well one day Rupert was coming down the stairs and he stopped on the landing to light a cigar and then he heard Sarsfield shout: "It's for your father to question me about your mother's fortune, Miss Fitzsimon, it has nothing whatsoever to do with you." And Rupert waited for a minute until Sarsfield had gone back into his office – you know men – they hate anything embarrassing – but when he went out down the steps, there was a young lady standing there on the pavement and Rupert said that she was Joseph's daughter, he thought. Looked like him, he said.'

'Was Rupert surprised?' The question came out mechanically, to prompt further revelations. It was obvious that Lucy had more to say.

'Not really, there had been talk about Sarsfield, before – you know – just privately among the solicitors.' Lucy lowered her voice and gave a quick glance at the curtained door. 'You know how it happens, murmurs at law dinners, on the golf course, that sort of thing. But, according to Rupert, if Anne Woodford's fortune, her dowry, had been embezzled, then it was certain that the husband, that Joseph, was in on it as well as Sarsfield. It's just the sort of thing that his father would have done,' added Lucy viciously. She was one who did not forgive easily.

'So Angelina Fitzsimon was asking questions about what happened to her mother's fortune,' said the Reverend Mother slowly.

'Of course Joseph had no right to it. It's not like when you and I were young. Nowadays women have control over our own money.'

'Unless they are shut up in an asylum, of course.'

'You nuns are so cynical,' said Lucy with a twinkle. 'I'm sorry about the girl, though. Was she pretty?'

'Very,' said the Reverend Mother. 'She had the blue eyes and the same chestnut-coloured hair . . .' She said no more. They both had their memories of that summer so long ago when the sea was always blue and the sun drew the scent from the gorse-covered cliffs.

'Well, I'll leave it with you. You'll say nothing about Rupert in all this business.'

Her tone was quite unconcerned, quite certain, and her trust in her cousin was absolute. She got to her feet, drawing the cosy furs around her neck and checking the angle of her close-fitting hat in the mirror above the cupboard.

'I must go,' she said. 'I daren't keep the chauffeur waiting any longer. Those servants rule our lives, you know.' She paused at the door and looked back. 'Of course embezzlement in a solicitor would be a very, very serious matter. It would ruin him for ever.' She gave one of her dramatic pauses and said impressively: 'I'd say that a man could kill to keep a secret like that.'

And then she was off, popping into the classroom before she went and exchanging a few merry words with the girls and left promising to send some pretty clothes that her grand-daughters had grown tired of. No doubt their fond grandmother would replenish their wardrobes at regular intervals.

Lucy, thought the Reverend Mother as she made her way back to the classroom, would have been a good grandmother for a lonely, worried girl, whose mother was missing from the family home. She sighed at the thought.

Just as she was thinking about this she heard the peal of a bell at the visitors' door and listened intently at the shuffling of Sister Bernadette's slippers – the lay sisters all wore sheep-skin slippers which kept their feet warm, and polished the shining wooden floors that they trod – an innovation of which she was proud, especially since she had managed to manipulate a wealthy cousin of hers, a hides and wool merchant, into donating the skins. And, as an extra bonus, some of the young lay sisters, many of them not more than fifteen, did enjoy

virtuously skating up and down the glass-like floors in order
to maintain the high polish.

And yes, it was Patrick. She knew his step by now. She
busied herself with her account book and just raised a head
when he came in. She was ashamed that she was so eager to
see him, so eager to use her brains on something new. She
was stale, she thought. The convent and the school ran like
clockwork. Her reputation in the city was so high that funds
flowed in – she had even recently set up a kitchen where the
older girls learned to cook with the ingredients that were
donated to them from the shops and market stalls. Tasty break-
fasts and nourishing lunches for half-starved children were
turned out by the fourteen-year-olds – by the time that they
left school, if they were ever lucky enough to have a house
with a kitchen, they would have learned to cook cheap meals
for their families, but, since most of them lived in one room,
there was little use for their skills in their present homes. Still,
it might help some to get jobs as servants in the houses of the
moderately well off and then they might get a chance to cook.

But she wanted to use her brain more than she was doing
and somehow she had found herself speculating on the death
of this girl – this Fitzsimon girl. Now that she knew the
surname her interest had become painfully intense. It was all
very well for Lucy to shrug her expensively clad shoulders,
but there was such a thing as responsibility and the death of
this girl had to be solved, no matter what the cost. Her thoughts
went back to that summer by the sea, picturing in her mind's
eye that long steeply descending grassy path that led to the
dark sandstone cave in the cliffs. Still, that was over fifty years
ago. At the moment the present was what counted and she
would do her best to get justice for Angelina.

'Well, Patrick,' she said graciously.

'I just called in to tell you that you were right about the
Fitzsimon girl being put down into the sewers,' he said. 'There
were a couple of her hairs caught into a rough piece of metal
at the side of the manhole cover.' He cleared his throat self-
consciously. 'I felt a bit like Sherlock Holmes – brought down
a big magnifying glass. Joe was most impressed.'

The Reverend Mother sat back and succeeded in setting her

mouth so that a smile of triumph would not spread over her face. She should, of course, modestly attribute the inspiration to God, but rejected the thought as a waste of time and a piece of hypocrisy.

'So what happens next, Patrick?' she asked.

His face clouded over. 'The superintendent thinks I should leave it alone – still thinks it's a suicide because of the pregnancy – says that we're understaffed at the moment – every man that can be spared from the barracks is out looking for this fellow who took a shot at the Bishop. There's a house-to-house search for him around here. Waste of time! He probably slipped through the crowd around the Cathedral and was most likely on the back of a motorbike as soon as the shot was fired and is now holed up in one of those deserted cottages in west Cork. Most of the Republicans are hiding out in these places.'

Probably, thought the Reverend Mother. Although it was more than seventy years since the Great Famine had devastated the countryside, many of the homes of those who had died or who had left the country had been kept in rough repair by neighbours who found the places useful to house a few lambing sheep or a cow and calf during the worst of the winter weather. It was rumoured that the Republicans had taken over lots of these, put tarpaulins beneath rotting thatch and nailed wood over broken windows. She thought again about the brilliantly clever little girl, the Eileen for whom she had hoped great things, hiding out in one of these places, and her heart moved in pity.

'I'm more interested in clearing up this murder business, Reverend Mother,' Patrick was saying. He looked at her appealingly and she responded to that appeal. Patrick, she thought, was worthy of her help. Every fibre in him wanted to solve this murder case – he knew that there was something badly wrong and his logical, analytical mind resented being fed the official line on this, but she, being world-wise and shrewd, also knew that it would be quite a feather in the cap of the young officer if he managed to solve a high-profile case like this and did achieve a conviction of murder against the person who had murdered a young lady like Angelina Fitzsimon. For various reasons, for his own sake, for assisting him on his struggle up from his background to his present position, but also because of events that had occurred long before he was born, the Reverend Mother had resolved to help him as much as she could possibly do.

'It's this business of the ticket to Liverpool, and the travel bag,' he said, without raising his head from his notebook.

'I know,' said the Reverend Mother reflectively. 'It doesn't seem to fit in with suicide.'

'She'd do either one or the other – plan to commit suicide, or plan to go to England; not both – and then there's the bruise on the throat. How does that fit with suicide? And what sane person commits suicide by jumping into a sewer when there is a river less than half a mile away?' He didn't wait for an answer to his questions, but snapped his notebook shut and put it and the pencil back into his pocket. 'I'd better get on,' he said. 'I'm supposed to be doing a house-to-house search.'

'I'll ring for Sister Bernadette,' she said.

'And, Sister, could you send a message to Dr Scher and say that I would be pleased to see him when convenient,' she said when the lay nun appeared. She saw Patrick's eyes go to her and she gave him a slight inclination of the head. Of course, officially she could not interfere, but there were more ways than one of obtaining information and she was not surprised when Dr Scher turned up half an hour later and didn't bother making pretence of visiting Sister Assumpta before asking to be conducted into her presence.

'I wanted to ask your advice, Doctor,' she said when the door had closed and she had listened for the sound of the soft slippers shuffling away, down the polished corridor. 'I wondered whether to pay a condolence call on the Fitzsimon family. They are, of course, relations of mine.'

She looked at him blandly and was pleased to see a spark of interest in his eyes.

'Yes, of course,' he said after a minute, 'the Newenham connection.'

It wasn't the linking up of dynasties that interested him, though. She was sure of that. All of these families in Blackrock and Montenotte were related – it was notorious that the merchant princes of Cork sought for mates for their children among their own class. No, Dr Scher was wondering why she had interested herself. She made herself wait and after a minute her patience was rewarded.

'Strange case,' he said meditatively.

She gave him a quick glance and then looked down at the table. She knew the effect of it. A flash from her green eyes, a lowering of the perfect oval of the face: it intrigued and stirred curiosity. Often she had used it to prise a substantial contribution to her school from a businessman and she was not surprised when Dr Scher said heartily: 'I'll drive you down there, Reverend Mother. Now, if you wish. I'm semi-retired these days – a few old patients, three hours a week at the university – the odd post-mortem for the civic guard, sure I don't know what to do with myself half the time.'

SEVEN

James Connolly, 1916:
'The worker is the slave of capitalist society: the female
worker is the slave of that slave.'

After leaving the convent grounds, Eileen departed the city on the back of a motorbike, her hair well tucked into her beret and her coat collar turned up against the wind and rain and her arms around the waist of a young former medical student called Eamonn. She giggled a little at the thought of what the Reverend Mother might say if she saw her as they sped through the wet streets and climbed the hill out of town, going south towards Ballinhassig. No conversation was possible with the wind driving in their faces and she contented herself with beginning to formulate an article for the *Cork Examiner*. No one quite understood whether the paper's owner had secret Republican sympathies or whether he just liked to sell his newspaper to all, no matter what their politics were, but he had proved surprisingly willing to take chatty articles and had paid well, so well that Eileen hoped she might get a new typewriter at some stage.

Ballinhassig village was about five miles south of Cork city. The Republican Party had been given the use of a farm just outside the village by an elderly farmer whose sons had all gone to America. John Cahill had been a belligerent Land Leaguer in his youth and had obtained this twenty-acre farm with the Gladstone distribution of the land. It had a far better house – a two-storey one – than his own cottage, but he had never liked it and had handed it over to the Republican Party and now it was used as a training camp.

It had everything that they wanted – it was located in the mountains, within the dip of a hill, remote and surrounded by trees. They had made a four-bedroom accommodation within it, cheerfully scrubbing, mending, painting and cleaning and chopping enough wood from fallen trees to keep it warm and dry, but best of all, the farm was on top of the half-a-mile-long tunnel of the Cork to Bandon railway and a vent came up in one of the fields. A steel ladder hung from top to bottom of the vent in one of the bends of the tunnel, and in the case of a raid everyone could disappear into the tunnel and hide in one of the alcoves there. Also, it had three different lanes leading to the farm so their comings and goings were not too noticeable. All in all, it was the perfect hide-out for an illegal organization.

'Listen,' said Eamonn as he switched off the engine of the motorbike when they stopped in the farmyard. There was a sudden sound of clicking that filled the silence.

'Eileen! Eamonn! We've got six new Lee-Enfield rifles!' A girl with very short hair came running out of the barn. 'Come and try them. We're going to have targets this afternoon when we get used to firing them dry. I've a bruise on my shoulder from it, but I'm getting the hang of it.'

'Prefer the pistol,' said Eileen, swinging her leg over the wheel. 'Anyway, I'd better report to the boss. You've cut your hair, Aoife.'

'I'll do yours if you like,' offered Aoife, and then with a glance at the house, 'Tom Hurley's here. He's waiting to see you.'

Tom Hurley was the chief of the three South Cork Units so Eileen went straight into the house. She had been composing a literary effort for the *Cork Examiner*, but the report that Tom would require from her would be something quick, simple and to the point. A man on the run wanted something different to a man sitting with his newspaper over his morning cup of tea. Eileen's lips twitched as she remembered the Reverend Mother talking to the top class about different styles of writing for different audiences and reading extracts from an eighteenth-century writer called Addison and then comparing them with the leading article in the *Irish Times*. Little did she know that one of her pupils would find her words so useful!

'Well,' said Tom Hurley when she entered the room. It was the first time that he had been here since they had painted this room and she looked around her critically, trying to see with his eyes the dazzlingly white limewash on the walls and the doors and windowsills painted a daring black. The thick curtains had been made from threadbare mouldy old blankets, found in the loft, boiled to a solid, felted consistency and then dyed a cosy dark shade of red and they looked great against the white walls. Eamonn had even cleaned a century's worth of soot from the iron crane in the big fireplace and the kettle that dangled from it was now only slightly blackened.

'Like it?' she asked with a nod around the room.

'No,' he said uncompromisingly. 'If there's a raid, they'll know that some prissy nancy boys from the city have been living here.'

'And girls,' murmured Eileen with a lift of her eyebrow. In fact, there were five girls and five young men in this unit. People like Tom Hurley laughed at the Cumann na mBan, the women's unit, saying that the girls were recruited to make the sandwiches, but the head of their unit, Constance Markievicz, was a better shot than any of the men. Eileen, Aoife, Máire, Kitty and Susie didn't allow any of this sort of talk in the house.

'One should take a pride in one's surroundings,' she said loftily. 'Remember what McDonagh said: "The fierce pulsation of resurgent pride that disclaims servitude . . ."'

'Come on, make your report,' he said irritably.

'Body of a girl – probably about eighteen – been strangled – no notice on her – nothing. It's nothing to do with us.' Eileen rattled out the words in a brisk, businesslike manner and removed her beret and gloves.

'How do you know that someone didn't move the notice before you arrived – the civic guard, for instance?'

'I spoke to the person who found the body; she used to teach me, Reverend Mother Aquinas of St Mary's of the Isle.'

He nodded at that. He was a Cork city man – had heard of the Reverend Mother.

'So, it's nothing to do with us, in your judgement?'

'No,' said Eileen decisively. 'Nothing to do with us. She was posh – wearing a satin dress.'

'Better get something out to the papers.' He nodded towards the typewriter sitting on a newly polished table by the window. 'We need to put our side of the story – did you see that long bit they published from the Bishop – seems to think that we are worse than Satan. Put something like: "The Irish Republican Army utterly deny any involvement in the murder of a young girl," etc., etc., etc. – you know what to write.'

'Yes, I do.' Eileen eyed him with disdain. 'And you don't think that the *Cork Examiner* is going to print stuff like that, do you? I'm going to make a good story out of it – a mystery, like Sherlock Holmes. "Who killed this beautiful young girl, dressed in a satin ball gown, a girl on the threshold of life? What scoundrel put his hands around that delicate neck . . .?"'

'All right, Dr Watson.' He got to his feet with a sudden grin. 'And get a few cows in here to shit in this prissy place, make it authentic, for God's sake,' he said over his shoulder.

EIGHT

St Thomas Aquinas:
Hominem unius libri timeo.
(I fear the man of one book.)

Bellamonte, the house in Blackrock, was just as the Reverend Mother had remembered it. Fifty-two years ago, she thought, as Dr Scher set the brake on his Humber in the covered-over space where, in the days of her youth, the carriages used to wait: it is fifty-two years since I have visited this house. It had been owned by Robert Fitzsimon, Edmund's elder brother, in those days. There had been a couple of sons, both killed in the first Boer War, a fortunate circumstance for Joseph who had inherited not only the Bordeaux property from Edmund but also the Cork property from Robert. It had been a great place for parties, she remembered. She and Lucy had always been invited, even while they were still at school, and she remembered both of them climbing carefully out of the carriage and balancing their crinolines in the draught that always blew up from the river. How many changes had there been to the world since that time!

Dismounting nimbly from the petrol-smelling car, she wasted no time in nostalgia, merely noting that everything was in excellent order, the white paintwork on the windows, the gleaming black paint, the polished chrome knocker and knob on the front door were perfect and that, although it was only March, already a gardener was hard at work in the hillside gardens which had been sculpted into six wide terraces, dropping one by one, down to the edge of the River Lee.

Inside was the same as it had been in her youth. White marble stairway, adorned with a crimson carpet, the same carpet, but no, it must be new, she thought – no carpet could have lasted over fifty years and still shimmer under the gas lamps with quite such an opulent gleam. She could have sworn, though, that there had been a crimson carpet there when she had been eighteen years old. They were shown into the library – and the serried ranks of Tennyson, Wordsworth, Walter Scott, Dickens and Thackeray, all bound in red leather and edged in gold, were just the same – all still in perfect order, as though they had not been touched since the day when they were delivered to add a touch of colour to the north-facing room. She had teased Edmund Fitzsimon about them, she remembered, once when he had been staying there with his brother, had threatened to set him an examination on their contents – he had been very tolerant of her schoolgirl sense of mischief. A nice man, she thought – very good to his wife, Angela, very understanding of her sorrow when she failed to conceive a child.

Just standing here in the library brought him back vividly to her – and yet he had been dead for over twenty years, dead and left his entire retail empire to Joseph.

The man who entered a few minutes later was different, though. Edmund Fitzsimon had been lean and tall, dark-haired, slightly aristocratic-looking – fitting in well with the landed gentry to whom he sold his wines, spices and teas. This man, Joseph he had been named, had a different look – short, stocky, intensely blue-eyed – unlike the almost navy colour of most blue-eyed, white-skinned Irish people, this man had eyes that were china-blue in shade and hair that was not of the usual light golden red, but was still, despite his age and a sweep of silver over the forehead and just above the ears, as richly red-brown as the hue of a horse chestnut. It should have been a shock to see him, but oddly she was now more concerned with the fate of the girl, Angelina. What had happened to that girl, she asked herself? And why was her father not looking more concerned, not looking more devastated?

And, of course, this was where the chestnut hair and china-blue eyes had come from – and perhaps explained her feelings of recognition when she had looked down into the dead girl's face, before she had noted the expensive gown and shoes.

And yet, no young girl closely resembles a middle-aged man with an aggressively bristling moustache and heavy bags of flesh beneath his slightly protruding eyes. He must be, she calculated, about fifty-three now. He had married well, Joseph Fitzsimon, she had heard that. He had wed a wife, one of the Woodford family, with a large dowry, who had presented him with two children within years of the wedding. An unfortunate marriage, though, in other respects.

Quickly the Reverend Mother banished these thoughts and rose to her feet holding out her hand. Dr Scher had made the introductions well and Joseph seemed flattered by her visit.

'We haven't met before,' he said pressing her hand slightly before relinquishing it, 'but I take it very kindly that you have gone to the trouble of coming to call on us. I understand that it was you who found my poor daughter.'

He hadn't shown much signs of sorrow about that poor daughter, according to Patrick and now she found herself scrutinizing him with interest. It was true that she had, in the past, avoided encounter with this man. Somehow, in her gathering of subscriptions for her various projects, she had always skipped the offices of Joseph Fitzsimon, slightly despising herself for cowardice, but at the same time knowing that anything which brought the past back and deflected her from her concentration on her chosen way of life would only serve to weaken her and make her mission less of a triumph.

'And your son?' she queried. 'How is he? This must have been a terrible shock for him, also?'

She did not mention the girl's mother. All of Cork, she understood, knew that she was in the lunatic asylum across the river, rumoured to be completely mad. How could this man have condemned his wife to eternal imprisonment with no family face to watch over her?

'I remember this library,' she said in a friendly way. 'It looks just as it was when I used to visit here, over fifty years ago.'

'Ah . . . yes,' he said, his gaze passing over the well-dusted rows of books with the appearance of one who did not know or care for them. St Thomas Aquinas, she knew, was reputed to say that he feared the man who had just one book, and she understood what he meant about the narrowness of outlook that could give. However, she thought, perhaps a man with one well-loved book might be a more rounded individual than the man who possessed hundreds and never opened any of them.

'Come into the drawing room,' he invited expansively. 'We are just having tea. Your colleague, Professor Lambert, is here, Dr Scher. He came kindly to sympathize with us when he heard the terrible news.'

The drawing room, also, was as she remembered it. Just as cosy as ever. Well-stuffed couches, and four armchairs – each with a padded foot-rest in front of it – all expensively upholstered, covered in red velvet to match the curtains that hung on the tall windows and in front of the door to the hall and ranged in a line in front of the fireplace. She remembered that marble fireplace, too. It was still as immaculately clean as she had always noted it to be – and a coal fire was glowing in its grate, sending out its heat to banish the cold and chill of this March day with its leaping flames reflected in the white stone.

For a moment she thought that the room was empty and then saw that one tall-backed chair was occupied by a figure who rose to greet them, brushing aside Joseph's effort to introduce him.

'The Reverend Mother and I are old friends,' he boomed in that voice which always seemed to be too big for his frame. He was a smallish man, rather overweight, and every time that she met him she forced herself to gaze straight into his eyes. Too many people looked away when confronted by the terrible port-wine stain that covered more than half his face and twisted the mouth out of shape. They met at various charitable committees and she thought him far more sincere and more dedicated than most who attended those affairs often in a spirit of condescension and for the sake of seeing their names on the newspaper. Professor Lambert was an immensely benevolent man and did great work for the St Vincent de Paul Society, distributing food, clothes and coal for fires among the poor of the city. It was rumoured that he had spent most of his inherited wealth and of his salary from the university on his charities.

'Ah, Lambert,' said Dr Scher, not too pleased, she noted with amusement, to have another medical man already in position and, judging by the few scraps of pink-iced cake on the silver tray, to have already consumed much of the afternoon tea provided.

When Joseph had installed the Reverend Mother in the chair

by the fire and went to fetch his son and to order fresh supplies of tea, Professor Lambert seated himself beside her, and she knew that he would, in the oblique Cork way, explain his presence in this house of mourning.

'A terrible business,' he said in a hushed voice and she agreed, murmuring the conventional, 'May God have mercy on her soul.'

'You found her, I heard,' he said, and added, 'Slipped into the river, I believe,' but he didn't appear to want an answer to this and went on, 'I still can't believe it. I saw her last night, you know – saw her at the Merchants' Ball.'

The Reverend Mother's interest was immediately engaged. She breathed a quick prayer that Joseph Fitzsimon would take his time about fetching his son and asked with an appearance of conventional politeness, 'How was she, Professor?'

'Seemed in good spirits,' he said; 'not that I could hear much that she said. Terribly loud band – that new-fashioned jazz – can't stand it – would split your eardrums.'

'How did she look?' Dr Scher moved away from the silver tray and came to join them. 'Did she look depressed in any way, Cyril?'

Depressed? If the man were to infer from Dr Scher's words that Angelina could have committed suicide, well, that didn't matter, thought the Reverend Mother. The essential was to get to the truth and now that Sergeant Patrick Cashman had been told by the superintendent to shelve the case for the moment, then she, Reverend Mother Aquinas, owed it to the dead girl to find out as much as possible about her last hours.

'I didn't notice anything much,' said the professor reflectively. 'Mind you, people will tell you that it's hard to get a word in when I start talking.' He laughed good-naturedly. He seemed unself-conscious, but that disfigurement must have given him a very unhappy childhood. She began to feel rather sorry for him and allowed him to fetch her tea, much to the annoyance of Dr Scher. He re-seated himself beside her and resumed his memories of Angelina's last night on earth.

'What was she like – I never met her,' explained the Reverend Mother, inviting him to expand.

'Angelina was a quiet, reserved sort of girl,' he said and his voice was warm with sympathy. 'She was never one who said too much, you know. And of course it was very, very noisy, there. Drums, saxophones, trombones and all sorts of discordant musical instruments. No,' he reflected, 'I can't remember anything that she said, that I actually heard . . . It was only when I received the terrible news that I thought back and I realized that she was very quiet that night; I could hardly coax a word out of her. I handed her over to one of my young students, nice lad, one of the Spiller family; I thought to myself that I was getting a bit old for the dancing game so I went upstairs and joined her father at pre-dinner drinks at his table and then moved on to one of my colleagues' tables, spread my company around, didn't go downstairs again until later on!' He smiled slightly at the memory of the convivial evening and then hurriedly re-arranged his face to the decorous lines of sorrow.

'Terrible, terrible thing,' he said.

'What was she like, as a person, I mean?' asked the Reverend Mother, sipping her tea and feeling impatient with the way most men seemed to repeat themselves.

'A nice girl,' he said mechanically and then with great sincerity, 'She was a very nice girl, Angelina Fitzsimon, a very good girl, Reverend Mother. You would have liked her, would have approved of her. Most girls of her age, these days, think of nothing but dancing and parties, but she put a lot of her time, and her money too, into the St Vincent de Paul. Worked in our shop in the Grand Parade, made up bundles of clothes for poor families . . . Her father wouldn't allow visiting their houses, of course, but she gave up two days a week to the shop and lots of poor women used to come in and she'd always find something for them – was really nice to them, too – she'd say things like – "I think this would suit you – you have such lovely blue eyes" – just as if she was a shop assistant, not someone doling out charity. I appreciated that. Brought in bags of her own out-worn clothes, and persuaded lots of her friends to do the same.'

Bags of clothes, thought the Reverend Mother, her mind going to that well-worn leather bag, with the slightly dowdy clothes inside it that Patrick had shown her. Angelina had checked it into the cloakroom at the Imperial Hotel – but why? And the ticket to Liverpool – the father had thought that the girl was eloping, but, if so, why not bring her best clothes, her silver hairbrushes, not the cheap, brand-new toiletries that had been in the oilskin bag.

She was still pondering this when Joseph Fitzsimon came through the door abruptly, almost dragging his son behind him. Both looked angry. There was a high flush in the two faces that were so alike. He muttered something when introduced to the Reverend Mother and she replied, giving him a gracious smile.

And yet, while she was expressing conventional phrases of sympathy and regret, she was thinking hard. She had seen that face before – not a masculine face – a face like Angelina's, a face with smooth white skin, blue eyes and chestnut hair – a face that was alive, not frozen and swollen into a death-mask. And yet she knew very few young ladies of the monied merchant princes' class, so it should have been easy for her to have identified it. Her troubled mind just could not recollect where she had seen it and this bothered her. Many of the elderly sisters in the convent during her reign had lost their memories and dwindled from occasional forgetfulness into senility. In no way did she want this to happen to her. She frowned slightly and saw the young man's startled eyes upon her. There was an odd guilty look about him, like a child caught out in a lie.

She would ask no questions, she decided. That would be straying beyond her role as conventional visitor. Instead she turned the conversation to her recollections of the house fifty years previously, to the dinner parties that she had attended.

'You must come and look over it,' said Joseph, instantly seizing a way of entertaining his guest while waiting for fresh tea. 'Cyril, I'll leave you to look after Dr Scher. Gerald, see what's happening about the tea, won't you? Will you come with me, Reverend Mother?'

Patiently he showed her the dining room, the library and the study and then led the way up the stairs towards the first-floor lobby.

'I remember the lobby,' she said with a smile. 'We used to

leave our cloaks there.' She laughed a little. 'That was over fifty years ago,' she said and was pleased to hear that there was no nostalgia, just a note of triumph in her voice. What a useless life she and Lucy had been leading then, she thought, looking back. Useless, stupid and pointless, when it came down to it. Competing with each other to ensnare some rich young man. What she had made of her life after that had been so much more worthwhile, so much more interesting. The decision to enter the convent had been the right one for her. And as for Lucy, had she made the right decision? Probably, she thought.

'You'll be surprised to see it now,' said Joseph with smile over his shoulder as she marched up the stairs behind him, disdaining the use of the handrail on the balustrade, still painted a pristine white – and she recollected the colour from fifty years ago. This was a house where little changed, where a carpet, when slightly worn, was replaced by one of the same colour and texture.

The lobby itself bore the same colours of red and white – red carpet again, red cushions on the pair of long slender sofas that were placed in the exact centre and the walls were painted white. Painted white as always, but now, fifty years later the colour hardly showed with the lines and lines of framed photographs, their shades of pale cream and pale brown outlined by the black frames. Her host took her to the early ones – none of her – she remembered none being taken at that house – and the endless posing and elaborately screened cameras of that era made the whole process tedious and memorable. There were some that she recognized though – Edmund Fitzsimon, his wife Angela, both of them – and neither too young – there they were, gazing steadily and sadly into the lens – even one of their cousin, Thomas Copinger. Odd to see them, she thought. Odd to see those people without life or colour – hair, eyes, all just distinguished by shades of dark and light – preserved for prosperity in pale shades of light brown – all pictures of people who were now in the grave.

'Here are some photographs taken of her recently,' said Mr Fitzsimon taking down a few of the framed photographs. He avoided using his daughter's name, noted the Reverend Mother, and he took his time to select that few. None showed an animated face; the girl stared steadily, and, she thought, almost fearfully, at the camera, posing with a tennis racket, holding a bunch of flowers, leafing through some music at a pianoforte, standing between her brother and her father, clipping rose bushes. Joseph Fitzsimon unhooked this one and handed it to her. A sad-looking girl, she thought, and then spotted a rather more cheerful one of the same girl, much younger and dressed in a school uniform.

'So Angelina went to school at the Ursuline Convent, did she?' she asked, recognizing the habit of the nun in the background. The Ursuline nuns had a school for young ladies down at the end of Blackrock quite near to the castle which overlooked the spot where the River Lee entered into the waters of Cork Harbour. She thought that she recognized the uniform. It was an expensive school – she had gone there herself and remembered that the fees were thirty guineas a term in the middle of the reign of Queen Victoria.

'Yes, that's her in her school uniform. She liked school.' There was a hint of regret in his voice, a trace of nostalgia, perhaps for the days when Angelina had been young and biddable.

'And who is this,' she said, looking at another spot on the wall and seeing the same well-shaped face and slender neck, the same air of melancholy, all bearing a great resemblance to the profile of the girl Angelina, though the face was half-shaded by a splendid hat.

Joseph Fitzsimon hesitated for a moment. 'That is not my daughter; it's her mother, my wife,' he said quietly. 'Taken a long time ago. She, she was not well, even then.'

An early photograph of Mrs Fitzsimon, thought the Reverend Mother. There were a few later ones further along on the line where she seemed to have aged and to look even more apprehensive. Quite a few also with different types of large feathered hats on one side of her head, or the other, the wide brim shadowing her face. In the flesh, Angelina was probably not particularly like her mother, they probably would not have shared the same distinctive colouring of chestnut hair and bright blue eyes, but in a monochrome photograph shape of feature and the underlying bone structure brought out a strong resemblance between daughter and mother.

Professor Lambert was in the hallway when they came down and took his leave with a cordial shake of the hand to both. When they re-entered the drawing-room there was no sign of Gerald Fitzsimon, but Dr Scher, tea tray at his side, was cosily ensconced in one of the vast padded armchairs in front of the fire. The Reverend Mother eyed him affectionately. Dr Scher always reminded her slightly of one of those comfortable-looking, well-rounded teddy bears that decorated the windows of Dowden's shop in Patrick Street at Christmas time. She remained standing, however. The time for a visit of condolence had elapsed; there would be others calling to the house – drawn there by a mixture of compassion and curiosity. She declined the tea and the cake decisively and was allowed to depart. The advantage of her cloth was its reputation for austerity – it saved her from much unnecessary tea-drinking and cake-eating.

'So what did you make of Gerald Fitzsimon?' she asked as they drove off.

'He only stayed a few minutes in the room after you left,' he said readily, but he glanced at her sideways and his brown eyes had a touch of mischief in them.

'So what did Professor Lambert say about him?' She knew him well enough to know that he would have prised information from his colleague. Few could resist Dr Scher's genial charm.

He jerked the steering wheel to avoid a dignified cat that stalked across the road and did not reply for a moment. When she looked at him she could see a struggle going on across his face. She smiled slightly to herself as she guessed that he would soon justify his conscience by telling himself that she was a safe repository for secrets. And he would be right. Dr Scher had given her many a piece of juicy gossip, of information about the great and the good of the city and she had inclined her head, made no comment and kept the matter to herself. In fact, she thought now, the older she got the less she said. She waited calmly, watching how he struggled with the gear lever and thinking that she might make a better driver than he was. What a great thing it would be to have a car for her community. All this reliance on taxis and on friends! A car would give her such liberty.

'Well, you'll never guess, but he was telling me that young Fitzsimon is not a model student by any means. In fact, he was the ringleader in that scandal about medical students stealing ether from the hospital. The students were all having wild parties and getting drunk on the stuff, bringing in girls, too.' Dr Scher's resistance had crumbled, as she knew that it would. 'And,' he added with a quick glance at her, 'there was a break-in at the bursar's office, just after the fees were taken in last autumn, and it was rumoured, according to Lambert, that Gerald was responsible and that Joseph, the father, paid up in order to save the police being dragged into it. Lambert thinks that he'll never get around to qualifying; he'll be on his father's hands for the rest of his life,' he added. Then he swung the wheel wildly and turned into the marina and spent a few minutes re-aligning his car.

I'm sure that I could do that better, thought the Reverend Mother, but long years of keeping her thoughts to herself made her sit calmly until he straightened all of his wheels and said with a relish unimpaired by his struggles, 'But, of course, he won't need to qualify, now, will he? His father has a reputation of being a bit tight with the money, but, as it turned out, Gerald will get the grandmother's money.'

'Grandmother?' queried the Reverend Mother.

'That's right.' Dr Scher nodded, and his chubby profile was alive with the interest of passing on a piece of gossip. 'Old Mrs Woodford, Gerald and Angelina's grandmother – she was even richer than I thought. Lambert was telling me. He got it from Curwen the solicitor. You'll never guess,' he went on eagerly, 'but she left thirty thousand pounds. I'd never have thought that she was as rich as that. And all her money to the girl. She left it to the girl not to the brother, apparently on condition that she did not marry before she was twenty-one – but, of course, now . . . now that the girl is dead, well, Gerald Fitzsimon is a very rich young man.'

He looked across at his passenger and the Reverend Mother resisted the impulse to snap: *Keep your eyes on the road!* It was amazing what indiscreet gossips these men were, she thought. However, she was honest with herself enough to know that she had not the slightest notion of checking him or of refusing to listen to his revelations. She agreed with Patrick. Angelina Fitzsimon's body, with its bruised throat, had the look of a murder victim, even if the eventual cause of death was drowning. No one, she thought, would deliberately go down to a terrible death through a manhole into the sewers.

And the ticket for the ferry to Liverpool, the ten-pound note, the carefully packed bag, full of clothing, and toilet articles, all of these seemed to point to flight, rather than to suicide.

She made no remark, therefore, about professional discretion and waited patiently while Dr Scher, with great gusto, indulged in a horn-blowing contest against a humble Ford that had been innocently travelling on its own side of the road.

'That will shake up his liver,' he said gleefully. 'That's the latest medical theory, you know, Reverend Mother! A shock a day and you will live for ever.'

The Reverend Mother bit back a smile, feeling that he should not be encouraged in his outrageousness.

'So Mrs Woodford was as rich as that, was she?' she remarked, steering him back on track, steering his mind, anyway, she thought as she watched his erratic progress on the road. 'And Angelina knew of the condition that she could not marry before the age of twenty-one, did she?'

'That's right. Apparently, the girl was told of the condition by the old lady herself in the presence of her solicitor. And she said that suited her,' added Dr Scher, after a moment of waiting for a reaction. 'Shows that she had no notion of getting married in a hurry,' he added.

'But now that Angelina is dead the money goes to her brother, Gerald, is that right?'

'All thirty thousand pounds of it,' confirmed Dr Scher. 'And when you think that a car like my Humber only costs about four hundred pounds – well, that young man is going to be in the clover for the rest of his life.'

NINE

St Thomas Aquinas:
. . . *oportet in intellectualibus non deduci ad imagination.*
(. . . it is important when dealing with matters of the
intellect not to be led away by the imagination.)

Patrick was uncomfortable and apologetic when he arrived at the convent next morning. Sister Bernadette, knowing by instinct that this matter was of deep interest to the Reverend Mother, ushered him into her study without checking for permission, and then withdrew without any of the usual offers of cups of tea. Patrick's face was tense, but his gaze was direct.

'I'm sorry that you have to be involved in this matter, Reverend Mother,' he said opening the conversation in an unusually blunt fashion.

'What's wrong?' she asked.

'It's the inquest,' he explained. 'I'm afraid that the superintendent thinks that you should attend since you found the body. He's a Protestant,' he added by way of explanation and the Reverend Mother bit back a smile.

The superintendent was a member of the old Royal Irish Constabulary who had been lucky enough to retain his job when the new nationalist civic guards were formed. There would be a certain amount of muttering at his subjecting someone like the Reverend Mother to the indignity of giving evidence in court. Little did Patrick know that she would have been furious if she had not been given this opportunity! The very idea that this girl's death was going to be brushed aside as a suicide, despite the bruise on the throat, despite the ether in the stomach, annoyed her intensely and made her determined to do her best to influence the jury. It would, she thought, be a new experience and she had no notion of asking the Bishop for permission. If the question ever arose she would declare very positively she understood that the Bishop had been incapacitated by the wound on his arm. In fact, she doubted whether any would venture to challenge her judgement.

'Very good, Patrick,' she said quietly. 'What time?'

'The inquest is set for Monday morning at eleven, Reverend Mother. We'll send a car for you.'

'No,' she said immediately. 'Dr Scher will be going and I'm sure that he will be happy to take me. I'll send a message to him and if you don't hear from me then you will know that the matter is settled.' She looked at him for a moment and then said, 'And what if the verdict of suicide is not returned?'

He returned her look steadily. 'Then perhaps I'll be allowed to get properly to work on the case,' he said and she could see from the swiftness of his response how frustrated he had been by the orders to cease his investigations. She wondered how to drop a hint about the strange will made by the wealthy Mrs Woodford and decided that this could wait until after the inquest. In the meantime she would turn the matter of Gerald Fitzsimon over in her mind. He had the means of procuring ether – though she was puzzled as to the reason why that had been found in the girl's stomach – and he had been present at the Merchants' Ball at the Imperial Hotel and he had a powerful incentive to kill his sister if it meant that he would inherit a large legacy from his deceased grandmother.

'What about the man who was said to have shot the Bishop?' she asked cautiously as Patrick rose to his feet with a preoccupied air.

'Not a sign,' he said and he spoke with indifference. She hoped that he was sensible enough not to have displayed the same lack of interest in front of the superintendent, who might be a Protestant, but who would be well aware that the Bishop of Cork was an important personage and that if the Republican Party could be seen to be able to take a pot shot of him in public, then it would undermine the authority of the civic guards force in the city. However, she said nothing but allowed him to depart about his business. She had faith in his ability and in his common sense.

Then she sat down at her desk to write a quick note to

Dr Scher before going into the senior classroom to give her daily lesson in English literature to the eldest girls of the school.

She had meant to set them a test on a passage of *Jane Eyre*, which they had been studying, but she sensed that they were restless – their houses had been visited and they had been questioned. This had caused a nervous tension that was almost palpable in the room. It would be dangerous to antagonize the civic guards – no family wanted that – but at the same time they had no illusions about retaliation shootings if any information was divulged – these happened all the time – between anti-treaty people, pro-treaty people, Republicans and Free-Staters. Cork was a dangerous place.

In any case, *Jane Eyre* was not proving a success. Charlotte Brontë had put her heart and soul into this quite autobiographical work, but Jane's problems with her aunt, the bullying from her boy-cousin and the burned porridge at her boarding school did not appear too serious to girls like these who had spent their teen years avoiding cross-fire in the streets and facing days when there was often literally no food in the bare rooms that they inhabited with their mothers and their numerous siblings.

On an impulse she picked from the shelf *Wuthering Heights*, bestowed on them by Lucy, and began to read this piece of Gothic horror aloud as best she could and to her surprise the classroom was very still and attentive. The young eyes were interested and there was a low buzz of comments when she put the book away just as the bell had gone for the end of the school day.

It was then that Nellie O'Sullivan put up her hand. 'Please, Reverend Mother,' she said politely, 'you know the way the man in the story found the little boy Heathcliff in Liverpool, well, my sister Mary went to Liverpool this week.'

'Did she, Nellie? That's exciting news. Well, I'm so pleased to hear that.' She managed to keep the note of surprise out of her voice. Ever since she had left school about four years ago, Mary O'Sullivan, the Reverend Mother had heard, had been hanging around the streets, doing what, she didn't like to imagine. Though she couldn't begin to surmise how either the girl, or her unfortunate mother, burdened with the care of ten other children, had found money for the fare, she was delighted to think that Mary had been put in the way of earning an honest living. She had been a striking-looking girl, quite different in appearance to Nellie – quite different with her . . .

And then the Reverend Mother stared straight ahead, her eyes on the girls filing decorously out of the classroom. She didn't see them, however. In her mind was the picture of the dead girl, Angelina Fitzsimon, lying on the stretcher, china-blue eyes open to the sky, and chestnut curls of hair over her shoulders.

And now she knew why the sight had been a familiar one.

She stood for a moment in deep thought, ideas flashing through her imagination and then made up her mind.

'I think I'll pay a visit to Mrs O'Leary,' she said to Sister Mary Immaculate, who was harassing some of the girls who lingered, chattering, on the doorstep. Thomas Aquinas had warned about the dangers of allowing the imagination to seduce the intellect, but often, she found, an imaginative leap was the first step to uncovering a truth.

'Oh, she'd love that. Poor thing, she's confined to a wheel-chair these days.' Sister Mary Immaculate was enthusiastic about this notion. When the Reverend Mother was out, she was in command and she enjoyed that very much.

Mrs O'Leary lived in Bishop's Street, only about a five-minute walk from the convent. In her working life she had been the chief maker of hats for Dowden's, the most expensive shop in Cork, and she had been very generous with giving left-over pieces of hat-making material for the sewing class in the convent school. The Reverend Mother's conscience reproached her that she had not been to see her more often. For such an active, gossipy woman this life, confined to a wheelchair and to the four walls of her sitting room, would prove quite a penance.

The flood waters had receded for the moment, she noticed, as she stepped out of the garden gate on the pavement. Parts of the roads still had large puddles and the drains bubbled ominously, but she was able to walk dry-footed until she reached Mrs O'Leary's house, with its neat lace curtains, well-painted front door and shining knocker. Mrs O'Leary was reputed to have put quite a bit of money away during her long years of employment and her three sons in America were always sending letters stuffed with dollars, according to Sister Bernadette, who was a great friend of the postman.

The door was opened to her by Catty Cotter, a past pupil; a bright girl, thought the Reverend Mother regretfully. Perhaps if only she might have had the chance to go to Liverpool . . .

And then she remembered the problem about Angelina Fitzsimon, and her thoughts about Mary O'Sullivan, and decided to deal with one matter at a time. At least the house here was warm and shining with cleanliness and there was a smell of savoury cooking in the background. Catty Cotter 'lived in', as they said, boarded in the house by night and worked there by day, with only one half-day a week in which to amuse herself and to visit her family. However, she was surely much better off spending her days and nights here than in the room where her mother lived, or on the streets and quays of the city, like some of her contemporaries.

The Reverend Mother thought that there was something to be said for domestic service in a caring home to form a bridge between the children's birthplace and their ultimate destination in England or in America.

'You're looking well, Catty,' she said with approbation, noting the neat apron, the clean dress and the washed hair.

'Thank you, Reverend Mother.' Catty ushered her into the parlour, evoking cries of delight from Mrs O'Leary and then whispered commands to Catty. The Reverend Mother sat down by the fire and arranged her thoughts until Catty brought in the inevitable pot of tea and slices of cake and then disappeared back into the kitchen.

'God bless you, Reverend Mother, how are you, at all? I heard you had a terrible shock. Found a girl, a dead girl.' Mrs O'Leary gulped down some of the bitterly strong tea and looked excitedly across at her visitor.

'That's right,' said the Reverend Mother and then, very quickly, before she could be sidetracked, 'The police say that she was one of the Fitzsimons – you know the family – the Fitzsimons of Blackrock.'

'Of course I do, indeed. Didn't I make hats for her, for Mrs Fitzsimon, God love her?'

The Reverend Mother nodded. 'I thought it was probably you. I saw lots of pictures of her when I was down at their place in Blackrock. I saw the hats.'

'Bellamonte,' said Mrs O'Leary meditatively. 'Bellamonte, that's the name of the house, wasn't it? Many a hat box I sent out to that place. In an asylum now, poor thing, did you know that, Reverend Mother?'

'I did, indeed.' The Reverend Mother allowed a pause to elapse. She had to fight a small battle with her lifelong custom of discretion, but the need for information was paramount in her mind at the moment. 'I wonder what happened to her,' she said as airily as she could manage the words.

'What drove her mad, you mean?' retorted Mrs O'Leary. Her legs might be crippled with arthritis, but her tongue was as quick as ever. 'Well, I can tell you that, Reverend Mother, and not a word of a lie – he drove her to it – that husband of hers. Nasty he was, I can tell you that. Did you notice the kind of hats that they were, at all, Reverend Mother?'

'It was the first thing that I noticed,' said the Reverend Mother, repressing the sudden desire to add: *and not a word of a lie*.

She need say little, she thought; Mrs O'Leary was in full flow.

'Well you'll have noticed that she had hats to go on the left side of her face and hats to go on the right side of her face.' Mrs O'Leary didn't wait for any corroboration but swept on. 'And I can tell you, Reverend Mother, that's very unusual. Most people – you mightn't know this, of course, being a nun and all that, but I can tell you, and it's God's own truth, everyone has one profile that's better than the other. But she wouldn't have it, Mrs Fitzsimon, and do you know why?' Automatically she cast a glance at the door, but Catty was singing tunefully in the kitchen to the busy sound of a scrubbing brush and so she finished off dramatically: 'It was *him*, the husband, that Mr Fitzsimon, he was hitting her. Nearly always had a bruise, on one cheek or on the other; the poor thing was embarrassed and ashamed and was trying to hide them. I had to make these big hats, with feathers, that would hide one side of her face and not let the world know what was happening to her. Poor thing she was ashamed – ashamed, I tell you. Ashamed! I'd shame him, if I had him, him with all his money! I'd cry it from the roof tops!'

The Reverend Mother felt that she should put in something here – something like: *I don't believe it!* But she couldn't quite bring herself to break her lifetime of reticence. Luckily Mrs O'Leary was a star performer and needed no supporting act.

'And I'll tell you something else about that fine gentleman,' she hissed, the sing-song Cork accent rising higher as her story unfolded. 'Low he was, and that's a fact. Low, I tell you . . . Down the quays, he'd be. He'd go with any of them girls, he would. Seen him myself coming out one of the houses in Sawmill Street. Furtive-like. And him with such a nice little wife. Should have been ashamed of himself. And his uncle a bishop!'

TEN

St Thomas Aquinas:
Umbram fugat veritas, noctem lux eliminat.
(Truth eliminates the darkness of the night.)

D r Scher turned up early for the journey between the convent of St Mary's of the Isle and the courthouse. The Reverend Mother was already waiting for him, wearing her best cloak. Wimple and bib were snowy white and stiffly starched and Sister Bernadette fussed around her with a clothes brush, removing a few microscopic fibres or traces of dust. The whole convent was pleasantly excited at the prospect of the Reverend Mother's appearance in the court-house and various nuns popped their heads out of classrooms as she passed down the corridor, wishing her luck and praying over her as if she had been about to join an expedition to Mount Everest.

'You're looking very smart,' she said graciously to Dr Scher as he held open the passenger door of the car. Usually he wore a grey suit, plentifully sprinkled with cigarette ash and shiny at elbow and knee, but today he was resplendent in a navy pin-stripe which looked shiningly new.

'I'm hoping that splendour of my apparel will distract from the hesitancy of my evidence,' he said once he had cranked up the car and taken his place beside her.

'Why will your evidence be hesitant?' she asked, watching how he double-declutched and wondering whether she was too old to learn to drive. She could just imagine how a car would be very useful to the community. Perhaps the new Ford factory on the marina would like to donate one. She began to imagine a few newspaper headlines. 'Firm donates . . . Henry Ford remembers the birthplace of his grandfather.'

'Because I'm a bloody old fool and past my best.' He suddenly shot the words out, distracting her from her composition efforts. And then he added a perfunctory, 'Sorry.'

She considered his profile – he didn't look particularly worried, she thought, but then chubby faces like his seemed to naturally fall into lines of contentment.

'What's bothering you?' she asked.

'The age,' he said explosively and punctuated his words with a musical toot-toot on his horn. A messenger boy on a heavy bike, who had just darted out in front of the Humber, stuck out a tongue at him and Dr Scher chuckled, his good humour restored. 'Not my own age – the girl's.'

'You thought that she was younger, when you examined her, that's right, isn't it?' she said as he swung the wheel of the car to direct it over South Main Street. 'I remember what you said.'

'I thought she was about seventeen when I examined the body and it turns out that she was almost twenty-one,' he said.

The Reverend Mother said no more, though she noted his hesitation. South Main Street was full of shoppers, shooting from one side of the narrow street to the other in their search for bargains to fill their baskets, and she had no wish to distract him from his driving. She thought about what he said, though. There had been a note of conviction in his voice and she knew him, by experience and by reputation, to be a clever man. She sat without speaking until they reached what she still thought of as Great George Street but which had recently, and rather quaintly, in this republican city, been renamed Washington Street to shift the Georgian emphasis from England to America. The river was rising again, she noticed. The water was already inches deep in the gutters and the wide street was beginning to disappear under it. The playwright John Fletcher had said something about the world being a *city full of straying streets*, and the odd expression had reminded her of Cork and its disappearing roadways when she had first read it over fifty years ago.

Dr Scher turned down the side street beside the courthouse and parked his car rather askew. He still wore a puzzled frown on his face. He took his round silver watch from his waistcoat pocket.

'We're early,' he said. 'Let's sit here for a while. It's freezing in there. Are you warm enough, Reverend Mother, there's a rug in the back. I can put it over your knees.'

'I'm very warm, thanks to that hot bottle at my feet,' she said, feeling sorry that she had not expressed her gratitude for his consideration before now. Her mind, however, was focused on the dead girl and Dr Scher's explosion had drawn another shadow away from the light of the truth.

'Tell me why you thought that she was only seventeen,' she said, looking directly at him. The rain had begun to fall again and the car was like a small warm room in which they could talk with complete privacy.

He hesitated for a moment, not looking back at her, but looking straight ahead of him. He had switched off the engine and the car was very quiet – as quiet and as private as a confessional box, she thought. Rather inappropriately, she acknowledged, with a half-smile to herself, as she waited for his answer.

She wondered whether he would cover up his involuntary exclamation with one of his usual self-deprecating jokes, but when he spoke it was with a simple directness which was a quality that she had always valued in him.

'I must have made a mistake,' he said. 'The father must know the age of his own daughter. But . . .' Now he looked her full in the face and continued quickly. 'But I couldn't have, I just couldn't – not unless I'm going mad or senile, or something. It was the clavicle – I can see it now in my mind's eye – it's all wrong – it has to be wrong – the clavicle wasn't properly connected – it's the last bone in the human body to be joined up.'

'The clavicle?' queried the Reverend Mother.

'The collarbone, Reverend Mother, the collarbone!' he said as impatiently as though she were one of his students. 'Sorry,' he said quickly, turning to face her. 'Children's bones aren't joined, you see – they have cartilage between the bones – gradually as they grow older the bones connect up and the cartilage disappears. The clavicle is the last one, but a girl's clavicle should definitely have joined by the time she is nineteen or twenty – Angelina Fitzsimon, according to her father, was coming up to twenty-one; she was, wasn't she?'

'So Mr Fitzsimon said.'

'And there is not the slightest chance that he lied – no reason for him to lie. And she was due to inherit her grandmother's money when she reached twenty-one – in a few months' time. Lambert mentioned that when we talked together when we were at the house and he knew her well from her work with the St Vincent de Paul Society, so he told me. He knew all about her, about the grandmother's will – and about the age of inheritance. So I must have made a mistake,' he added, when she said nothing.

The Reverend Mother looked at him. The car windows had completely steamed up by now, but the gas lamp beside the courthouse shed a faint, watery light into the interior of the car.

'Talk me through the post-mortem,' she commanded. 'Imagine that I am one of your students.' Women were now able to study medicine, she thought, and was pleased that times had changed like that, but regretful that she had not had the chance. She would, she thought, have made a good doctor. She esteemed it a higher skill than that of a teacher and of an organizer – and she had to tell herself that these days she was more of an organizer than a teacher. Still, she could not regret her decision to enter the convent; the life had suited her, had given her an arena for her talents, had brought a deep sense of satisfaction and of fulfilment with it.

And then she switched her mind rapidly from the past possibilities and concentrated on the present.

'Just describe her,' she said quietly.

She could see by the dim light that he had shut his eyes and the childishness of the gesture brought out a feeling of affection for him. He was a gossip and could be indiscreet, annoyed her slightly sometimes by his inveterate habit of making silly jokes, but she was fond of him and she trusted him and now listened with attention.

'The body of a girl, aged approximately seventeen,' he began, still with his eyes, tightly shut. 'She showed signs of malnutrition in the bone structure of the wrists, in the slightly bowed bones of the legs and in the teeth, which were pitted and stained. The hair was clean – bore traces of soap – but it was thin and rather brittle. She was well below average in weight. The stomach contents were interesting: she had eaten about a quarter of a pound of porridge a few hours earlier and had swallowed probably about a glassful of ether.'

Dr Scher opened his eyes and fixed them intently on the Reverend Mother. They continued to stare at each other – thoughtful luminously green eyes fixed on the pair of startled brown ones, beneath bushy eyebrows. The Reverend Mother was the one to break the silence.

'You could be describing a girl from the slums, Dr Scher,' she said, her voice even and without surprise.

'So I'm wrong,' he retorted, rubbing his glove over his face. She waited until he had secured the handbrake before replying.

'No,' she said thoughtfully, 'you may not be wrong.'

He was silent for a moment and then said in a puzzled way: 'So you think that Joseph Fitzsimon neglected his daughter, didn't feed her properly . . . What am I going to say at the inquest? I've had a list of things from the sergeant that shouldn't be mentioned – like the ether in the girl's stomach, or . . .'

The Reverend Mother reached for the door handle. A car had just pulled off the road and had parked in front of theirs and she could see Patrick and the superintendent climb out of it. It was time that they went into court.

'You will tell the truth, nothing but the truth, Dr Scher,' she said and half-smiled at the triteness of the words as she waited for him to come around and assist her from the car. 'Though perhaps *the whole truth* might be a bit indiscreet,' she added as he opened the car door for her.

'Talk fast and use plenty of Latin words and medical terms,' she advised more helpfully as, with his supportive arm outstretched to brace her on the climb from the car to the pavement, she avoided the water welling up from the drains and stepped across on to the stone pavement and turned to greet the two men from the car in front of them.

'Good morning, Sergeant,' she said formally as she straightened herself.

'Good morning, Reverend Mother,' Patrick said. 'May I introduce the superintendent?'

He did it well, she thought, feeling obscurely pleased that he had introduced the superintendent to her as though she were the more important of the two. She wondered who had taught him that easy manner – had it been part of the curriculum during the few weeks' training which the young men destined to be civic guards in the new state had received in Dublin before taking up their duties all over the country? He held himself well, too, though not tall. With a sudden pang, as she followed him up the white marble steps, she wondered what his skeleton would show of early malnutrition if he were picked up dead in the streets of Cork.

He trod resolutely under the marble pillars of the portico and through the fifteen-foot-high wooden door held open by a court official and then turned back to introduce Mr Sarsfield, the solicitor representing the Fitzsimon family, to her.

The Cork Courthouse was not the same as it had been in her youth as, after a fire, it had been rebuilt in 1895 by William Hill, the architect and Samuel Hill, the building contractor. It was well designed with an open courtyard to its centre in which the bar room was located, providing the barristers immediate access to the two main courtrooms, and was an impressive-looking building – a neo-classical courthouse with Corinthian pillars, she seemed to remember reading. The Reverend Mother had never been inside before and looked around with interest at the magnificent building with its wonderful open space in the centre and the windowed dome above casting light down on the busy figures that hurried to and fro.

Mr Sarsfield, elaborately garbed in morning dress – striped trousers, cut-away coat – no wig – only a lowly solicitor, of course – greeted her effusively, but soon left them, and took himself across the court in order to whisper in the ear of one of the lawyers wearing a wig. Rupert was there, smoking his usual cigar, which he quickly extinguished before coming across and taking her by the hand.

'Lucy sent me, told me to make sure that you are all right,' he said with his pleasant smile.

'And to tell her all about it when you come home,' she supplemented and he laughed but did not deny, patting her hand reassuringly and leaving her in the care of Patrick.

She looked after him as he crossed over to speak to another solicitor. He seemed popular and very at ease. It had been a good match; she thought. The secret would have been safe with Edmund and Angela Fitzsimon – Joseph was to be brought up as their own child. Rupert still knew nothing; she guessed and then banished the thought of the summer from her mind. That was a time of her life that she preferred to forget. How could she have been so stupid!

'You'll be the first witness to be called,' said Patrick, and then with a concern which touched her, 'You're not nervous, are you?'

She considered this matter for long enough for him to feel that she was taking his question seriously.

'No,' she said with a smile. She didn't like to tell him that she was quite looking forward to it, nor that her mind was bubbling with ideas. Well, Dr Scher would give his evidence and then the court could decide on its verdict. She hoped that it would not be a verdict of suicide, though.

'Patrick,' she said earnestly in his ear, 'you must do your best not to allow them to say suicide. It's not fair to the girl – and not safe for other girls if this man escapes.'

She saw his eyes narrow. He was turning her words over in his mind.

'Girl?' he queried, and then, 'Do you mean Angelina Fitzsimon? Miss Fitzsimon?' he amended.

I'm not sure whether I do, thought the Reverend Mother and wished that they had more time to talk together, but already the court official was calling on everyone to sit down. She thought of all those vulnerable girls that passed through the doors of her school and of her worries for them when they were turned loose on to the streets of Cork.

The crowd had no sooner complied with this order, the cosy groups of lawyers, witnesses and bystanders all moving to their seats, when there was a roar of: 'All rise!' and everyone stood as the coroner entered and took his seat.

The Reverend Mother listened with interest to the opening statements and then the lawyer called out her name.

There was a stir in the court and many heads turned. She was well known in the city and it was rather dramatic to

have a Reverend Mother called to give evidence for the
finding of a body. She walked sedately down the middle aisle
and took her place at the stand, raising her right hand and
swearing to tell the truth, the whole truth and nothing but
the truth and added the 'so help me, God' in sonorous, grave
and reverential tones which hushed the whole court to the
degree that the proverbial pin could have disturbed the
silence.

The lawyer took her through her recollection of the morning
as delicately as though he were talking to his elderly grandmother and she kept her answers as short as possible.

'Just tell us in your own words what you saw when you
unlocked the gate between the laneway and the path to the
chapel,' he said encouragingly.

Now's my chance, thought the Reverend Mother.

'I saw a dead girl, a very thin girl, dressed in a satin gown,
and I saw a bad bruise on the front of her throat. I sent immediately for Sergeant Patrick Cashman as I thought that she had
been strangled, had been murdered,' she said and felt pleased
at how the words 'strangled' and 'murdered' rang out.

The lawyer had frowned a little at the word 'murdered' and
she saw him take a quick look at the coroner. His Lordship,
however, said nothing. One of the Magners, she thought, as
she glanced at him. He had been a baby when she had become
a nun and she felt a certain perverse satisfaction at picturing
him drooling in his perambulator beside their tennis court.

Patrick was called after she had been thanked and allowed
to sit down, a court official even coming forward and escorting
her carefully back to her seat.

'Look at you – the queen of the court. An escort back to
your seat! They never do that for me,' grumbled Dr Scher in
an undertone.

'Shh,' she said. She was anxious to hear what Patrick said.
He was standing up very straight and appeared quite unshaken.
The barrister took him through the morning from the message
that arrived by the gardener to the convent, to the summoning
of Dr Scher and the arrival at the lane where the body lay. He
described the bruise on the throat in rather more technical terms
than the Reverend Mother had done, using the word 'trachea'

and saying that some of the small bones had been broken, which seemed to impress the jury as, one by one, they all scribbled the word on the pads that had been provided for them. He pointed out that there had been significant traces of sewage caught in the clothing and described his visit to the cellar in the Imperial Hotel and how he found some of the dead girl's hair caught in the manhole when he examined it with the aid of a magnifying glass. There was some excitement among the gentlemen of the press, as the coroner described them. At least the Republican Party had a woman press officer, thought the Reverend Mother scornfully and then sighed over the image of her well-educated Eileen hiding out in some derelict cottage.

When Patrick came to the stage when Dr Scher had begun the post-mortem, he paused.

'Thank you, Sergeant Cashman,' said the coroner. 'We'll hear about that from the doctor. Any questions?' he asked looking from the court lawyer to the barrister representing the Fitzsimon family, but they shook their heads.

'Call Dr Scher,' said the court official.

Dr Scher bustled down the aisle, stepped into the witness box and swore the oath without hesitation. He started off very rapidly: 'Body of young female; had probably been in the water for about twelve hours; death was caused not by manual strangulation, despite marks on throat, but by water in lungs; drowning,' he said with a brief glance at the amateurs in the body of court and at the reporters in the gallery and then a lot of long, technical, medical terms to which the coroner made a great show of nodding wisely. To the Reverend Mother's relief, Dr Scher said nothing about the girl's probable age. She was glad about that. No point in displaying the hand too quickly at this stage. He didn't talk about ether in the stomach, either and also omitted the interesting reference to porridge – surely a strange dish for a young lady's tea. The reasons for ruling out strangulation had to be explained to the jury at the request of the coroner and they all looked most interested and scribbled madly.

But then at the end the bombshell was dropped. *The deceased was pregnant, probably about in the first trimester/three months.*

There was a stir of activity from the press gallery. From the corner of her eye, the Reverend Mother looked up, and saw the pencils flying. Some exciting headlines being composed, she thought with amusement, thinking of the eventual fate of most of these flights of fancy, once the proprietor of the newspaper got to know about them. She saw Joseph Fitzsimon's eyes go to the gallery also and guessed what he was thinking.

What had his childhood been like? she wondered. His early life in Bordeaux before Edmund and Angela were killed in that train crash should have been a good one. Then, after that, when he came to Ireland, the education that he had received was the best that could have been given as he had spent eight years as a boarder at Clongowes Wood College, the most expensive school in Ireland. Edmund and Angela had both been gentle and nice people, warm-hearted and generous. She would never forget how kind they had been to Lucy and to herself during the year which they had spent in their home in Bordeaux. Even after their deaths, Joseph would have had a comfortable life with Edmund's brother, Robert, back in Ireland – the family had a house by the sea, she remembered, as well as the one in the prosperous suburb of Blackrock. He would have been very much younger than Robert's sons, spoiled, perhaps, over-indulged, certainly petted and given his own way.

'Any questions?' The coroner looked towards the counsel for the bereaved family and the bewigged gentleman jumped to his feet and proceeded to earn his fat fee by trying to get Dr Scher to admit that the death could be suicide. Great excitement in the press gallery – pencils flying again, whispering between the heads seen above the benches; a couple of young journalists got to their feet and went to the doorway, obviously planning to be the first back to the office with the news. The Reverend Mother sighed to herself. Whosoever was the girl lying quietly in the coffin in Doolan's funeral parlour, her death would be attended with far more fuss than was usually given to thin, undernourished, pregnant young girls who were fished out of the river in the city of Cork.

Dr Scher was proof against all of the well-paid lawyer's

hints, insinuations, demands, fits of mock anger, appeals to his sensitivity, to the sympathy that he should feel for the father and family of the dead girl. He repeated monotonously and with a show of impatience the words *hyoid bone, manual strangulation had been attempted shortly before death, samples of the girl's hair found in the manhole at the Imperial Hotel had been matched with hair samples clipped from the body,* and *the victim was in the first trimester* until the coroner got tired of the whole business and asked whether the counsel representing the family had any fresh questions.

'You may step down, Dr Scher,' said the coroner eventually and Dr Scher stepped down out of the witness box and walked slowly back to his seat with the air of a man who has been through a battlefield.

The superintendent was called last of all and he made the best of a bad job, hinting that the civic guard were investigating possibilities of a homicidal maniac breaking into the Imperial Hotel and luring the girl down into the cellar, but his heart was not in it. It was apparent to the Reverend Mother that he had begun the proceedings with the almost certainty that the verdict would be suicide and now, because of Dr Scher's stubbornness, had been forced to anticipate a verdict of murder. She watched him critically as he stumbled through assertions that the coroner would not like him to divulge anything that could injure that enquiry in any way, and finished with the assertion that the civic guards would do all that was possible to find the guilty person if murder was suspected and that an arrest would shortly be announced – unless, of course, that it proved to be suicide.

And then the jury were dismissed to their deliberations. They took only a few minutes, which was surprising, and they came back with the verdict of 'murder by person or persons unknown'.

There was a buzz of excitement from the press gallery and then, as a solid body, they all started to edge towards the door as the coroner summed up, expressing the court's sympathy for the bereaved and sorrowing family and purporting to have confidence that the police would soon have an announcement to make.

'Lucy said that she would phone you this evening, Reverend Mother,' said Rupert appearing at her side. 'You must come out and see us some time. I'll send the car to you any time you want. Lucy said to tell you that something has occurred to her.'

ELEVEN

St Thomas Aquinas:
Sicut enim maius est illuminare quam lucere solum.
(It is better to enlighten than merely to shine.)

'I need to talk to Patrick,' said the Reverend Mother in a low tone to Dr Scher. 'Would it be possible to have a word with him in your car?'

'Come back and have lunch with me,' said Dr Scher with his usual enthusiastic hospitality. 'I'll go and ask young Patrick to join us. After all, the man has to have his lunch. We can discuss the post-mortem first of all, just to give us all a good appetite.'

'That's very kind of you,' she said with a nod. Dr Scher's house would be ideal. And lunch sounded a good idea. She hated to rush into things. It would suit her better to feel her way cautiously.

'Pity you can't go to the pub like a normal human being,' grumbled Dr Scher, but she had the impression that he was rather pleased to be offering hospitality. She watched him go across to Patrick, who was standing beside the superintendent, and saw to her satisfaction that Dr Scher had the tact to address some remarks to Patrick's superior.

They were back in a moment, Dr Scher telling Patrick that he had to sit in the back as 'Her Ladyship' liked to sit in the front and keep an eye on his driving.

'Went well,' he said, as he daringly pulled out right in front of the superintendent's car and did a spectacular turnaround in the middle of the street, to the annoyance of several lawyers who were desperately trying to safeguard their expensive cars from contact with the shabby Humber.

'So you won't be out of a job for a while, lad,' he added over his shoulder at Patrick as he clashed the gears noisily. Patrick did not reply and when the Reverend Mother glanced over her shoulder at him, she saw that he was staring through a hole that he had rubbed free of mist on the window beside him. His face, she thought with satisfaction, was concentrated and intent.

Dr Scher lived in one of the Georgian houses on South Terrace, handily positioned just two doors down from the synagogue, though the Reverend Mother doubted whether he was particularly religious, judging by some of the outrageous jokes about God with which he endeavoured to shock her.

The house itself was cosy with a large anthracite stove in the hallway giving a welcome gush of warmth as they came in and the comfortable study into which he ushered them had another blazing, though slightly smaller, stove set within the ornate fireplace. Dr Scher was in his element now, the perfect host, chairs pulled up to the fire, extra cushions, orders and counter-orders flying to the amused and indulgent housemaid, a brave attempt to get the Reverend Mother to drink some brandy on purely medical grounds, and then eventually they were all seated with the promise of a tasty lunch in twenty minutes at the latest. The housemaid firmly shut the door on them all and Dr Scher turned a bright face to his two visitors.

'Well,' he said.

'I was thinking about the Woodfords, my memory is that they were considered immensely rich – I'm just going back into the past, I suppose,' said the Reverend Mother apologetically.

Dr Scher flashed his spectacles at her. 'Still are . . . immensely rich,' he said.

'It's just surprising,' she went on, 'that Angelina's mother is in the lunatic asylum – check by jowl with the poorest of the city.'

'You think only the poor suffer from mental illness?'

'I think that Reverend Mother is surprised that the poor lady was not placed in a private nursing home,' said Patrick hastily, though she could have told him that she needed little protection against Dr Scher's teasing.

'Simple answer to that – the old lady, Mrs Woodford, had been senile for the last couple of years of her life – Mrs Fitzsimon, Anne Woodford, was in a private nursing home when Mrs Woodford made that will, but she had, I think, been certified as insane at that stage – a doctor cousin of Joseph Fitzsimon – man called O'Connor.'

'And presumably Mrs Woodford changed her will at that stage,' mused the Reverend Mother. She was surprised that Mrs Woodford had not insisted on having her own doctor examine the poor woman, but perhaps the deadly senility had begun to overwhelm her even by this stage. 'And she, perhaps, wanted to make sure that Angelina took her time over choosing a husband and was not pushed into anything by her father before she came of age.' She looked interrogatively at him and Dr Scher smiled warmly and gave a congratulatory nod.

'Not that I want to suggest that she decided to leave her fortune to her as yet unmarried granddaughter, rather than to her married, but insane, daughter to be looked after by her grieving husband, you understand,' he said smoothly. He sat back in his armchair. The light from the lamp flashed back from his spectacles, leaving his face looking bland and uninformative.

'But she was an only child, wasn't she, this Anne Woodford, Angelina's mother?' The Reverend Mother was conscious of a slight feeling of shame that she appeared to be flaunting her knowledge of the rich families of the city, but assuaged her conscience by remembering that her fund-raising would never have been so successful if she had not kept herself up to date with all the details of the wealthy.

'And?' Dr Scher raised an eyebrow and stroked the sparse grey hair from the top of his skull.

'Didn't her father leave her anything? Hadn't she got means of her own, over and above anything her mother could leave her?' With a fortune like the Woodfords', it would be surprising if everything was left to the wife and nothing to the only child, the daughter.

'What would she want with anything? She was a married woman, wasn't she? Married to a wealthy man, too. Men manage these affairs so much better than women.' Dr Scher gave her a teasing look.

'There's such a thing as the Married Women's Property Act,' suggested the Reverend Mother, noticing that Patrick looked from one to the other like a spectator at a tennis match.

'True, true.' Dr Scher appeared to have finished, but she knew better, and waited.

'You might want to have a chat with that lawyer of theirs, Mr Sarsfield,' he said after a sip from his brandy glass. 'My information is that he handles both trusts – the one for the mother's money and the one for the grandmother's legacy to Angelina. Cowen was the Woodfords' lawyer; but it wouldn't be in his hands now, more's the pity. Cowen is an honest man.'

'So Angelina's money, as well as that of her mother is handled by Mr Sarsfield,' mused the Reverend Mother. Rupert had said that same thing to his wife, but she would not dream of betraying Lucy and hoped that she sounded as though the idea was a new one to her.

'These trusts,' she said aloud. 'They are a source of discontent and sometimes of corruption.' Her own father had done the same for her once he knew that the cancer was incurable; though her fortune had been tiny in comparison with the money which Angelina Fitzsimon had been due to inherit from her maternal grandmother. She smiled to herself, remembering how much, at the time, she had resented this; feeling, as the young do, that it would be an eternity until she became twenty-one. But of course once she had taken her final vows the money had been swallowed up into the convent coffers. She remembered resenting the fact that she had not been allowed to present it publicly and with a certain amount of drama. And then she sighed at the memory of how full of conceit she had been then and also how naive and silly.

Still, she could say truly that she had never regretted the direction in which life had taken her. It would not have suited her to meekly defer to a husband and to pretend that his judgement was better than her own. Even though over the years she had learned to subdue her instinct to display her brain power and, now, like St Thomas Aquinas, preferred to illuminate, rather than to shine, nevertheless she would never have been content with a life where she would have had to feign stupidity.

'So if anyone was to murder Angelina Fitzsimon, then it would be the brother who would profit.' Dr Scher moved forward to tip a generous scuttle-load of anthracite on to the fire.

'The RIC training manual, which we still use, says that investigating a murder involves looking at means, opportunity and motive,' said Patrick, breaking into the conversation for the first time. He, too, had declined the brandy on the grounds of being on duty and he sipped his soda water dutifully, though he didn't look as though he enjoyed it. Would have preferred something sweet. She had often seen this in the children of the poor – the deprived childhood led them to crave sweets of any kind.

'And those that had opportunity must include all that were at the Merchants' Ball,' he went on. 'Father, brother, potential fiancé: Mr McCarthy from India and then of course there was Mr Eugene Roche – possible lover – excuse me, Reverend Mother.'

She ignored this. 'I suppose we are looking for a man in this case – thinking about the hands that squeezed the throat, the lifting of the heavy metal cover of the manhole, pushing the body down into it . . .'

'Much easier for a man to give her the ether, also,' said Dr Scher. 'It's natural for a man to carry over a glass to a girl.'

'I wonder why he gave her ether. Why do you think, Doctor?'

'That's an easy one, my boy! Isn't it good to see a young fellow so innocent? He'd give her ether so that he could bend her to his will, make her allow him to steer her off the dance-hall floor, take her downstairs, pretend to be taking her to the cloakroom, getting a glass of water to make her feel better, anything like that. Or else just seduce her, I suppose. These medical students make cocktails from it.'

'And then when he got her out of sight, he could strangle her?' Patrick was keeping to the point in a tenacious way that reminded her of a small terrier she owned when she was about eight or nine years old.

'Funny he didn't make a bit more sure of her, she was a very fragile girl, very thin.'

'He might have thought that he had done the job.'

'You don't think that he would have checked to see whether she was still breathing.'

'You'd be amazed how stupid people can be – might have had quite a bit to drink. In my experience,' said Patrick, in an elderly fashion which made her want to smile, 'wits fly out when drink enters in.'

'Not one of those fellows that have taken the pledge, not one of those Father Matthew boys, are you?' asked Dr Scher with deep suspicion.

'Ask me that when I'm not on duty.' This easy-going conversation with Dr Scher was good for Patrick, decided the Reverend Mother, listening to the bantering conversation while conscious of a ridiculous feeling of maternal pride when she thought back to the undersized bare-legged little boy, dressed in filthy and torn clothes. If he were to solve this murder, he would be in line for promotion and that provided an additional driving reason for her to involve herself in this mystery.

'So you think that he, our murderer, might have thought that he had killed her and that he just had to dispose of the body – would have to be someone who knew the Imperial Hotel, wouldn't it?' Dr Scher mused over this and took another sip from his brandy glass.

'Probably, but not certainly – might have just planned to leave the body in the cellar and then came across the manhole.'

'Mind you, if he left the body in the cellar, he would run a massive risk. The amazing thing was that there was no search for Angelina Fitzsimon, that she could just disappear like that from a dance where her father, her brother and her future fiancé were all present.'

'Remember how dark it was, the policeman on duty said that it was just candles – they had turned off the gas lamps and then the jazz music would have kept everyone's attention – the building was rocking with it, so I've heard,' said Patrick.

Interesting the hint that Dr Scher dropped about the solicitor, thought the Reverend Mother as the maid came in that moment with a loaded tray and proceeded to cover the small round Pembroke table with a well-ironed table cloth, taken from a drawer beneath its centre panel. Amazing the gossip that went around the South Mall! However, gossip was one thing and action was another. There would be nobody left alive who felt it was their duty to check on what was happening to Mrs Fitzsimon's fortune from her deceased and extremely wealthy Woodford father. And as for the legacy to the granddaughter – Angelina had seemed to be a strong-willed and determined girl with a social conscience very unlike that of the majority of girls of her age and of her class, but she had been under twenty-one and subject to her father's rule until she attained that age. She picked up the *Cork Examiner* tucked into the newspaper rack beside the fire and ran her eyes over the headlines. Yes, the news of the death was there, a small discreet paragraph, calling it an unfortunate accident and making it appear as if the girl must have fallen into the river by accident. No mention of the Merchants' Ball – the proprietor would have been present at that – and elsewhere in the paper there was the usual list of attendees – there was no mention, either, of the police involvement, or of the time and date of the coroner's inquest. And then her eye was caught by an article further down, under the provocative byline 'A Patriot'.

It was a good article. It described, very fully, and very movingly, the body lying out in the floods and the rain; the elaborate satin gown in neat juxtaposition with the miserable fate of the body; it detailed the police response; touched on the father's place in society, gave a brief description of the house in Blackrock (from the outside); and then it moved on to statistics of the amount of drowned and murdered bodies dragged from the river every year or found dead on the streets and finished up by implying subtly that the police response to the murder of Miss Angelina Fitzsimon, daughter of the well-known businessman Joseph Fitzsimon, was of a very different order to their response to a suspicious death of a denizen of Barrack Street or of Cove Street.

'Bit of a socialist, that fellow – calls himself a patriot but he's a good old-fashioned socialist,' said Dr Scher looking over her shoulder. 'Used to be one of them myself when I was young, but now I just look after my own comforts! Come and have lunch,' he said abruptly, 'that freezing courthouse will be the death of me if I don't get something warm in my stomach – don't know why they don't heat it – I bet old Magner wears two pairs of long johns under those judge's robes of his.'

Reverend Mother left the paper lying open on the rug in front of the fire. She wondered whether Patrick would be

interested to read it and then decided not. He had chosen his
path and he would allow nothing to deflect him on his way
up from and out of the class into which he had been born.
She agreed with Dr Scher: he was correct in stating that the
writer of the article was a socialist, someone who felt that
society was unfair, and she suspected that Dr Scher, also,
despite his protests, still felt that. The doctor was wrong,
however, in his choice of pronoun for 'A Patriot'.

In fact, she had recognized the style, slightly flowery, from
almost the first sentence and had felt absurdly proud of the
author. The building of clause upon clause, the juxtaposition
of images, the delicately chosen alliteration, even a well-placed
colon and an appropriate semi-colon gave her pleasure and
she felt in a very good humour as she joined the two men at
the table and began to tuck into a delicious soufflé omelette
and some excellent brown bread. She resisted the temptation
to tease Dr Scher about his well-rounded figure and listened
patiently to the arguments and counter-arguments between the
two men.

Patrick was in favour of the notion of Gerald Fitzsimon
murdering his sister for the sake of the substantial legacy that
he would immediately receive from his grandmother's estate
as soon as the death was proved. He allowed his omelette to
grow cold as he took out his notebook and make a note of all
the painstaking checking that he planned to do.

'I'll get a man on to interviewing everyone that was there
that night and see whether anyone saw him dance with his
sister or even hand her a drink. And I'll go to see the solicitor
myself and find out the terms of the will. And then I'll get
another man on the job of interviewing the servants at the
hotel. Surely it would be odd to see anyone in full evening
dress going down to the cellar. They went up to the first floor
and down again readily – the bar for the Merchants' Ball was
upstairs and the ballroom on the ground floor – but none of
them would have a reason to go down to the cellar.'

'There is a lift,' murmured the Reverend Mother, savouring
the crisp outside to her omelette and remembering her days
as a child, innocently pressing the button for the first floor on
a pretence of seeking out the bathrooms and then shooting

instantly down to the much more exciting cellars. 'And a lift, you know, can rise and then go down and no one is the wiser.'

'Oh! I see what you mean.' Patrick looked slightly daunted, but went on with his list, murmuring to himself while he did so. 'And this Eugene Roche that they mentioned. Would he be a professor, Dr Scher?'

'Just a lowly lecturer, like myself,' said Dr Scher. 'Don't let that solicitor fellow, don't let that Sarsfield talk you down, Patrick. He's a great hand at that. Would have you saying black is white before you could blink.'

'And then there is the tea-planter from India,' went on Patrick, still writing quickly. There was a slight look of resentment on his face. He had not liked Dr Scher's suggestion that he might be easily taken in by the solicitor. 'Why should he murder the girl – that was a nice match for him?'

'The strange thing is that the father said they were going to be married before he went back to India – before the girl reached the age of twenty-one – that would mean that she didn't inherit and that the money would go to her brother.'

'Perhaps he favoured the boy – didn't worry too much about the girl – just picked out a good husband for her. Some families are like that – wanted to establish a dynasty – rival the Murphys and the Beamishes and be top dogs in the city . . .' suggested Dr Scher.

The Reverend Mother allowed them to talk on. The idea that had come into her head was so fantastical that she wanted to allow it to simmer, to allow her own brain to turn it over in peace before irrelevancies could be argued and could distract her from the facts.

It was just as Dr Scher deposited her at the convent gate after he dropped Patrick off at the barracks that a question came to her.

'Did you look at her nails when you were doing the post-mortem?' she asked when he had secured the hand brake.

'Her nails?' He turned to look at her with genuine surprise. 'There was nothing strange about her nails,' he said and then nodded wisely. 'I see what you mean. You were wondering whether she had put up a fight, had scratched the man, perhaps marked his face, but you're forgetting, aren't you, she was wearing gloves, these long, tight gloves that reached right up beyond her elbow. She couldn't have got those off in a hurry.'

'That's right,' said the Reverend Mother, but he had already got out and was bustling around to open her passenger door. Dr Scher, she thought, had been slightly obtuse. She glanced at her own nails, clean, short, but well kept – the nails of someone whose only manual work was to hold a pen or a piece of chalk. Hands, she thought, could betray their owner quicker than a face.

So she went in to the news, from Sister Bernadette, that there had been a huge row between Nellie O'Sullivan and Sister Mary Immaculate and that Nellie O'Sullivan had shouted that she was leaving the school, that, in any case, she had found herself a good job in Paddy's bar on Albert Quay and then she had rushed out of the classroom and slammed the door behind her. And that half an hour later a scared younger sister delivered to the convent door a hastily brown paper-wrapped parcel containing the gym slip, whose hem had been turned up, a blouse and a matted cardigan.

And that Mrs Rupert Murphy was waiting to see her, but had gone into the classroom, and was, giggled Sister Bernadette, discussing clothes with the senior girls there.

TWELVE

St Thomas Aquinas:
Sic ergo summum gradum in religionibus tenent quae
ordinantur ad docendum et praedicandum.
(Thus the highest place in religious orders is held, therefore,
by those who are dedicated to teaching and instructing.)

Lucy had been as good as her word. As soon as the Reverend
Mother appeared, one of the excited girls was despatched
to summon the chauffeur. He was a big, broad-shouldered
man but he staggered slightly under his burden.

'Your room? Or the classroom?' Lucy's eyes sparkled.

'The classroom: put four of the desks together, girls,' said
the Reverend Mother decisively and ignored the disap-
proving look from Sister Mary Immaculate who was lurking
in the corridor waiting to complain about Nellie O'Sullivan.
The expensive trunk was placed on the desks and the girls
crowded around. Lucy, in her element, kept a hand on the
closed lid and counted heads. 'Nine,' she said. 'I thought
that there were ten of you.'

'Nellie O'Sullivan had to go home early; perhaps one of
you could pick out something for her,' said the Reverend
Mother smoothly. She suspected that they would not see Nellie
again. It was surprising that she had stayed as long as she did
and if she had some sort of job, even working in a public
house, it was unlikely that they would see her again at school.

The clothes that Lucy had brought were very tasteful.
Well-cut skirts, cotton blouses, easy to wash, and jackets in
deep blues, browns, purples and dark greens. The sort of thing,
thought the Reverend Mother appreciatively, that a girl could
wear if going for an interview for an office job. For a fleeting
moment she thought about Eileen and then dismissed the
thought. Eileen had chosen her own pathway and who was to
say that she had chosen wrongly.

'What would look good on Nellie?' she asked one of the girls and Lucy immediately intervened, picking out, once she had heard about the brown eyes, a pretty skirt, very short, and a stylish short jacket in brown tweed with a pale pink blouse to go with it.

'Let's leave them to it,' suggested the Reverend Mother, rather regretting that the classroom had no mirrors, but that the girls resorted to examining themselves in the windows with the day darkening outside and also in seeing their reflections from the approbation in friends' eyes. Sister Mary Immaculate had peeped in at the discarded gymslips that littered desks and chairs, and then, in disgust, had gone off to supervise the teaching in the next classroom.

'Come and have a cup of tea with me,' suggested the Reverend Mother and Lucy followed her down the corridor and into the study where a bright fire blazed on the hearth and Sister Bernadette had just finished arranging an afternoon tea, fit for such a distinguished guest, on a small table between two easy chairs.

Lucy sat down gracefully, waiting until the door had closed behind Sister Bernadette before stretching her hands out to the fire and saying pensively, 'Do you know, I've been thinking about Ballycotton all day.'

The Reverend Mother said nothing. She had not seen Ballycotton for over fifty years but it still remained vivid in her mind's eye – the harbour, the cliffs, the Copingers' house where she and Lucy had spent most of their summer holidays.

Thomas Copinger had been Lucy's guardian. He had been her dead father's partner and was a man with a family of young children. The deadly tuberculosis which had carried off her own mother had also killed Lucy's mother – both sisters dying soon after the births of their daughters – and twelve years later Lucy's father had succumbed to the same disease, and had left the girl orphaned. It was surprising perhaps, she thought, that in view of the friendship between the two girls, Lucy had not been left to the guardianship of her father, but perhaps Lucy's father had felt that the motherly Victoria Copinger would be maternal towards his orphaned daughter and would steer her through the social scene when she came to a marriageable age.

It had not worked out like that.

She and Lucy had spent most of the year at the Ursuline Convent boarding school in Blackrock and Christmas and Easter at her home, but every summer they had spent in the Copingers' holiday home in Ballycotton. Mrs Copinger was fully occupied with her young children so it was left to her husband to entertain the two very much older girls. It had all seemed such fun, then. Going out in Thomas's boat, swimming in the icy waters of Ballytrasna Bay, climbing the cliffs, discovering caves, lighting fires on the beach; when was it that they both fell in love?

Both with the same man.

And, of course, it was almost inevitable. All around there were families with young children, or else a few solitary priests reading their missals on the cliff walk – there were no young boys of their own age, or even young men – most young people went to the more fashionable seaside resorts – places with dance halls, bathing machines – no, there was just Thomas, more than twenty-five years older, but dazzlingly handsome.

And ready for a little fun with a pretty young girl, while his heavily pregnant wife struggled with their large family of young children.

And oddly, it was not with the appealing, blonde, kittenish Lucy, but with her cousin, not pretty, tall, with heavy-lidded green eyes and black hair which in the damp sea air, half an hour after the application of the curling tongs, fell in weighty straight masses across her shoulders.

And she had flaunted her conquest. Had delighted to lie beside him in the beach, had allowed him to dry her wet hair, even to rub her goose-pimpled legs with a rough towel when she came out of the sea.

But that had been that. Even at seventeen, thought the Reverend Mother looking back to 1870, even at seventeen she had a strong will, a strong sense of her own value and the knowledge that her father would not approve made her instinctively dodge Thomas's outstretched arm, from time to time, to deny him playful kisses, to place Lucy between them when they walked the cliffs, to hang a towel over the entrance to the cave where she and Lucy changed into their bathing smocks and trousers, to refuse to go sailing alone with him . . .

Only afterwards had she realized remorsefully that she had tipped Lucy into his arms.

She still remembered every minute of that day, could see the cliffs – the sea below them, azure blue breaking into creamy foam around the sharp, pointed rocks – black when wet with water, but deep rose-red, the colour of unopened apple blossom, in the heat of the sun. That old red sandstone of Cork broke into the sharp angular shapes and the tall pointed entrance to the cave was like an asymmetrical triangle. It went back very far, right back into the cliff.

'Do you remember the day when you spotted the lizard, there sunning itself on the side of the cliff?' Lucy's voice broke into her thoughts, uncannily almost reading them, though, perhaps, in talking about Joseph, it was inevitable that both should think back to that late summer's day.

'And I insisted on taking it back to show to the children.' She could remember it well, could remember her feelings, her jealousy that he had placed a finger under Lucy's chin and had dropped a kiss on her blonde curls. Her insistence on giving the children the lizard had arisen from that rather than from any kind feelings on her part. Neither she nor Lucy had taken too much notice of the younger ones that summer.

Lucy heaved a sigh. 'And it all happened that afternoon.'

'I know.' She had instinctively known at the time that something was going to happen; had looked back when she reached the bend on the cliff walk and had, for once, not looked forward to feast her eyes on the sight of the two islands, but had turned back. They had been just at the entrance to the cave, Thomas and Lucy, both figures dwarfed by the enormously tall entrance. And she had not seen them for hours.

She had pondered for the whole afternoon on what they had been doing. Even while she joined with Thomas's children in making a house and garden for the lizard and catching flies for it to eat she had been speculating on what might be happening.

It had been her fault. She had felt that afterwards. Lucy was the younger of the two and she had promised her father to look after her when they had first gone to boarding school together.

Perhaps that enforced promise had brought a certain jealousy with it. She had been jealous of Lucy's prettiness. Had she been ignorant of Thomas's intentions; of his lack of control, lack of decency, or had it been a case of her just not wanting to know? That was a question that she had never managed to answer. She brooded on it for a moment until her thoughts were interrupted by Lucy.

'Tell me about Joseph's girl, about Angelina. What was she like?'

'A very nice girl, it seems,' said the Reverend Mother, reverting instantly to the modern world of 1923. 'She was very good to the poor, very charitable, so Professor Lambert told me. She worked in the St Vincent de Paul shop. I'm sure that you would have liked her.'

'She was my granddaughter,' said Lucy sadly and then, after a minute, 'Well, who murdered her, then?'

'The police,' said the Reverend Mother demurely, 'will do their best to find out that.'

'Nonsense,' said Lucy energetically. 'Rupert says that super-intendent is a fool and the other one is too young.'

'He was a pupil of mine,' said the Reverend Mother. 'I have confidence in him.'

'One of yours, was he?' Lucy looked interested. 'I suppose you have him feeding out of your hand. You needn't try to pretend to me, Dottie.'

The old familiar nickname made the Reverend Mother smile. It was a long time since anyone even called her by the more stately name of Dorothea. In public, Lucy and she were punctilious with their 'Reverend Mother' and 'Mrs Murphy'.

'Anyway, you've got far more brains than any of those men. You always had brains. You were the one that first thought out that Bordeaux plan. I thought that I would go out of my mind when Thomas wouldn't do anything.'

Thomas Copinger, like his son after him, had married a rich wife. Lucy's news had filled him with horror, almost with terror. He pretended to disbelieve her, denied that what they had done could have made her pregnant, threatened to tell everyone that she had been out all night with one of the young fishermen, had absolutely refused to have anything more to do with them and had told them they would have to leave his house by the end of the week.

'Do you know, I was seriously thinking of throwing myself over the cliffs when you came up with your Bordeaux plan?' Lucy's well-rouged mouth had tightened to a hard line as she gazed into the fire, but she passed a hand across it, allowed her features to assume their usual pleasant aspect and then said lightly, 'Of course, I always knew that you were clever, but that was pure genius.'

It had been a sudden flash of inspiration. They had been sitting, the two of them side by side, in a little secluded dip in the cliffs, hidden from the path above by a large gorse bush, she had her arm around her cousin, listening to the sobs in a slightly detached way – things were, she had thought, too bad for easy comfort. It had been a foggy day and the lighthouse that crowned the cone-shaped island flared its beam across the water and, as if the light had illuminated her mind the thought suddenly flashed upon her. Angela and Edmund Fitzsimon, their cousins out in Bordeaux, who managed the French side of the wine business, had given up hope of a baby. She had heard that said. They were rich, kind, and could have been ideal parents, everyone said that, but Angela had failed to conceive after ten years of marriage, ten years of hoping and praying. What could seventeen-year-old Lucy do with a baby? But to them it would seem the most wonderful gift in the world.

'Lucy,' she had said bracingly on that foggy morning. 'Stop crying and listen to me. You and I are going to learn to speak French fluently. We are going to spend a year in Bordeaux.'

And it had all worked out. Nothing was said. They both went back to Cork. Her father, quite unsuspecting, thought it was a wonderful idea, an inspirational way of rounding off their education and he was confident that he could persuade Thomas Copinger to agree on Lucy's behalf – and of course met with no opposition! As soon as they arrived in Bordeaux she had packed Lucy off to bed and then told the story. Edmund and Angela were touched by the plight of the childlike Lucy, shocked, also, when they heard the whole story that night; though looking back on it later, she thought that they had not been surprised at Thomas's behaviour. But, above all, they were only too delighted to have a baby of their own blood. Nothing would be said; Thomas was a father of five young children; there could be no scandal. Lucy would have her baby and then would get on with the rest of her life.

A nice couple, Edmund and Angela, she thought. What a terrible pity for Joseph that they were killed in that train crash while he was still quite young. Robert had taken the young child back to the Fitzsimon house in Blackrock, but his heart was not in childrearing; Joseph was left to a nanny and a governess and then after the death of Robert's own sons in the first Boer War was packed off to boarding school while still quite young. Not the best of upbringings, she thought now and then her memories were interrupted by a chuckle from Lucy and she looked across at her cousin enquiringly.

'I was just thinking what a wonderful thing a crinoline was. I was saying that to one of my granddaughters the other day when she was laughing about that portrait of me that was painted after I got married. "Wait until you start a family, young lady," I said to her. "Those skirts won't hide an inch. I could go up to the last month and no one the wiser," that's what I was telling her. It was a bit of luck, too. Do you remember me? No one noticed anything. And you, you clever thing, had the idea that Angela should shorten the laces on her crinoline so that she could look as though she were expecting.'

It had all been done very discreetly – the midwife was a very young nun from a nearby Bon Secours hospital and convent in Bordeaux. Edmund had donated large sums of money to the babies' ward in the hospital and Sœur Marie Madeleine had sworn to keep the secret as sacred as one told in the confessional. The two girls had returned to Ireland as soon as Lucy had recovered and that had been that. Their ways had parted soon afterwards. Lucy had fallen in love with young Rupert Murphy – or was it the other way around? In any case, she had two beautiful little blonde girls by the time that Angela and Edmund were killed.

'And you went into the convent.' It seemed more of a statement than a query and the Reverend Mother did not reply. There were certain questions that had never been aired between them. She had never asked Lucy why she did not offer to adopt Joseph after the train crash and Lucy had never asked her why she had taken the decision to become a nun. Both, perhaps, felt that the answer was known – and possibly both were wrong in their surmise.

'I never saw him as a child, you know,' said Lucy in a low tone. 'I think that he must have been about thirty years old when I saw him first. And I hated him when I saw him. He was the image of his father.'

'But the girl, Angelina.' There was no point, thought the Reverend Mother, in dwelling on the past.

'Killed by her father, I wouldn't be surprised,' said Lucy smartly. And then, though her cousin had said nothing, she went on with her usual decisiveness. 'Joseph is nothing like the Fitzsimons. He is like his father, like Thomas Copinger. Money is everything to him. The girl, according to Rupert, was stirring up trouble, was enquiring about what happened to her mother's fortune, if she succeeded, Joseph could have lost that and then old Mrs Woodford's money was to go to Angelina. Rupert told me that, also. So there were he and his son with an expensive lifestyle and there's not the same money coming in as before the days of all of those troubles with so many big families going back to England and shutting up their houses and their estates – that's what Rupert says. There wouldn't be the tenth of the entertaining done these days. So Joseph, without his wife's fortune, might not be able to keep up the house in Blackrock. And Angelina was asking questions about that fortune. Of course he killed her, waited his opportunity to have a lot of people around, to have others to throw the blame on to; that would have been the way his father would have done something, that sort of person doesn't care what he does as long as he himself is safe,' she ended, speaking decisively, forcefully, but without bitterness, almost like someone who prides themselves on knowing how men act.

It was a convincing notion, though somewhat startling. Joseph Fitzsimon, from Patrick's observations, was emerging as a man without much feeling, a man who could place his wealthy wife in the lunatic asylum and then use her fortune for his own ends. Did he care about his daughter? He hadn't appeared to show much sense of loss or of sorrow, neither at the house when she had visited, nor, according to Patrick, when first confronted by the dead body.

'What would he have gained from it?' she asked.

'Security, continued source of funds,' snapped Lucy. 'You're so innocent, you nuns. You don't realize the importance of money.'

I think about money all of the time – more than I think about God, thought the Reverend Mother cynically. She was under no danger of overlooking its importance, though she had not realized that the recent wars had so threatened the wealth of the merchant princes of Cork city. It would, of course, have been possible for Joseph to have approached his daughter in the dimly lit, noisy hall, to have offered her something to drink that had been laced with either, to have persuaded her into the lift, half-strangled her, taken her down into the cellar and pushed the body into the sewer beneath.

And yet, somehow there was a feeling within her that the whole story had not yet been uncovered.

Thomas Copinger, she thought, must have been a man of strong carnal appetite if he had carelessly seduced and impregnated his own seventeen-year-old ward, although he had a wife and family close by. It had been a dim understanding of his nature, of his mood that day which had frightened her and kept her away from him, had made her turn back from the cliffs when she could almost sense his arousal.

Later she had judged herself harshly, had thought that there had been a lot of angry jealousy in the way in which she had gone away from them that day.

But there had been no excuse for his actions – Lucy was his ward, a young girl, almost a daughter. Looking back and judging him later, he had been, she thought, a man without scruple, a man for whom his own wants, his own desires were paramount and who did what he wanted to do without the slightest compunction for the hurt which he inflicted. His reaction to Lucy's panic-stricken realization of her pregnancy: to deny everything and to warn her that he would spread a story about her and one of the young fishermen all around Cork if she dared to name him, had been despicable.

It could be, she thought, that his son, Joseph, had inherited this obsession with self, with money, with satisfaction of his appetites, no matter what the cost to others.

Joseph may have had a strange gestation time in the womb, she thought, with a grain of compassion. He had not been wanted by either his father or by his natural mother. Lucy had been filled with moods: emotions of depression, grim anger and, sometimes, abject fear during the months when she bore this unwanted baby concealed beneath the wire circumference of her crinoline and perhaps that would have an effect on the developing child. Never once had Lucy expressed any interest in the infant; just looked forward to shedding her burden. It had been a long and difficult birth and it was Angela who bore the newly born baby away from the heavily chloroformed young mother, Angela who bottle-fed the baby, who sang to him, cuddled him, cared for him, while Lucy kept to her bed and seemed to want to be treated as an invalid for the couple of months following the birth.

And that almost breakdown had lasted until she and her cousin had returned to Ireland and Lucy had immediately blossomed into new beauty and had captivated the very young Rupert Murphy.

THIRTEEN

St Thomas Aquinas:
Utrum in Deo sit voluntas malorum . . .
(Whether in God there is the will for wickedness . . .)

D r Scher's Humber drew up outside the convent gate
just as the younger children were going home from
school. The Reverend Mother was at the gate. She
liked to stand there at that time of the afternoon. It gave an
opportunity to any parent who wanted to voice a concern about
a child, or to quietly ask for a loan of some clothing, it also
gave her a chance to chat informally with the mothers about
their children and it made sure that no undesirables were
hanging around the school gates looking to befriend unac-
companied children. Child prostitution, she was aware, had a
strong presence in a city of poverty-stricken families. There
was, she often thought compassionately, a strong instinct within
these women to make sure that their children had food to eat,
cost what it might, and this provided an opening for the
perverted and the wicked.

She noticed that Dr Scher had a young man in the car with
him, not anyone that she knew, but he was probably another
doctor as he was dressed in a white coat. He seemed, she
thought, to be asleep. His hat was off and his head, adorned
with crisp red curls, leaned against the passenger window in
an abandoned posture.

She waited until the women had gathered up their children
and had departed and until she had checked that any unescorted
children were safely under the wing of a neighbour and then
she went across to the car. The young man with the red hair
still slept deeply.

Dr Scher jumped out immediately. His face was full of
triumph.

'I'll bring him in,' he said, before she could say anything.

'I'd say that he could do with a good breakfast – been up all night.'

It was two o'clock of the afternoon, but she did not argue. She just went back into the convent, met Sister Bernadette and said: 'Dr Scher and his friend have been up all night in the hospital. Do you think, Sister, that you could bring them something to eat, something substantial, bacon and eggs, perhaps.'

As she could have guessed the kind woman's face lit up at the request and she disappeared instantly towards the kitchen. She went back to the car, looked dubiously at the sleeping man, hoped he wasn't drunk, but said: 'Bring him in, Dr Scher.'

It took a bit of good-humoured taunting from Dr Scher before he managed to get the young man on his feet. Even still he walked in a manner of an automaton, groping his way, touching the gate and even the top of the sooty, unlovely hedge of laurel as he made his way towards the front door to the convent. Once in the Reverend Mother's study he lapsed back into sleep again, relaxed in the visitor's armchair and snoring loudly.

'Who is he?' asked the Reverend Mother. She did not bother to lower her voice. It was obvious that the young man would not be easily awakened.

'His name is Munroe – Dr Munroe – he works in the Eglinton Asylum, the lunatic asylum,' added Dr Scher giving the name that most Cork people gave to the immense and menacing long line of a grey and red, angular-faced building on Sunday's Well, high up above the River Lee.

'I do some work there occasionally, just the odd night, here and there,' he said, sounding almost apologetic – Dr Scher liked to appear hard-boiled and cynical. 'This is a nice young fellow, not as hardened as most who bring themselves to work in that place.'

'Let him rest for the moment.' The Reverend Mother noted with pity the dark shadows under the eyes and the continual twitch of the cheek muscles. When Sister Bernadette pushed open the door so that she could wheel in the trolley, he jumped to his feet immediately, shouting, 'Yes, what's the problem?'

'Relax, have a drop of whiskey,' said Dr Scher. He took

one of the tumblers, emptied the water from it into the fireplace and poured out some golden brown liquid that came from a bottle, produced from his pocket. He held it to the young man's lips in the way that a mother would hold milk to the lips of a suckling child and the red-headed young doctor drank it obediently.

And then he blinked blue eyes at the Reverend Mother and gave her a bewildered stare.

'Where am I?' he asked as she placed a small table beside him.

'Have something to eat,' said Dr Scher and pushed a plate of bacon and eggs towards the young man, making sure that he took knife and fork into his hands.

'He's exhausted,' said Dr Scher in a low voice. 'Very few are willing to work there, these days. I met him coming out and declaring that he won't go back. He will, of course, just like I will, though I swear that I won't. These poor people up there have to be looked after. He's a young Englishman,' he added.

The Reverend Mother said nothing, just buttered a few slices of soda bread and after some thought, spread them thickly with marmalade. Sister Teresa, the cook, always made her marmalade with the maximum amount of sugar. It would be good for this exhausted, drained young man. When he had finished his bacon and eggs and had tilted some of the whiskey down his throat she fed him, piece by piece, the bread and marmalade. There was, she was glad to notice, some colour coming back into his cheeks and the dazed eyes had begun to focus. There were a few sugar buns on the tray and she split one, buttered it and handed it to him. It was the ultimate sugar boost and he smiled, pushed the whiskey aside and swallowed a cup of hot, strong tea.

'You'll make me fat,' he said, looking up at her.

'The Reverend Mother is interested in Anne Fitzsimon and her daughter, Angelina.' Dr Scher, she thought, had perhaps come to the point too quickly, but then he was probably used to the utter collapse and exhaustion that had startled and frightened her when she had first seen the young doctor.

'You're from England, are you?' She put the question in

order to give him a moment to think a moment to recall his
senses and to focus his mind on the institution that he had
just left.

He grinned in a boyish fashion. 'Scotland – do you mind?'
he said with mock-reproof and she smiled back at him. His
eyes were becoming alert and he replied good-humouredly to
her queries about why he was in Cork, explaining how his
father at been an officer at the naval base at Haulbowline in
Cork Harbour and how, as a schoolboy, he had become addicted
to sailing. Had his own boat moored at Crosshaven – a present
from his father, bought when he had qualified as a doctor.

'Cork is the second biggest natural harbour in the world,
someone told me that once,' said the Reverend Mother, glad
that he was beginning to relax. 'Dr Scher tells me that you
know the Fitzsimons – mother and daughter, is that right?'

'You wanted to talk about Angelina Fitzsimon, or was it
about her mother,' he said, looking from one to the other.

'Angelina Fitzsimon is dead,' said Dr Scher. The Reverend
Mother thought that she would not have used quite such
brutality, but she understood that these men dealt with a reality
outside her experience.

'What!' The doctor half-rose to his feet, swayed and then
sat down again. His voice had remained soft and subdued and
the Reverend Mother, on the alert for raised voices, which
might attract attention, took no alarm. Dr Munroe was used
to the unexpected, she thought. He dealt with crises day in
and day out.

'Dead? Was it an accident? Or was she murdered?' he asked
thoughtfully and watched Dr Scher bow his head. And then
unexpectedly, he added in a very low voice, 'I'm not altogether
surprised.' He looked all around him, almost fearfully.

Dr Scher hitched his chair a bit nearer to him and leaned
across, placing a hand on the other man's chair.

'What do you know about Anne Fitzsimon?' he asked.

'The mother?'

'That's right. She's been in the asylum for ten years – I've
looked up the notes.'

'What's wrong with her?' The Reverend Mother saw that
she was intended to ask that question.

'Everything,' said Dr Munroe, focusing on her. 'Everything that would be wrong with you, or rather your niece or grand-niece, if she were dragged away from her children, shut up in a madhouse and given cupfuls of laudanum every time that she wept. And allowed no visitors,' he added.

'I see,' said the Reverend Mother. She absorbed the explanation without surprise. The thought flashed through her mind that this could have been a terrible threat that Angelina's father held over her.

'How could that have happened?' She asked the question, just as she asked many a question – purely because she knew that she was expected to ask it; but she could guess what had happened.

'Easy enough.' Dr Munroe took a bite from the bun that she had placed on the arm of his chair and then another and another, swallowing each one rapidly. The Reverend Mother crossed the room and put some more on a plate, placing one securely into his hand and putting the others on the hearth at his side.

'God, I was hungry,' he said. 'I don't think I've eaten since yesterday, or was it the day before? It was a bad few days and nights, anyway. What were you asking? Yes, it's easy enough to have someone shut up in an asylum – if you've got the money, and got the power. Do you know two out of three inhabitants of the asylum are women and do you know the diagnosis that is down for most of them – hysteria – and what's hysteria? You tell me that.'

'You tell me,' said the Reverend Mother good-humouredly, but she could hear a note of impatience in her voice. She wanted to get back to the question of Angelina.

'No, I can't,' said the doctor unexpectedly. 'I can't because it isn't a disease. Everything was much easier when I was training – we cut up a madman once – it was you, wasn't it, Dr Scher? You brought him in, sawed through the skull and let us all see the brain – all shrivelled up. He wasn't suffering from hysteria, that old man; he was just mad; his brain had rotted away.'

'I remember,' said Dr Scher in a low voice. 'But bring us back to Mrs Fitzsimon. You said that she was not allowed visitors.'

'I sneaked the daughter in – was sorry for her.'

'You knew her, knew Angelina?'

'Met her, met her with her brother. Played tennis with her on one Sunday when I wasn't working. He introduced us. Lovely girl. Not a bit like him.'

'So you know Gerald Fitzsimon, do you?' put in the Reverend Mother. 'I understand that he is studying for your own profession, isn't he?'

'Pretending to,' said Dr Munroe cynically. 'Been at it a long time and not made much progress. He started the same time as I did, but didn't move on too quickly.' His eyes looked around the neat parlour and then returned across to the closed door. Even so, the young doctor dropped his voice.

'In it for the drugs, young Fitzsimon; easy enough to lay your hands on them. Some of those professors are pretty careless. And, of course, if you have the money to buy – like Gerald has – well, you can buy direct from the suppliers – get the stuff before they turn it into laudanum. I know there is a law saying that only pharmacists can sell it nowadays, but believe you me they're not the only source, if you need it badly enough.'

'Opium?'

'That's right. You can get it down the quays if you have the money for it. Give us another glass of that whiskey. I probably should go back up there to the asylum, but I have to go home and have a kip before I do that.'

'Just tell me something first. How did Miss Fitzsimon get into the asylum to see her mother, if all visitors are forbidden?'

'Because I am a fool for a pretty face.' The young doctor was looking more relaxed now. He swallowed some more whiskey and leaned back in his chair, gazing up at the ceiling, with a slight smile on his lips, thinking about Angelina, or else thinking about sailing on Cork Harbour, perhaps. A rich man's amusement, but it would be better than taking drugs; healthier, too. Even in her young days there was a yachting club in the harbour. She wondered whether he had ever taken Angelina out in his boat.

'But that's not doing her justice to call her a pretty face.'

There was a sudden energy come into the tired voice. 'Did you ever meet her?'

The Reverend Mother thought back to the stranded figure lying in the convent gateway, red-brown hair like seaweed tangled by the tide, blue eyes, dull with death, staring up at the grey sky above. And yet there was something else depicted at the back of her mind: a different girl; a girl full of life and spirit, full of energy and of intelligence, a girl such as she had been once. Rapidly she suppressed the image.

'No, I don't think so,' she said briefly.

'It's a funny thing, but when I met her first a word came into my mind and that was *noble*.' Dr Munroe gave an embarrassed laugh. 'Like one of those Roman matrons. She was a very nice girl and a very clever girl. And, by Jove, she had courage. She had read up about the Married Women's Property Act and had been cross-questioning her father about what had happened to the fortune that the mother had inherited from her father, the girl's grandfather.'

'One of the richest men in Cork,' said Dr Scher respectfully.

'Even went down to see the solicitor on the South Mall – Sarsfield, I think was his name, and cross-questioned him, and she tackled dear Dr O'Connor, the one who certified the mother, tackled him herself, asked for details of her mother's illness and of her treatment. She . . .' He looked around furtively and then whispered, 'You won't tell anyone about this, will you, but I "borrowed" a nurse's uniform for her, she used to slip it on in my room and then she would go off with my keys in her hand and take her mother out of that prison-room of hers, take her down the gardens, try to get her interested in planting things, doing a little bit of digging – we're supposed to encourage the patients to do that sort of thing – not that any of us have the time for it – anyway, Angelina did that with her mother – anything to try to postpone the time when she would start to cry for her laudanum. Was at it for months until dear Dr O'Connor recognized her! The mother, Mrs Fitzsimon, had a fit, then, almost literally, screaming and yelling at the doctor to get away from her daughter and trying to stop the other nurses from dragging her away. Went berserk! And then, of course, she started howling for her medicine, so they slipped her a cup of laudanum and that was that.'

'Would you say that Mrs Fitzsimon is insane?' asked the Reverend Mother, noting with interest the annoyed look came upon Dr Munroe's face.

'Look here, Reverend Mother,' he said daringly, 'you seem a sober and sensible type, but I can guarantee that if I got you to take laudanum for a week, you'd find it hard to get off it. If it's been the only thing between you and despair for ten years; why then it would be impossible to do without it for too long. The only thing you can do for someone like that is gradually lengthen the spaces between administering the drug – can be done, but it's a long, hard road. I explained that to Angelina.'

'And she accepted it?' queried Dr Scher.

'Oh, yes, I told you. A very intelligent girl. Had a lot of patience – she told me that she found she could stay patient while she was with her mother because she was rehearsing in her mind what she would say to the fat lawyer in South Mall – he was by way of being her mother's trustee, you see. She told me about a few of the questions that she had put to him.'

A smile came over the lips of the young doctor and then it disappeared.

'Dreadful to think that she is dead: I can hardly bear to think of it!' He rose to his feet. He had not repeated his first words: *I'm not altogether surprised.* Now that he was fully awake and more in his right mind, he probably would not. But did he suspect Gerald Fitzsimon, or the solicitor, or someone else even nearer to Angelina – like her father, Joseph Fitzsimon, perhaps?

'I'd better be getting home,' he said. 'Thanks for the food and for the drink.'

'Take the bottle with you; plenty more where that came from.' Dr Scher nodded to the half-bottle of Midleton's whiskey.

'No, I won't; it might be like laudanum for me. You're in trouble when you start using alcohol or drugs to keep you going during the long nights,' he said, suddenly sounding quite elderly. The Reverend Mother walked with him to the front door and Dr Scher followed. They all stood there for a moment, looking at each other. And then he was off, walking with a quick, springing step and disappearing out of the door in an instant. Dr Scher looked at the Reverend Mother when he came back into the parlour.

'Sarsfield,' he said, echoing Lucy's words, while he carefully put the half-empty bottle back into his pocket. 'That's the solicitor – and now that's a name that we haven't properly considered. He had been at the Merchant's Ball too; the name was on young Patrick's list. Hadn't danced with Angelina, though. Not surprising, perhaps, given what young Munroe has said of the interviews that she was reported to have had with the solicitor who should have been looking after her mother's interests.'

It was funny, thought the Reverend Mother, as she turned the matter over in her mind. If this was a murder of someone from the slums Patrick would be looking at who knew the girl; who had quarrelled with her; were there two men after her? Who was drunk on that particular night?

It probably was, she thought, a simpler process.

In the case of Angelina Fitzsimon – well, it was a different world. A world with she was familiar, but where Patrick, and even perhaps Dr Scher, was not so much at home. It looked to her as though money – earned wealth or inherited wealth – and status in the precarious class structure of the city might have been at the root of her murder.

Dr Munroe had sketched a portrait of a strong-minded, spirited girl who was determined to get justice for her mother, to restore her inheritance to her, and to free her from the asylum and from her addiction to laudanum; a girl who had the courage to tackle her father, her father's physician and her family solicitor about the wrongs done to the unfortunate woman. The Reverend Mother was taken by that portrait and her heart swelled with strong feelings of kinship towards that brave and courageous girl. She thought back to Lucy's words and wondered whether it could be true that the father had killed a daughter like that.

Or could it have been the brother, Gerald? Perhaps the Copinger inheritance of ungoverned passions and a love of money had gone down from father to son and then to grandson.

It was no wonder, she thought, that Thomas Aquinas spent so much time debating about whether God allowed, even willed, evil to have its place in the world.

FOURTEEN

St Thomas Aquinas:
Qui omni congregationi sit, sicut in societate habet
partem ut pars at totum.
(Whosoever is of the whole community has a part to
play in that society.)

The funeral of Angelina Fitzsimon took place on Saturday morning. The Reverend Mother had wondered whether Dr Scher could attend on a Saturday, but he had sent around a message the night before to tell her that he would pick her up at half-past nine.

'And the postman had a bit of news about Nellie O'Sullivan, Reverend Mother,' said Sister Bernadette. 'He said that she was serving drinks last night in Paddy's Bar on Albert Quay – all dressed up, she was. He hardly knew her.'

'Going the same way as that sister of hers,' snapped Sister Mary Immaculate, who had just come in with a list of books to be ordered.

'To Liverpool, is that right?' asked the Reverend Mother mildly. 'I understand that was where Mary O'Sullivan went.'

Her deputy sniffed, but did not venture to enlighten her superior to any greater degree and Reverend Mother went back to her accounts in a forbidding fashion which informed both sisters that she did not wish to discuss the matter further. She kept her head down until they left the room, but then lifted it and stared at the opposite wall.

The accounts could wait; the murder had to be solved. She put them aside, bowed her head into her hands and began to think hard. By the time that Dr Scher arrived to drive her to the funeral her clear mind had formulated a number of questions.

The cemetery down in Blackrock was full – full of the great names of Cork. They were all there, all very well dressed in shining shoes, expensive broadcloth and starched shirt fronts with starched, snowy-white handkerchiefs peeping from breast pockets. An elderly canon performed the service, a couple of other canons assisting him, then the coffin containing the body of an undernourished, painfully thin young girl was buried beneath a marble angel who kept watch over the hallowed remains of the Fitzsimon family.

'*Old money*,' said Dr Scher's voice in her ear, and she nodded. His father had been a jeweller who had made the journey from Russia, or was it Lithuania, to Manchester and then, for some strange reason, to the city of Cork. Old money would have been reverenced by the jeweller – these would have been the people who patronized his shop and allowed him to accumulate enough to educate his son and send him on to university – but, of course, old money in the case of Irish Roman Catholics meant only a few generations away from the peasant farmer. The starched handkerchiefs were not produced at the graveyard. Angelina's relations and family friends watched dry-eyed. Perhaps the announcement of the illicit pregnancy had absolved father and son from any excessive show of grief. They stood stony-faced as the coffin was lowered down into the prepared hole and then turned away as the earth was shovelled over it.

And then the important business of the day began.

The great and the good lined up to shake the hands of the bereaved family, father, brother and a cousin; and then joined the other long line which had, at its head, a young reporter from the *Cork Examiner* with a shorthand notebook. A sharp-looking young man, well spoken and with a good instinct for future success, he never once annoyed anyone by asking them how to spell their names, or put any questions about 'double ts', 'en' or 'an', whether it was 'Mc' or Mac' or whether the Murphy standing before him was representing Murphys the Brewers, Murphys the Skins (as the owners of the tanning factory were known) or indeed Murphys the Sausages. He nodded respectfully at each name as if to say that he had immediately recognized its owner and disposed of those 'representing . . .' with a quick flourish of his busy pencil. The Reverend Mother's eyes were attracted towards

Patrick and she heard him say to the superintendent: 'I'll give our names to the reporter, sir, while you are condoling with the Fitzsimon family.'

He moved away quickly before a reply could be made – no reply was needed. Of course, the superintendent wanted his name in the paper. It would be the first thing that he would look for on Monday morning – as would everyone else who was present today. And it would be expected of his subordinate that he would attend to important matters like that.

Patrick, she noticed, didn't need to queue up. As soon as he approached, the young reporter waved an astute pencil at him, entered a few hieroglyphs into his notebook and nodded him away. She herself had the courtesy of an almost bow of acknowledgement and she had little doubt that her name also would appear – representing the convent of St Mary's of the Isle. Amazing how important it all was to people, but perhaps it was important because it ensured their place in the community was openly recognized.

'Know everyone, these fellows,' said a friendly voice at her shoulder, and she looked around and then saw Professor Cyril Lambert. 'He had my name and "representing the St Vincent de Paul Society of Cork" before I opened my mouth. It's a gift, I suppose. Wish I had it. I'm always offending people that I should know by passing them by on the street without even a nod. Does that ever happen to you, Reverend Mother?' And then as Patrick joined them, he asked him the same question.

'I can't say that it ever does,' said Patrick after a moment's thought. 'But there are a lot of people who should know me and who slide away without a nod the minute they see me.'

Professor Lambert laughed uproariously at this mild joke, throwing his large head back in amusement. Joseph Fitzsimon turned his head at the sound and looked across grimly and then quickly away in an embarrassed fashion. The professor put a hand across his mouth.

'Oh, dear,' he said. 'That was rather insensitive of me. And yet, do you know, Reverend Mother,' he said with sincerity, 'I deeply mourn her, probably more than most who are here – not many girls of that age would spend such a lot of their

free time helping the St Vincent de Paul Society. All the ladies
subscribed for a wreath for her and we put a card saying "from
the poor of Cork" on it. We felt that was appropriate. And I've
written a letter to the *Cork Examiner* expressing my sorrow,
and my appreciation of all that Angelina Fitzsimon did for
those so much less fortunate than she. It should be in today's
paper.'

'That was kind,' said the Reverend Mother appreciatively.
Everyone who was anyone in the city of Cork read the *Cork
Examiner* from cover to cover. This letter would pay a fitting
tribute to the girl who had everything, but still was moved to
pity by those who had little or nothing. She looked at the
professor, noticing how all that approached near to him tended
to sidle away when exposed to the flaring pimpled skin across
his face – it was, she acknowledged, hard to be natural with
someone as disfigured as he, but nevertheless the effort had
to be made. He was such a kind man who spent his inherited
money on making life more bearable for the poor of Cork.
She made up her mind. This was a man who could tell her
some more about that elusive figure, Angelina Fitzsimon.

'Do you think that I could beg a lift back to the house from
you, Professor, if you are going there just now,' she asked.
Long years as a Reverend Mother had made her accomplished
at asking small favours and he immediately and enthusiastically agreed and went off to fetch his car, telling her that he
would wait for her at the gates to the cemetery. She sent a
message to Dr Scher by Patrick – she could see him deep in
conversation with a man whom she guessed, by his deeply
tanned face, to be the tea-planter from India. Let him worm
out the gossip about this projected marriage. She would indulge
herself in understanding a little more about the personality of
the dead girl.

Professor Lambert's car was not in any way as comfortable
as Dr Scher's. Still, she told herself while edging irritably
away from the ill-fitting window behind her neck, he was
popularly reputed to spend most of his salary on charitable
works. He was the president of the St Vincent de Paul Society
and responsible for much of the fundraising initiatives, related
to the Crawfords, she seemed to remember, but the Crawfords

had been prolific breeders of large families, and old money doesn't last as long as pride in family.

'How did you first meet Angelina Fitzsimon?' she asked as they drove away. At least he was a competent driver and they bounced along in his tinny little car at a sensible speed and remained on their own side of the road.

'She came to see me, I had taught her brother and she made that an excuse when introducing herself. She came to my office in the university. She was a very nice girl, very serious, very determined. Clever, too, I would have thought, much cleverer than the brother.'

'I suppose,' said the Reverend Mother acidly, 'it never occurred to anyone that she might have made the better doctor if she were the one to study medicine.'

He gave her a startled glance, but then nodded. 'She may have done. You're probably right. She was very interested in disease. In fact, she helped me a lot with my notes about tuberculosis in Cork. I was collating the sufferers into a house by house, and street by street . . .'

'But she didn't visit houses; you said that, didn't you?' Angelina, thought the Reverend Mother, had had the courage to defy her father and to visit her mother in that living hell to which he had consigned her. Surely a girl like that would not hesitate to meet the people who tried to live their lives while being ground down with such poverty.

Professor Lambert gave her an uneasy glance and then turned back to the road again. 'Her father would have been very against anything like that,' he said obliquely and she did not pursue the question – in fact, she was sorry that she had asked it and began to placate him with praise of the work done by the St Vincent de Paul Society, telling him about various pet schemes of hers to educate the poor of the city in order to extract them from the fate that seemed to be theirs from the moment in which they were born.

'But, of course,' he pointed out, 'while this is wonderful for some, for the clever girls, you are omitting, on the whole, to change the fate of those who are not interested in education or who are unintelligent or light-minded. If they are a Crawford, or a Woodford, or a Barry, but they are not too academic, then they play tennis, listen to jazz, go to the cinema, to parties, but if they belong to the slums, then it is just the last straw in sinking them to their fate. Work needs to be set up for these people. Have you ever seen the line of dockers down on the quays, all queuing up, standing there from morning to night, hoping against hope that they will be the ones chosen for an unloading job . . .?'

'I suppose you're right,' she said, struggling against a feeling of irritation. She was used to praise, to people telling her how wonderful she was. No one had ever dared before to tell her that she was not doing enough. She thought of Nellie O'Sullivan and sighed. Nellie had got a job in a public house, but how long would that last, and what would it fit her for in the future?

'Thomas Aquinas said justice should be for all – that to be part of the community meant that you were responsible for that community,' she said, forcing herself to be fair to him – the odd girl, the one in a hundred, like Catty Cotter educated in cookery in the kitchen that she was so proud of, might get a job with someone like Mrs O'Leary, but what was she doing about the ninety-nine who could find nothing in their native city? She put the thought aside for the moment and said, 'Tell me some more about Angelina – she seems an interesting girl.'

'Angelina Fitzsimon was something special, you know,' he said, and the gravity of his tone and the deep voice in which he uttered the words touched her heart.

'Why?' she asked, imbuing the monosyllable with a touch of indifference.

'Well, how many young ladies of her background would concern themselves with the poorest of the poor?' he said. 'She was a wonderful girl. I don't pretend to know of all of her thoughts, of everything that went on in her head – and I suppose like all of us she could have been easily led astray by a plausible tale, but she was a person of integrity and honour.' His voice shook slightly and it was apparent that the idea of the murder of this girl had upset him greatly.

'You make me sorry that I never made her acquaintance,' said the Reverend Mother and her sincerity of tone slightly alarmed her.

Luckily, he saw nothing strange in her fervour. 'Probably

I, and my assistants at the St Vincent de Paul, saw the real Angelina,' he said earnestly. 'It was difficult to get to know her properly, though. She was a reserved girl and she – one should not say this, perhaps – but she was quite unlike either her father or her brother. I would not be surprised, Reverend Mother, if she wanted to get away from them.' And then he stopped and she got the impression that he felt he had said too much as his lips closed tightly and he spoke of common-places until he reached the house where Angelina had grown to maturity.

He allowed her to get out by herself and she missed Dr Scher's gallantry as she pushed open the awkwardly hung front passenger door and struggled on to the flagstones. They were among the many to return to the house from the funeral, but an efficient butler appeared almost immediately and ushered them inside.

The funeral meats were spread out on the large long table in the dining room and the folding doors were thrown open between that and the drawing room. She remembered that table, remembered meals at it when she was young girl, remem-bered the easy conversation, the deference with which Robert and his brother, Edmond, and Angela, also, treated her father and their fond indulgence of his motherless daughter and especially of Lucy, the pet of them all. This was over fifty years ago, she thought, but the Royal Navy patterned blue-and-white china had still survived and was piled high with small and delicately designed morsels which could be eaten with the hand. The table was lined down the centre with decanters of various types and blends of strong liquor and already the servants were bringing in steaming teapots and coffee pots.

'Did Angelina's father approve of her charitable works?' she asked after accepting a hot cup of deliciously scented tea from a polite parlour maid, well outfitted in lace apron and cap. They withdrew into the alcove formed by a bay window and her question, she thought, would be unheard.

The professor gave her a slightly comical look, half mischiev-ous and half appraising.

'Well, fathers have great notions for their daughters, especially when they are only daughters,' he said in the diplomatic tones of one used to living with two cultures – those who have and those who have nothing and desperately need some charity from the first class.

'I see,' said the Reverend Mother, taking a cautious nibble from one of the sweetmeats enticingly displayed on the small table beside them. She could see, and the side of her that still remembered her own girlhood as the indulged daughter of a wealthy merchant could just imagine how Joseph Fitzsimon had not wanted his daughter to become involved in anything that might spoil her matrimonial chances. It was, she thought, trying to be fair, hard to blame him. These merchant princes of Cork city were practising and assiduous Roman Catholics to the man. There was none of this new and dangerous talk of birth control – families were large – fourteen or fifteen children that lived to maturity were not in any way unusual where there was plenty of money to feed the offspring and procure them medical attention in the case of illness. But of course, many of their sons had fought in the army and navy during the Great War and had been killed. This meant that there were plenty of girls in the matrimonial marketplace, to put it crudely.

Any girl that was different, that had odd interests like spending much of her free time and money in ministering to the poor, in collecting clothes for them, in talking to them, finding out their dreams and their aspirations – well, a girl like that might well not have found favour with the gilded youth of Cork city.

Like this boy, here, she thought as her eyes went to the figure of Gerald Fitzsimon as he entered the room. He would, she remembered, be about twenty-three years old. He was a handsome boy who had inherited the red-brown hair and the bright blue eyes of his father and was, perhaps, a good four or five inches taller. She had noticed that about the merchant princes of Cork – all of peasant origin. Generation by generation, good feeding had added inches to their offspring.

Professor Lambert's eyes followed hers.

'I wonder whether he mourns his sister,' he mused and then looked at her as though slightly shocked at his own words. 'Of course he does,' he said eagerly replying to his own question.

'It's just that age. Sometimes, they make a point of hiding their feelings.'

There was no doubt that Gerald Fitzsimon was hiding his feelings – if, of course, he had any. He had a sullen expression on his face as he gazed haughtily around at the visitors who had attended his sister's funeral and had been invited to partake of a meal, according to the custom, before they set off on the journey back to their own homes. He was a striking-looking young man though there were dark circles under his eyes and a few odd-looking lines of strain around his mouth. The few people who came up to him, murmuring the usual condolences, seemed to move away hastily leaving him gulping down his whiskey and staring morosely at the rain-sodden garden through the side window, near to theirs. The Reverend Mother made up her mind and, with a murmured excuse to Professor Lambert, she moved to his side.

'You're Gerald, Angelina's brother,' she said in the fatuous tones assumed by the elderly. 'I knew your grandfather,' she added and waited for his response to this. The boy's nerves were on edge. Her attention was sharpened by the start he gave and the way he suddenly turned on her, spilling a drop of the whiskey he had just about lifted to his lips.

'My grandmother,' he stuttered and she wondered whether he just didn't listen to elderly women, or whether his mind, at the moment, was focused on his Woodford grandmother and on the fortune that was now his. She didn't bother to correct him, just gave him a warm smile. 'You look very like your father, and your grandfather,' she told him. 'I would have known you anywhere.'

His eyes seemed to show a slight desperation and he looked around for an excuse to leave her, but she was too quick for him.

'And where did you go to school?' she asked, standing squarely between him and the window and keeping her eyes on him so that, without blatant rudeness, he could not get away from her.

'At Clongowes, up in County Kildare,' he muttered. 'Would you like me to get you . . . ?'

'Clongowes,' she cried enthusiastically. 'With the Jesuits – how you must have enjoyed that.'

'Not really,' he said abruptly. He had a slightly dissipated look around the eyes, though his skin was tanned and healthy, she thought, watching him tilt the last of the whiskey down his throat, and signal, abruptly, to the parlour maid for a fresh glassful. 'I hated it, actually,' he said in a tone of such rudeness that she guessed he had been drinking even before the funeral took place. 'Don't most people hate boarding school?' he queried, taking another sip from the glass and facing her belligerently.

She left that question unanswered, though it was, she thought, a good one. It was interesting that Joseph had sent his son to boarding school just as he had been sent by his guardian, Robert Fitzsimon. What made them and others like them, who had wonderfully warm, comfortable, well-cared-for houses, library, billiard and table-tennis room, tennis court, everything to keep sons and daughters happy, send their children off to boarding school to be, in the main, unhappy there, while the children of the poor stayed in the miserable, overcrowded, damp, cold houses where homework and study was an almost impossibility?

'You would have preferred to stay at home?' she asked politely while he downed the rest of his whiskey.

He scowled at her. His inhibitions were fast vanishing with the alcohol that he was consuming. Soon she might see that real Gerald Fitzsimon behind the facade of young-man-about-town.

'Not here,' he said with disgust. He shook his glass as though to see whether there were any drops remaining and then looked at her defiantly. 'I hate this place, too,' he said. 'There's only one place in the world that I like and that's Crosshaven – I've got a boat there, not a very good one – I'd like to buy myself a decent one, now . . .'

'You like sailing?' Like his grandfather, she thought. There was always a new and better boat that such men craved. Well, he would have had to make a great success of his profession or else marry money – sailing was an expensive hobby.

Now, of course, with the death of his sister, he was master of a good fortune. Woodford money was in a different category to the modest inheritance which would come to him eventually from his father.

'I remember going out on a trawler for an all-night fishing trip,' she said, chatting easily about the sea and telling him about her childhood holidays.

She had been talking in order to allow him to open up, but it almost seemed as though the image was unbearable to him. He muttered something about getting her a sandwich and made his escape. She gazed after him thoughtfully. For a moment, the sullen, spoiled-boy look on his face had lifted and had been replaced by look of such yearning that it had almost hurt her to look at him. Was he thinking back into childhood holidays – was he remembering his sister, just two years younger than he? The look on his face had definitely been of longing, but then it had been replaced by a fixed mask of despair.

The Reverend Mother stayed where she was in the slightly withdrawn window alcove but looked straight across at Professor Lambert who was now wandering beside the laden table in the centre of the room and nibbling here and there like a pony put out to grass. He came as quickly and as directly as though he had been reeled in by her fishing line and once he had joined her she wasted no time.

'You taught, or is it "teach", the Fitzsimon boy – that's right, isn't it?'

He looked at her curiously. He was, she noted, quite unself-conscious about his terribly disfigured face. She supposed that over the years he had come to terms with the port-wine stain. 'Gerald?' he queried. 'Yes, that's right.' He gave his booming laugh and then hushed himself quickly again. 'Well, nominally, anyway. His name is down for my lectures. I'm Professor of Pathology – mainly I deal with diseases of the lungs and chest – these are my interests.'

'But not Gerald's?'

'No,' said Professor Lambert, 'though, to be fair, I don't think he attends many lectures at all.'

She absorbed this silently. Dr Scher had said more or less the same thing.

'So why is he studying medicine?' she asked. 'Why not something that he is interested in? Is there anything that he is interested in?' Probably, she thought, the boy's record at school was poor and the medical course was too hard for him. It was,

she thought impatiently, a stupid system where a boy of medi-
ocre ability, pushed by his father into studying a difficult subject
like medicine, would be accepted by the university and children
with brains would be rejected because their parents did not
have the money to pay the fees and to maintain them.

'I don't think he's interested in anything except sailing,' he
said. 'Someone told me that he has a yacht down in one of
those east Cork fishing villages. Will spend days and nights
on it, one of my students told me; all by himself, too, which
is a bit strange. I'm a rowing man, myself, or I used to be
and it was the companionship as well as the fresh air and the
exercise that attracted me. We used to row on the River Lee
– from the University down to Blackrock Castle and then back
again.' He looked down at his broad chest and heaved a theatrical sigh and then said, 'Whenever you are ready, Reverend
Mother . . . I live in South Terrace, you know. I can easily
drop you back to St Mary's of the Isle – no trouble at all.'

As they drove along the South Terrace he showed her his
apartment, up on the top floor of a house only six or seven
doors down from Dr Scher's place.

'Never been in private practice – nothing but a university
lectureship and a professorship was good enough for me – pass
on the knowledge, I suppose – influence the next generation.
That place has plenty of room for me – I'd rattle like a pea
in a place the size of Scher's; don't know why he keeps on
the whole house just for himself – hasn't got a wife or a child
to fill it,' he said slightly scornfully. 'Nice fellow, though –
young people like him.' He seemed to add those words in a
slightly perfunctory manner, but the Reverend Mother did not
respond. Her mind was busy with Gerald Fitzsimon. A liking
for yachts and for remote fishing villages would not lead to
any career for a young man of the merchant class of Cork. It
would be little wonder if his father were to become impatient
and withdraw him from his medical studies which appeared
to engage so little of his time and put him to work in his own
retail business. In fact, if Joseph had done so, that might have
been the best thing for Gerald, especially since the Woodford
fortune from the maternal grandmother had been destined for
his sister, not for him.

'This is most kind of you, and I know you must be busy,' she said as they arrived at the gates to the convent. She did not ask him in – she wanted to have some space in which to think her own thoughts, so got out quickly as soon as he stopped and waved a brisk farewell. He drove off with a faint toot-toot of the horn and she made her way meditatively through the gate and up the front pathway to the convent.

All was quiet within her kingdom. Saturday morning school classes were over for the day and the sisters, teacher, novices, pensioners and sacristans were at their midday dinner when she arrived. She slipped past Sister Mary Immaculate with a mutter about a lunch having been provided at the house of the dead girl and she went along to her study. She had, she knew, some very earnest thinking to do.

She had reached its threshold and was just about to open the door when the faithful Sister Bernadette destroyed her peace.

'We've had all sorts of excitement here, Reverend Mother,' she said dramatically. 'The police have been doing a door-to-door search of the whole area. They even had the cheek to call in here – I sent them off with a flea in their ear – you can depend on that! They're searching for Eileen O'Donovan. You'll never guess. They're saying that she's the one who killed that poor girl that you found in the lane – that she's the one who murdered Angelina Fitzsimon.'

Patrick came around at four in the afternoon. He was full of apologies that the convent had been disturbed and was, she thought, seething with wounded pride that the matter had been taken out of his hands and that his superior had ordered the search of the neighbourhood, without a word to him, just before they had both set out for the funeral. The Reverend Mother gathered that the superintendent wanted to be able to assure the family, and, even more importantly, the *Cork Examiner*, that active and sweeping measures had been taken to rid the city of a murderer. The lamplighter, she guessed, had given in his evidence, not naming the Republican Party – something that might have brought death to him and to members of his family, but laying emphasis on seeing a well-known figure, dressed not in the comely and suitable shabby rags and defining shawl over the head and shoulders, but in the heavy wool breeches, jacket and beret of the rebels.

Patrick had, of course, known about Eileen O'Donovan although she would be about five years younger than he. There had been a mixture of excitement and outrage in the neighbourhood at her emergence from the chrysalis of respectable poverty into the exotic uniform of the Republican Party. The rumour that she was the author of the article for the *Cork Examiner* would have been enough to point the finger at her. The body, obviously described before the arrival of the police, might have been enough to condemn her. The Reverend Mother's presence at the scene would have been immediately whitewashed out of the records. She wondered whether to summon the superintendent, but decided to wait until Monday. If Eileen were arrested before that, then she would take action immediately. In the meantime, she sat down on her chair and began to think about the murder of Angelina Fitzsimon and all the ramifications of relationships within those families who had once been so familiar to her.

FIFTEEN

St Thomas Aquinas:
Ita vivunt in scaenis quomodo concordia sidera – bellum cum plerique sine paulisper ire vix aliquis scit animabus eorum?
(How is it that the billions of stars live in such harmony – when most men can barely go a minute without declaring war in their minds against someone they know?)

I t was the smell of blood that alerted the Reverend Mother. She had taken the key to lock up the chapel after sundown – it formed a good excuse for her to get outside the convent and to refresh her mind by pacing the gravelled path of the shrubbery of Portuguese laurels and ugly privet which had been established in the Victorian heyday of the convent gardens and was the pride and joy of their present gardener, who continually clipped back every rebel branch.

It had come on to rain though, almost as soon as she had stepped out of the side doorway – not a soft mist, but a heavy downpour which, together with the bitter wind from the east that snatched at her veil, made walking impossible and forced her to do without her evening stroll and go immediately towards the chapel for shelter. There would be flooding again soon just when high tide coincided with this cold east wind and heavy rain, she thought, as she pushed open the chapel door and closed it carefully behind her, omitting the customary dip of the fingers into the holy water and going straight through the little porch and into the main body of the church.

And that was when the smell of blood came to her nostrils. It was surprisingly strong, overpowering the incense and the candle grease. Only one light was still illuminated, the red globe over the altar, but it seemed to show that the chapel was empty. She stood for a moment, looking around, feeling puzzled.

Something else was amiss. The small table that stood to the

side of the altar showed up bare and dark brown, stripped of
its usual linen cloth. And the steps leading up to the altar,
made from the finest Italian marble, had little round red spots
marring their immaculate surface.

Without hesitation the Reverend Mother snatched a cande-
labrum from the altar and held it up, following the trail to the
small room where the priest robed every morning before Mass.

'You should have stayed within the altar rails if you are
looking for sanctuary, Eileen,' she said and then moved forward
instantly as the girl swayed. She put an arm around her and
asked, 'Are you badly hurt, my child?'

'Bit of trouble,' said Eileen. She turned a face that strove
to be nonchalant towards the Reverend Mother, but was drawn
with pain and deadly white. She looked as though she were
about to faint. She sank down on a chair and bowed her head.

It was an emergency and without hesitation Reverend
Mother raided the cupboard for the sacred communion wine
and angled the bottle towards the girl's mouth. 'Drink some,'
she said authoritatively and was relieved to see a little colour
come into Eileen's face. There was an ominous stain still
spreading on the white tablecloth which Eileen held to her
arm and the Reverend Mother seized the priest's stole from
its place on a wall hook and bound it firmly over the bulging
cloth.

'What happened?' she asked, relieved to see a little colour
come back into the girl's face.

Eileen took another swig of the communion wine before
answering. 'Good stuff,' she murmured, 'you'd better take it
away, Reverend Mother, before you get me drunk.'

Reverend Mother accepted the bottle and waited for an
answer to her question.

'We had to get Jimmy Logan, the lamplighter fellow, out
of the barracks,' she said after a minute. 'Not just for his own
sake,' she added as the Reverend Mother stifled a snort. 'He's
the type that loves to give information and he'd probably give
it to the civic guards as quickly as to the Free-Staters or to
ourselves. The trouble is that the things he says and the things
that he will swear to in court can do a lot of harm. We got a
message to say that he was singing like a canary, fingering

me for the murder of that girl.' She shifted slightly, biting her lip and suppressing a groan as the Reverend Mother tightened the knot on the embroidered stole.

'Was it a knife wound?' asked the Reverend Mother, deciding not to go into the politics or the ethics of the raid on the barracks. This was not the time for a pious lecture.

'Bullet, I'm afraid,' said Eileen. 'I'm sorry that I came here, Reverend Mother – I'll be off when I feel a bit stronger. That stuff in the bottle is great. If I had a bit more I might be able to walk. One of our lads, Eamonn, is great at digging out bullets – was a medical student – at least, he did a year in pre-med. He does it with his pocket knife – dips it into iodine first, of course.' There was a wobble in the voice, which its owner strove to make sound nonchalant and the Reverend Mother was not deceived.

'How did you get here, Eileen?' she asked gently.

Tears started into Eileen's grey eyes. She gulped and made a huge effort to control her voice.

'I'm crazy,' she said shakily. 'You wouldn't believe it, Reverend Mother, but a bullet in the arm really hurts and do you know the first thing that I thought – well, I wanted my mam – like I was a little kid again.' With that she broke down and sobbed. The Reverend Mother eyed the communion wine and decided that the God of St Thomas Aquinas would intend her to use her common sense. She took off the cork again.

'Just a small drink, now, Eileen. I certainly don't want you inebriated,' she said in brisk tones.

Either the drink or the matter-of-fact words seemed to work. Eileen swiped her face with a rather dirty hand, had a quick gulp, gave a watery smile and continued her story.

'And then I came to my senses. I couldn't bring the civic guards down on top of my mam – she has enough to put up with – so I came in here. I thought if I had a bit of rest I could be on my way once it gets dark . . .'

Her voice faded away. Her face, by the light of the six candles, was even whiter than ever. The Reverend Mother looked out of the small window. Already the light was fading. There was no doubt that another storm was brewing.

'Wait here for a moment,' she said. 'I'll find you a bed for the night. You can sleep in my study and no one will be the wiser. Just wait until the sisters have gone to bed and then I'll smuggle you in. You don't mind the dark, do you? I'll have to blow out the candles or someone is bound to see their light and come asking questions.'

She wished that she could tuck Eileen up in a bed straight-away, but it would be too risky. She touched the girl's cheek and was alarmed to find how cold it was. Eileen needed warmth. She chose a heavily embroidered dark red chasuble from the cupboard and wrapped it around the girl. It would not be worn by the priest until Good Friday and any murky stains could be got out of it by then. She would, she planned, hand it over to Sister Bernadette in a nonchalant fashion just after the Palm Sunday rituals on the week before Easter and ask her to check that it was in good order. Hopefully any stain would be put down to a spilling of wine by a careless altar boy, or better still, by the priest himself.

'Wait here until I come back,' she said to Eileen, but she took the precaution of locking the church door when she went out. The girl was headstrong and stubborn; and seventeen, she knew from her own experience, is a time when one thinks one knows best.

But when she got back to the convent she began to change her mind. It was not as late as she had thought – Eileen could not be left there in that cold chapel for another few hours – and there was no doubt that the bullet would need to be dug out of her arm. She had no faith in the young Republican who was so handy with his penknife, even if he did use iodine, and had gone through the pre-med year at the university. With a sigh she went to the phone in the back corridor, picked up the receiver and asked the exchange for Dr Scher's number.

He was in. For a few minutes she had worried that he would be out, that he had not gone back home after the funeral, but once the housekeeper knew that it was Reverend Mother Aquinas on the phone she changed her official voice, which doubted whether the doctor was at home, and said obligingly that she would get him.

He sounded sleepy when he came to the phone, but the

Reverend Mother ignored that. She was impatient of people who felt that they had to have these little after-supper naps.

'I'd like you to come over,' she said and then wondered what to say next. Sister Bernadette, of course, would have an ear open so she had to be careful. 'I just want to discuss something with you,' she went on, carefully. 'You got home safely from Blackrock, did you? I heard that there has been trouble in town today.' She chattered on, talking about her conversation with Professor Lambert and his praise of Dr Scher's ability to operate successfully in any conditions. 'I heard a story that will amuse you,' she said carefully. 'I've heard of a young man who digs out bullets with a penknife – used to be a medical student for a year, I believe, but then he gave it up. What do you think about that? Should he be trusted to deal with a case, what do you think?'

There was a long silence and then a sigh. 'You'll get me hung,' he said resignedly. 'See you in ten minutes.'

Well, at least he is quick-witted was her thought as she hung up the phone and went upstairs to the linen cupboard. There was plenty of spare clothing there. The Reverend Mother got out a habit, a wimple and a veil. There was also a bag for soiled linen so she packed the articles into that and strolled downstairs frowning in a manner which she knew would deter Sister Bernadette from asking whether she could help her in any way. The Reverend Mother was known to be charitable with donations to impoverished families and hopefully this would pass without remark.

By a piece of luck she met no one and went out through the rain, towards the chapel, carrying the bag in one hand and an enormous umbrella in the other. Eileen was looking very faint, but she revived enough to giggle at the nun's garb. Her dashing military-style coat was soaked with blood and it did not seem wise to remove the stole that was binding her arm to her chest so in the end they had to be content with draping the habit – luckily a large size – over everything and taking trouble to fix the wimple and veil as authentically as possible.

'Can you walk?' asked the Reverend Mother, looking at her anxiously.

'"You can do anything if you want to badly enough," that's

what you used to tell us,' said Eileen. 'I used to believe you,'
she added bleakly.

What a lot of nonsense we tell the young, thought the
Reverend Mother, but she just smiled and held her hand out,
keeping it firm and steady as Eileen staggered a few steps.
When they got out of the chapel, and once it had been locked
up, she put up the umbrella, shielding both of their faces, and
tucked her arm firmly into Eileen's, supporting the girl. Many
nuns walked like that, compensating for the loss of family
by their affection for their fellow members of the religious
order. The appearance of the two of them going arm-in-arm
through the convent garden would not excite any attention in
the semi-dark with the rain falling and she steered a path to the
side door into the convent.

'Wait for a second,' she whispered, thrusting the umbrella
into Eileen's right hand and pushing the door open. To her
annoyance she felt her heart beating very fast when the figure
of Sister Mary Immaculate came bearing down on her. She
didn't hesitate for a moment, though.

'Ah, Sister, I was coming to see you. Could you prepare
reports on the senior class for me for Monday morning,' she
said, making her voice sound slightly cold. 'I'd like to have
some notes on each girl's strongest point as well as their
weakest.' Her mind had gone to her conversation with Professor
Lambert – perhaps she was overemphasizing the academic at
the expense of the practical. She would have to think hard
about the purpose of education – it shouldn't just be a butter-
making process where the cream was allowed to rise to the
surface, to be turned into the golden product that had made
Cork rich, while the remaining skimmed milk was an almost-
waste product.

Sister Mary Immaculate received her command in sulky
silence and turned away without any of the usual standing around
and gossiping endlessly. The Reverend Mother stood very still
until she heard the leather soles tapping on the staircase leading
up to the nuns' dormitories, then went quietly down the corridor
and opened the door to her study. There was a leather couch in
the room and she moved it to a position where its front was
to the fire and its back to the door. She placed a cushion for a

pillow and fetched a rug from the cupboard. Only then did she go back to fetch Eileen.

When the sound of the doorbell came to her ears, she felt very tense. She would have loved to have gone to the door herself and usher Dr Scher in as quickly as possible, but that would have been too great a diversion from her usual behaviour so she sat at her desk with her account book open and hoped that Eileen, on the couch, would lie still until Sister Bernadette had departed.

Dr Scher's medical bag was so much part of him that Sister Bernadette did not seem to have taken any notice of it. He was giving her details of the funeral, seeming to remember all of the names effortlessly and she was enjoying that – Cork was a small city and these names were familiar to all of the residents – Sister Bernadette exclaimed at every representative of the various dynasties. She eagerly offered tea, but to the Reverend Mother's relief he put her off with a reference to the huge meal that had been offered at the funeral feast, down at Blackrock.

Eventually she was gone, and with slightly shaking fingers the Reverend Mother quietly turned the key in the lock. By the time she turned around Dr Scher had gone around the couch and was standing with his back to the fire looking down at the patient, who stared up at him defiantly.

'This is the person who writes the column on the *Cork Examiner* that you admire,' said the Reverend Mother in the tones of one performing a social duty. 'Dr Scher; A Patriot,' she added and saw comprehension dawn on his face.

'Right, having made the introductions, let's just have a look at you,' said the doctor as Eileen, with an impatient hand, dragged off the wimple and veil. It took longer and a lot of lip-biting before she was free of the floor-length habit and then came the agony of removing the coat. Dr Scher suggesting cutting it, but Eileen was alarmed at that and insisted it wasn't hurting her to take it off. There was an oozing of fresh blood, but eventually the arm was free and Dr Scher bent over her, feeling her forehead and pulling down an eyelid to peer into the socket.

'You've been drinking,' he said, sniffing her breath.

'That was the Reverend Mother!' Eileen, rather faint, but still indomitable, giggled and said demurely, 'She kept pouring communion wine down my throat.'

'Nuns! You can never trust them with the bottle!' exclaimed Dr Scher with such comic emphasis that Eileen giggled again. 'I could give you a whiff of ether, but it might be a bit much on top of the alcohol. Can you bear a bit of pain?'

'Yes,' said Eileen resolutely. 'I don't want ether. I have to be on my way soon. Don't give me anything that will make me woozy.'

'You'll stay the night, and until Dr Scher says that you can go and that is an order,' said the Reverend Mother sternly and then was almost unbearably touched to see a couple of tears ooze out from Eileen's tightly shut eyes.

She bore the pain well as Dr Scher's sharply pointed knife and tweezers did their job and she stayed very still while the arm was being bandaged. 'Brave girl,' he said gently when he had finished. 'Now a glass of water, Reverend Mother and she can take a few aspirins. She can have a few more before she goes to sleep tonight and I'll be around to see her first thing in the morning.'

'Come at five minutes past ten,' commanded the Reverend Mother, and then when he raised an eyebrow she condescended to say: 'Mass is celebrated at ten o'clock in the community chapel.'

He gave her an amused smile and saluted in a military fashion, but she ignored him. She was concerned about Eileen, who seemed to be drifting in and out of consciousness.

When he had gone Reverend Mother abandoned her pretext of work and sat beside the girl. Eileen dozed and then twitched violently a few times in what seemed to be a nightmare, but a touch on her hand woke her and she fell asleep again quite quickly. At ten o'clock she awoke feverish and thirsty and the Reverend Mother gave her a couple of aspirins. They didn't seem to work very well, though, and Eileen was holding her bottom lip between her teeth and had her hands tightly clenched.

'Try to relax, Eileen,' she ordered and Eileen nodded obediently.

'A fellow I know says that he has a great way of relaxing and that he always uses it if he's winged by a bullet.' she said in a voice that she strove to make sound unconcerned.

'Thinks about his medical studies?' queried the Reverend Mother.

Eileen giggled. 'No, this is a different lad,' she said. 'He says that he imagines a pub and that when he goes in, the first thing he sees is a great, big blazing fire and the second thing is the counter completely covered with glasses of Beamish stout – and each one of the glasses has a head of froth on it and he goes along the counter, drinking each one of them, real, real slow – that's what he says. And by the time that he comes to the back row on the counter he's usually asleep – that's what he says. Doesn't work with me, though,' added Eileen. 'I suppose the problem is that I don't like Beamish stout, much.'

She shifted restlessly on the couch. She looked close to tears and the Reverend Mother sought for something to distract her thoughts.

'Do you remember the body I found,' she began, and then stopped. This was something that might distract Eileen, but it certainly wouldn't be a peaceful image, which would lull her off to sleep. Then she thought of the dress and knew what to do. She remembered the time when there had been a pitched battle between the Republicans and the Black and Tans auxiliaries, right on the street outside the convent. Sister Philomena, normally a rigorous disciplinarian, whose usual response to the most alarming battle noises was 'Keep your head down and get on with your sums', had melted at the terrible distress of the young children under her care and had put them sitting, squashed into the corner of the room, furthest from the windows, had herself sat on the floor in front of them, spreading out her voluminous skirts, like a mother hen, and had told them the story of a fairies' banquet, to which, normally a very truthful person, she swore that she had been invited to for her seventh birthday by the Fairy Queen herself. Lost in the wonders of fairy cakes iced with pink and blue, of jelly and cream in tiny acorns and of sweet honey-flavoured drink delivered in miniature buttercups by some orange and brown striped bees, the children stopped listening to explosions and to the rat-tat-tat of the rifles and were soon eagerly contributing suggestions to the banquet.

'You remember you asked me what the dress on that girl was made from and when I told you that it was satin, it reminded me of something,' she went on. A story was something that she prided herself on telling and so she embarked into a description of how, before her first ball, she had gone to Dowden's department shop and had picked out the most beautiful gown.

'It was satin,' she said, her voice quiet and reminiscent. 'It had been made in London by the famous designer Mr Charles Worth. He made wonderful dresses from satin. It was his favourite material.'

'Satin,' repeated Eileen and it seemed as though her tongue caressed the two syllables with a slightly sibilant sound. 'What did it feel like?'

'Very smooth, almost as smooth as glass when you stroked it with your hand – different though when you wore it – it seemed to glide – it's different wearing satin to wearing silk – silk rustles, satin just sort of . . .'

'Slithers,' Eileen put forward.

'That's right, that's the way it goes when you walk in it, it slithers along with you.'

'What colour was it?' Eileen's eyes were fixed on her with an intensity that made her search her mind for the details of that wonderful gown.

'It was chartreuse,' said the Reverend Mother – her tone, she noted with amusement, was almost reverential, but that was the way that she had felt about it then. 'The most beautiful shade of green, green with a sort of lemon glow from it,' she went on and saw Eileen nod and probably store the new word for future use.

'Would have looked good on you – you have those kind of eyes,' she said kindly.

'And the skirt,' went on the Reverend Mother solemnly, 'the skirt was floor-length, and six foot across the diameter – just like a big circle on the floor – and I wore a crinoline under it, I think it was five hoops of whalebone, held together with tapes – started just above my waist . . .' Her voice went on describing every detail, of lace and embroidery, while her mind went back to those months in Bordeaux and to Lucy's words about the crinoline concealing her pregnancy.

'And when I put the dress on over the crinoline and looked in the mirror – we had no gas lamps in the bedroom, then, but since I was getting ready for a ball I had twenty-four candles – and so the light from the candles seemed to be reflected from the sheen on the satin and instead of the dress being one colour, it just looked as though it were woven from forty shades of green and lemon.'

The Reverend Mother let her words tail out gradually. Her thoughts went from that first ball – she had danced with Richard McCarthy first of all – and with Thomas Copinger, and then he had danced with Lucy while she looked on from the side-lines. That dance was very clear in her mind and in order to banish it, she went on talking about the precious lace and the shaping of the bodice, of the necklace of emeralds and aqua-marines that her father had bought for her, of the shoes made from satin and dyed to match the dress. By then the black eyelashes had come down over the grey eyes. Eileen had dropped off to sleep. She waited for a few minutes, then rose carefully and got out a notebook. She was compiling a list for the Bishop of some of the worst cases of deprivation that had come to her notice in the school. She did this every year and every year he thanked her effusively and praised her efficiency – but, of course, he did nothing. And yet, she thought, he was a man of influence.

Eileen woke an hour later. She lay for a moment looking around her in a bewildered fashion and then seemed to remember. The Reverend Mother was touched to see the look of relief that came over her face once she realized where she was. Since Eileen admitted to being a little thirsty, she made tea for both of them from the small spirit lamp that she kept in her room in order to refresh herself when working late.

Eileen, she thought, five minutes later, was looking much better. There was a tin of biscuits – left over from the numerous Christmas presents that were showered upon the Reverend Mother – in the bottom of the cupboard. She was pleased to see the girl tuck in hungrily, demolishing the chocolate-coated ones in three bites. She began to look alert and more like herself, so the Reverend Mother chanced a question, again.

'Eileen,' she said, 'do you recollect when you came upon me in the lane on the morning of the last flood, when the body was there, was that the first time that you had seen that girl?' Eileen, she remembered, was also seventeen years old. Of course, by the time that she left, only a few of the most promising, the most intelligent of the year group remained in the school. The others had left at the statutory age of fourteen or even before that. Perhaps she would not remember these. It was only the old, she thought, who remembered youth properly.

Eileen looked up at her and her glance was clear of fever and quite penetrating. 'I didn't kill her, Reverend Mother,' she said. 'Why should I?'

'I know that, but I wondered whether you recognized her in any way?'

Eileen frowned. 'Yes, funnily enough, I did, I did in the beginning,' she said, hesitantly, 'and then I knew that I couldn't have, when I looked at the dress. Satin,' she added, impressing the word on her memory. 'I don't suppose I ever saw her before in my life.'

'Yes, but if you forget about the dress, think back to the face? Did it mean anything to you?'

Eileen closed her eyes. Her face looked suddenly very weary now and she almost seemed drowsy and relaxed.

'Never mind,' said the Reverend Mother softly. 'You go to sleep. Don't worry. The door is locked and I'll spend the night in the armchair here, beside you.'

The Reverend Mother roused herself at six o'clock. She left Eileen sleeping behind the locked door to the study while she went into her bedroom, washed and made sure that she was neat and tidy for the Sunday morning, while planning carefully her next move. Sunday was the holy day of the week and Sunday morning brought its rituals within the convent. It would be important not to scandalize any of her nuns.

'Sister, I am going to twelve o'clock mass at the south

chapel.' She ignored Sister Mary Immaculate's startled expression – the only occasion when the Reverend Mother went to the parish church of the area was when the Bishop was present, confirming the children from the schools on the south side of the city. 'I shall leave you in charge, here,' she went on and was gratified to see the expression of self-importance come over her subordinate's face. I dislike this woman intensely, she thought and wondered whether it was something that should be mentioned at confession and then decided against it. Thomas Aquinas, she had been glad to read, had taken it for granted that there would always be enmity and antagonism between different human beings. Only the stars, he had thought, were able to go on their way without warfare.

The convent was completely empty, when Dr Scher's ring at the door came at precisely five minutes past ten o'clock. He raised his eyebrows when the door was opened to him by the Reverend Mother.

'I am honoured,' he said ironically. 'Have you run out of minions?'

She ignored that. She had a favour to ask and she wanted to ask it out of Eileen's hearing.

'You have a nice big house, there on South Terrace, don't you, Dr Scher?' she said. She wondered whether to mention that Professor Lambert thought that it was much too big for him, but then decided that might not be good tactics. These old bachelors were often as touchy and gossipy as old maids. There was no telling whether the two men might not be secretly quite antagonistic to each other. 'Do you think,' she asked tactfully, 'that your housekeeper would mind having a quiet visitor for a few days – that's probably all that it would take, wouldn't it?'

'You mean me to aid and abet your illicit concealment of a person wanted by our friends, the civic guards,' he said annunciating his words very primly.

'They'll never even think of you,' said the Reverend Mother robustly. 'Anyway, it's a shame to have that big house empty and just one man in it. Eileen will be no trouble to you. Give her a book and you won't know that she's there. And you can discuss Karl Marx with her.'

He looked around the empty hall and she could see him look slightly puzzled.

'The Sisters are all at Mass,' she explained. 'We could take her over there now and no one would know a thing about it.'

'You never thought of joining the Republican Army yourself, did you? I can see you master-minding a raid on the armoury at the barracks, or something like that.'

'But you'll do it, will you? I can't think of any other way of keeping her safe.'

She knew what he meant and felt obscurely pleased by his words. She often had thought that she had a good brain for organization. It was odd that as a nun she had such scope for stretching her brain and acquiring new skills. At the age of seventeen she could never have guessed how much she still had to learn and how fulfilling her life would be within the walls of the convent.

He didn't answer her question but went into her study and put his hand on Eileen's forehead. 'How does the arm feel this morning?'

'Sore,' said Eileen with a grimace. 'Aches a bit.'

'It will do, for a few days, but the fever is down. You won't die.' He looked down at Eileen's breeches and at, on the floor beside her, the blood-stained military coat, with the pistol protruding from the pocket, and grimaced.

'We can dress her in these things.' The Reverend Mother picked the large habit, the veil and the wimple from the neatly folded pile on the chair. 'I've packed a couple of linen night-dresses for her in this bag. Your housekeeper needn't know anything about who she is.' He had, in the past, she knew, kept a severely ill patient in his own house until a hospital place could be found for them. His charity towards the poor and the sick was well known in Cork.

'Oh, very well,' he said testily. 'But no guns, young lady! You can leave that pistol here with the Reverend Mother. She'll look after it. I'm a pacifist myself.'

'Take this rug out to the car; we'll follow in a moment.' The Reverend Mother stored the pistol on a high shelf, just behind a large Bible.

Once he was out of the way, she got Eileen to dress in the

nun's habit, arranged the wimple, pinned the veil – the girl's own boots would not be seen under the long flowing skirt.

'I'll return your clothes in a couple of days,' she promised, wondering how to get out bloodstains as she stuffed them into a bag and put it into her cupboard. Sister Bernadette would know all about stain-removal, but that military-style coat could not be entrusted to her. 'Let's go,' she said as soon as the girl was ready.

Eileen made a convincing nun, with a saint-like profile showing beneath a linen-swathed forehead. She said nothing, but she seemed steadier on her feet and her grey eyes were not as full of pain as they had been yesterday. Side by side they walked to the car – there was no one on the street outside – most of their neighbours would be at Mass in the convent chapel – and the steady rain would put off any purposeless street strollers. Nevertheless, the Reverend Mother kept her well shielded within the enormous umbrella.

By a piece of unexpected luck the housekeeper and the maid were both out at Mass when they came to the house at South Terrace. Dr Scher unlocked the door, ushered them upstairs, went back downstairs allowing the Reverend Mother to get his patient into a nun's cotton nightdress and then into bed, before appearing with a glass of lemonade and telling Eileen to take some pills with it.

'She'll sleep now,' he said after a few minutes while they both stood and watched the girl's eyelids droop over the white cheeks.

'I'll take the nun's clothes back to the convent; that will save you a few explanations,' said the Reverend Mother. 'You're very good. There's no one else that I could ask a favour like that of.' She made the words as warm as she could, but her mind had already left Eileen and had gone back to the puzzle about the dead girl who had been washed up into the convent's side gateway.

'You'll have something to eat before you go,' invited Dr Scher.

'No, I won't,' said the Reverend Mother going towards the door. 'I have to go to Mass in the South Chapel. Don't bother getting your car out. The rain has stopped and I'll enjoy a walk. Anyway, I have an umbrella. You stay here and look after your patient.'

St Finbar's Church, the South Chapel as it was always known, had the usual crowd streaming to participate in the ritual of the once-a-week Solemn High Mass with its majestic organ, the singing, the incense and the altar liberally manned with priests and deacons. It served a very large area, including among its parishioners the middle and upper working class as well as the very poor. The problem of the natural divisions of the classes was neatly solved by placing a pair of trusty parishioners with collection plates, well extended, at the door to the main body of the church and gallery whereas there was open access, with no money demanded, to the side chapel where the poor congregated.

The Reverend Mother was immediately recognized by a wandering deacon and ushered towards the gallery. She was somewhat embarrassed to discover that she had come out without a purse, but the man with the collection plate stepped adroitly out of her path and she climbed the steep steps and took her place in the front row as that seemed to be expected of her.

She was immediately conscious of the smell that rose up and remembered the words of Lucy's trustee, Thomas Copinger, when he had said: 'I never go to the gallery in the South Chapel – the smell of the shawlies down below would knock you flat.'

Thomas, she thought, thinking back dispassionately with the wisdom of age, was not a particularly nice person. He would, she realized with a shock, now be almost a hundred years old if he were still alive and yet his image as a vigorous man in his forties, the bright hair and even brighter eyes, was still vivid in her mind.

No one in the side chapel moved when Mass was over and the people in the gallery started to pour down the stairs and to mingle with the less distinguished from the main body of the church. The Reverend Mother bestowed a few vague smiles whenever she saw anyone looking at her and turned towards the door leading to the enclave of the poor. She had spotted a face that she knew and was determined to exchange a few words.

'Well, Nellie, you're looking very well, and how is the new

job going?' she asked in friendly tones when the girl came out. Nellie had her younger sister Lizzie with her. Lizzie must be about ten, thought the Reverend Mother, but she was dressed in a younger child's party dress – quite filthy, but it had once been rose pink with layers of frills and some expensive smocking on the chest area. At the sight of the Reverend Mother, Lizzie escaped back to Mrs O'Sullivan, who, her shawl pulled well over her head, yanked Lizzie away quickly and she was left with Nellie who was eyeing her with a mixture of apprehension and defiance.

The praise of her dress, however, seemed to lull her suspicions. It was well cut, made from good quality tweed, the hem neatly turned up and Nellie was so proud of it that she kept her coat dangling over one arm while she explained in a loud whisper that it had come from the StVincentdePaul man – running the name into one word.

'It's lovely,' said the Reverend Mother with sincerity, 'and that colour of pink really suits you, Nellie, goes well with your brown eyes.' And then carelessly, as though she had only just thought of the matter when about to depart, she said over her shoulder: 'Have you heard from Mary yet?'

Nellie shook her head. 'No, we haven't, Reverend Mother. Me mam's disappointed but I told her that Mary would have plenty to do without wasting time writing letters. She'd have to find herself a place to live and a job to keep her going.'

It was true, of course. All emigrants had a struggle when they left their native country for an alien environment. Often families never heard from them again and had to console themselves with imagining how prosperous and happy their lost children might be at that very moment – and no doubt it was true in some circumstances. There were some Irish people who did well in England or America.

Nevertheless, as she walked slowly back to the convent, the Reverend Mother had a strong feeling that the O'Sullivan household would never hear from their eldest again.

SIXTEEN

The Inland Revenue and Customs and Excise were merged
to form the Revenue Commissioners in February 1923.
Tax arrears were collected with difficulty as many taxpayers
had not made payments for years and some tax offices
had been burned down after 1919.

The Grand Parade was still flooded on Monday morning, though the waters had gone down a little. Patrick eyed it from the puddled surface of a pavement in Washington Street and decided against braving it on foot. There was a murky hue to the water and the smell was bad. Solid lumps that floated on its surface might have been mud, but were more likely to be sewage. A few enterprising men had old-fashioned traps and horses for hire so he raised a hand as one drew near and looked at him enquiringly. He didn't fancy getting his highly polished leather boots soaked in that stew.

'The Imperial,' he said as he climbed in and the man gave a resigned sigh and clicked to his horse to walk on. The Imperial Hotel was situated about half a mile down the South Mall and if the Grand Parade was bad, then the South Mall would be worse.

'Should be going down by tomorrow, sir,' he said as turned back into the flood water again. 'One more high tide and then we'll be rid of it – that's what people are saying. It's a crying shame, isn't it? The Lord Mayor and the City Council should do something about it – it's the poor that suffer – that's what people say, anyway,' he added, rapidly shifting the blame for his Republican sentiments to the nebulous 'people'.

Patrick made no reply. He was busy turning over his thoughts. Silent, Angelina was described as – well, that fitted – after all, the girl must have taken a momentous decision to leave her father's house and take the boat to England. She would have had a lot on her mind, would not have felt like indulging in light conversation. She must have been, thought Patrick, soberly, both worried and frightened. It seemed curious to him to think of a rich girl like Angelina, having to undergo these feelings.

'The Imperial, sir.' The taxi driver pulled up his horse with a great splashing of water and waited until it had subsided before opening the door for his passenger. Patrick gave him an extra-generous tip before stepping out on to the wooden walkway which the staff of the Imperial Hotel had laid down across the pavement so that their guests arrived with dry feet.

A city tailor-made for the rich and the important, thought Patrick as the doorman hastened to the edge of the walkway, ready to lend a hand if necessary. The marble steps were covered with oblongs of rubber-backed sisal carpet pieces to make sure that the fog did not cause anyone to slip. He was ushered in, the doorman kindly offering him the use of a beautifully laundered warm padded towel to wipe the fog from the closely woven wool of his greatcoat, before he handed his card to the man behind the desk with a request to see Mr McCarthy from India.

Mr McCarthy was still at his breakfast in his private suite when Patrick was escorted up to him. The room was so hot that not a trace of fog or damp could penetrate its warmth.

'Sergeant,' he said, mumbling the word, and then wiped his mouth. 'Excuse me; sit down, will you, terrible weather, isn't it? Can't wait to get back into the sun!'

'Yes, you must miss India, Mr McCarthy. Have you been out there for a long time?' Patrick took a seat before the fire and strove to feel at ease.

'Forty years, Sergeant, forty years, a great place, India; made plenty of money out there, worked hard, of course.'

Of course, thought Patrick; and now the tea-planter was thinking of whom to leave the money to. He had come back to his native Cork to pick himself a wife.

'You've heard about the death of Miss Angelina Fitzsimon,' he said coming to the point quickly. 'I am the sergeant in charge of the enquiry and I would just like to ask you a few questions about the young lady.'

'Yes.' He buttered a slice of toast, spread it with marmalade and swallowed in it greedy gulps.

'You went to the Merchants' Ball on Monday night, of course. May I ask, how many times did you dance with Miss Fitzsimon?' Patrick didn't know why he asked that question, but he was curious to know about the girl's evening. The result of most of Joe's enquiries seemed to be that few people remembered seeing her.

'Just the once.' Mr McCarthy wiped his sticky hands on a starched napkin.

'Just the once,' repeated Patrick. After a minute's hesitation he forced himself to probe further. 'I understand that you were unofficially engaged to be married to Miss Fitzsimon. May I ask when you proposed?'

'That was before I went up to Dublin, I had a talk with her father – I went up there for a week. Investigating new markets for my tea. We've expanded the plantation back home so I could be exporting double the quantities by next year. Only came back there on Monday afternoon – good train service between the cities, these days – the country is quietening down after all the nasty business – all of this Republican affair.'

'And was Monday night the first time that you met Miss Fitzsimon again after you came back from Dublin.'

'That's right.' There was a slight frown on the tea-planter's sunburned forehead and Patrick pursued the matter.

'You found her in poor spirits, perhaps,' he ventured politely.

'That's right. She seemed different. I pressed her a bit – well, you know, we were more or less engaged – her father was keen – she was saying nothing, just a whisper, here and there – you know the way that women are – I tried to snatch a kiss in the shadows and then she said that she felt sick. I took her to sit down and I asked her out straight whether she was willing for our engagement to be announced that night and she just whispered, "No, not yet." And then I told her that she had had long enough to think about it and it was either yes or no at this stage.'

'And what did Miss Fitzsimon say to that, sir?'

'Whispered she felt sick, put her hand to her mouth, pressed her hand to her mouth, so I went to get her a drink of water, and damn me, when I came back she had vanished. Gone off to the cloakroom to be sick, I suppose.'

'So what did you do then, sir?'

'Well, I'd had enough. Don't like it when girls start feeling sick for no reason. You know what I mean. I've had plenty of experience in my time – haven't lived like a monk, you know, Sergeant. I thought about it and then I began to guess. She had looked funny, looked different, you know. Something wrong, I thought. I've had plenty of girls, you know, Sergeant . . .'

The old goat, thought Patrick, but he waited.

'So I went upstairs and told Jos Fitzsimon that it was all off; told him my suspicions, too. After all he was the father – should be looking after her – she'd lost weight, they often do with that morning sickness, but she was bigger up here. Felt different all in all.' The tea-planter pointed to his chest. 'Something about the face, too, not so healthy-looking, not that you could see too much in that bad lighting – romantic, I suppose they thought – all those candles.' The scorn in his voice was palpable. He cut through a sugar bun and swallowed it with a gulp of tea.

'So, how did Mr Fitzsimon take your guess, sir?'

'Pretended not to believe a word of it, but he looked a bit white around the gills – ugly customer, that fellow, I think. Kept pouring out the whiskey – didn't know that I have the hardest head around. No good trying to make me drunk. I'd made up my mind. Not going to father any by-blow. In any case, plenty of pretty young fillies in Cork – no need to take damaged goods. Wasn't my baby, anyway, Sergeant, you can take my word for it; if she was pregnant, I had nothing to do with it. Much too busy.'

'I see. So what time was it that you left Miss Fitzsimon?'

'After nine, I'd say. They had just started their meal, but Fitzsimon called the waiter to bring another plate for me. Trying to soft-soap me, he was.'

'And did you stay with the Mr Fitzsimon for the rest of the evening?' Patrick was not surprised when the tea merchant shook his head.

'Not me – the atmosphere was a bit tense once he saw that he couldn't talk me around. I told him straight that I might be wrong about the pregnancy, but in any case, I didn't think that we were suited. She was a bit too reserved for me. I had been a fool not to see it earlier. Thought she'd thaw out once I got the ring on her finger, and, to be honest, I was thinking more about this business trip to Dublin than about the girl. Almost forgot all about her until I came back and then I thought, dammit, I must get this business sewn up. But then, when I danced with her and got those suspicions, I thought to myself that I could do better and that I'd better cry off before I'd committed myself too far.'

'So you didn't stay at the Fitzsimon table?'

'No, people upstairs on the balcony were wandering around a bit in between the courses – ten courses; you wouldn't believe it, would you; big eaters these Cork businessmen, you know, so I took the opportunity to get away from Jos. Went off and chatted to another customer – plenty of people to see – Joseph Fitzsimon would calm down eventually – it was in his interests to keep in with me – no one else could supply him with the variety of teas that I could ship over.'

'I see.' Patrick rose to his feet. 'So you saw no more of Miss Fitzsimon after nine in the evening?'

'That's right, Sergeant. Must say that I'm sorry if she threw herself in the river on account of what I said, but what will be will be. Might all be for the best in the long run, what do you think, from what I hear?'

'Mr McCarthy, Miss Angelina Fitzsimon was almost strangled, according to the police doctor – her throat was badly bruised. The coroner's court gave a verdict of murder. Someone pushed her body down through a manhole in the cellar of the Imperial Hotel and it went from there to the river.' Patrick looked down steadily at the man.

'Still think that it was probably suicide. Must be hard to know after she had been in the water for hours – under a drain, too, according to what Fitzsimon told me. Probably smashed up against a piece of grating, or something.'

'So Mr Fitzsimon discussed this with you.' Patrick understood why McCarthy had been so frank with him. Probably surmised that he would hear all about the tea-planter's suspicions of a pregnancy, and his rejection of Angelina from Fitzsimon, himself.

But he hadn't.

Joseph Fitzsimon, reflected Patrick, had not said a word about the withdrawal of the tea-planter's offer of marriage, and he had also kept silence about the accusation of pregnancy.

As he went down the stairs after the interview, he told himself that despite the flooding he would venture to cross the South Mall and get on to Morrison's Island and make his way by means of the bridge over to St Mary's of the Isle. He would have a word with the Reverend Mother about Mr McCarthy.

'I honestly don't think that he had anything to do with it,' he said half an hour later as he swallowed Sister Bernadette's tea and unburdened himself to the Reverend Mother.

'Is that instinct or reason?' she asked him with a slight smile and he welcomed the question. It made him trace his thought processes.

'It's reason, Reverend Mother,' he said as seriously as though he were seven years old again and had been asked a question in his catechism. 'A man who kills a woman because she is pregnant will, in my experience, probably do so for three reasons.' He held up a hand and counted matters off on his fingers. 'One; that he is mad with fury because of her betrayal – well, having talked with him, I'm pretty certain that McCarthy did not care anything for Angelina Fitzsimon. He seemed quite indifferent to her. The second reason,' and Patrick doubled down his middle finger, 'would be if he were scared that she would betray him by revealing her pregnancy to her father or to a jealous wife – well, he wasn't married and her father wouldn't care – would just hush it up by a quick marriage and then the child would be declared to have arrived early.'

'And the third reason?' queried the Reverend Mother.

Patrick took a quick swallow of his tea. 'In this job,' he said after a moment, 'you get to know people. I've seen lots of men who could be tipped over into killing someone, and he would not be one of them. I just don't think that he would be the type for violence. Wouldn't get his hands dirty; might cheat, lie a little, but not violence. I just can't see it. Smooth sort of man,' he said after a minute's thought and the Reverend Mother nodded her head to his experience. The city, she thought, was a violent place – the power of the gun and the fist ruled above the power of the law. Patrick knew all about that. She decided to trust to his judgement. In any case, her own reasoning, if correct, would mean that the tea-planter had nothing to do with the death of the girl. She bowed her head and tucked her hands into her sleeves.

'You're probably right,' she said. 'The truth about this murder,' she said thoughtfully, 'is probably something quite different.' She rose to her feet and smiled at him, holding out her hand. 'Thank you for keeping me informed, Patrick,' she said. 'Somehow I feel that this poor dead girl is part of my responsibility as well as yours, since I was the one who found her.'

And then as he went to the door, she spoke again.

'May she rest in peace,' she said, quite unexpectedly, and Patrick was reminded of the superstition that he and other boys had held that murdered people would rise from their grave at night and seek through the city to find the person who had killed them. Perhaps this poor murdered girl would not rest until he had done his duty and found the murderer. He subdued the thought instantly as fanciful, but as he walked back to the barracks, he swore to himself that this murder would not be left unsolved just because people with large houses and larger bank balances were involved.

SEVENTEEN

Civic Guard Handbook:
'Most uniformed members will not carry firearms.
Standard policing should be carried out by uniformed
officers equipped only with a wooden truncheon.'

When Patrick went back to the barracks, he found the superintendent fulminating over the *Cork Examiner*. 'Republican rag!' he snorted.

Patrick said a dutiful 'Sir' following it up with an inaudible mutter. It didn't matter. The superintendent didn't want to hear his opinion, anyway. He melted down the corridor to his office, sorted out a few notes, gave Joe a few more tasks to do at the shipping office, the bank and the Imperial Hotel and then decided to visit the university. He could, he thought, pick up a meat pie in South Main Street on his way.

The Western Road was still a little flooded, but the pavements were dry so he made rapid progress. He walked up the road thinking about some of his friends at the North Monastery. Many of them, though from no better homes than himself, had desperately wished to win the Honan Scholarship, just one single scholarship for the whole of the province of Munster! They had spent nights and days studying for it in a frantic attempt to attend university. Patrick, he thought, looking back at his young self, had put that aside, calculating soberly the odds against it, bearing in mind the numbers who so desperately wanted to win it. A position where he earned money would be good enough for him, he thought, and once he had successfully sat his School Certificate he had started work at a tailors' establishment, keeping their account books in meticulous order, and issuing beautifully penned bills and, better still, assiduously and tactfully haunting clients until the money owed was paid. Then he had joined the RIC – ignoring the taunts and mockery of those around him. When the advertisements for a newly formed civic guard service had appeared, he had applied at once and had got the job. Now all he had to do was to make a success of a high-profile case like this murder and he would be well on the way to be trained for a more senior position: to be an inspector was his dream.

Reluctantly, his mind went to the Reverend Mother. She wanted a finger in the pie; he knew that. He would, he thought, not ignore any helping hand towards the fulfilment of his ambition. Somehow there was something about that elderly woman that made him sort out his thoughts and impose a logical structure on the masses of remembered words and impressions.

The thought lent him energy and he pounded along the pavements and did not draw breath until he reached the beautiful hump-backed bridge that spanned the southern branch of the River Lee at the entrance to the college and passed beneath the magnificent grey stone archway.

The former Queen's College, now University College, Cork, was built of limestone. There was good stone available in Cork – rose-red old Devonian sandstone on the east side and superfine, very white limestone to the west. Shandon's steeple was built of the sandstone on the north and the eastern side and the limestone on the southern and the western side; many buildings in the city combined the two stones, but it was the limestone on its own that had been chosen for the building of this first university of the south. It was a good choice and it had weathered in its first almost eighty years of life until now it looked like one of the colleges in pictures of Oxford or Cambridge University.

Where Finbar taught, let Munster learn was engraved in fancy letters below a shield bearing the tri-part emblem of Cork: a ship and two castles; the heraldic lion of England, and the three crowns of Munster.

The lower grounds where the river ran were still flooded but the roadway leading up to the college had been well built with good drains on either side of it so the surface was dry. Patrick marched up grimly, conscious of his uniform and ignoring jokes and teasing glances aimed at him and went through the archway at the top and into the quadrangle. It was crowded with young men, wearing gowns over heavy over-coats, all chatting animatedly.

'Could I possibly see Professor Lambert?' he asked the porter, showing his badge with assurance.

'Yes, sir. What name, sir?' The porter stood up to answer him and was leading the way out down the stone corridor almost before Patrick had proffered his name.

'Through here, Sergeant.' The porter took him through the Aula Maxima. They went down the corridor side by side, without a word spoken, until they reached a door with a brass plaque that bore the name of Professor Cyril Lambert. The porter rapped, opened the door almost immediately and announced:

'Sergeant Cashman to see you, sir.'

'My sins have found me out,' said a deep voice, slightly amused. Seen close up, Professor Lambert was younger than he expected, although he had glimpsed him at the funeral. Like most people, he thought, he had looked aside quickly not wishing to stare at the disfigurement. Not an old man, but only in his early forties, big voice for not a very tall man. He looked clever, thought Patrick, forcing himself to look him in the face as the man rose to his feet and held out a hand.

'Take a seat, will you, Sergeant.'

The place was cosy – small enough to be heated by the coal fire that seemed to banish the traces of the damp air that still lingered outside of the window. Patrick introduced himself and explained that he was investigating the murder of Angelina Fitzsimon.

'You knew her well, Professor?' He had decided on a straightforward approach in those interviews. In a city as small as Cork, everyone would know his business.

'Yes, I knew her.' The professor did not enlarge on that. He seemed shocked, reticent.

'Have a whiskey,' he said then.

'Not me, sir, we're not allowed to drink on duty,' said Patrick. 'But you take one, please.' And then as the man poured out the liquid – from a nice cut-glass decanter, he noticed – he thought he would start on the questioning quickly. The college bell had just chimed the quarter hour and the professor might have a lecture at ten o'clock.

'You said that you knew Miss Fitzsimon well?' he stated.
'Perhaps you could . . .'

'I knew her, poor, poor girl, but I wouldn't say that I knew
her that well,' the professor interrupted. 'I met her a few
months ago . . .'

Patrick carried on. 'I understand from Mr Fitzsimon that
you told him you danced with his daughter at the Merchants'
Ball. How did she seem to you – depressed in any way –
anything like that?' And if the man were to infer from his
words that Angelina could have committed suicide, well that
didn't matter.

'I didn't notice anything much,' said the professor reflectively. 'Angelina was a quiet, reserved sort of girl. Come to
think of it, she was extra quiet that night; I could hardly coax
a word out of her. I handed over to one of my young students,
nice lad, one of the Spiller family; I thought to myself that I
was getting a bit old for the dancing game so I went upstairs
and joined her father at pre-dinner drinks at his table and then
moved on to one of my colleagues' tables, spread my company
around, didn't go downstairs again until later on!'

'Perhaps you can help me with another matter. Gerald
Fitzsimon is one of your pupils, isn't he?' Patrick made a
mental note to see young Spiller. Grain merchants, the Spillers,
he thought. 'Was Mr Gerald Fitzsimon downstairs dancing?'

'Yes, he's the right age for it,' said the professor. 'It's a
good idea, the Merchants' Ball – dancing and music downstairs, eating and chatting upstairs; young and old have a good
time, but ne'er the twain shall meet.' The smile vanished from
his face and his voice was grave when he said: 'But when was
she missed? I stayed to the very end and I would have noticed
if there had been a hunt for her.'

'I understand that Mr Fitzsimon and his son went home
separately. Each thought that Miss Fitzsimon was with the
other.'

'Poor girl. I suppose now that I am thinking back there
was something a little odd about her on Monday night. She
hardly seemed to be listening to me. I think perhaps that I
could go so far as to say that she appeared, if not distressed,
to have something on her mind, something worrying her. The

music was very loud when we danced together and I couldn't hear her very well.'

'So you thought that she might be better with . . . with someone else?' Patrick had been going to say *someone nearer her own age*, but decided that it might not be tactful.

'That's right.' Professor Lambert smiled. 'I could see her thinking that she had not got all dressed up in a gorgeous dress in order to dance with an old man like me – so I grabbed young Spiller.'

'Perhaps you could introduce me to Mr Spiller, Professor?'

'Yes, of course. He should be at my next lecture if the young layabout has got himself out of bed in time.' Professor Lambert opened a large cupboard, put on his overcoat, buttoned it up and then took out a black academic gown with flowing sleeves and added it as a top layer. A fine dust of chalk whirled around the room for a minute and then settled down on the tops of the furniture. A nice man, thought Patrick, clever, too, by all accounts. According to Dr Scher, Professor Lambert was a foremost physician in the field of tuberculosis – consumption they called it in Cork – and that he had saved lots of lives that would have been lost by other, less-skilled doctors. It was surprising that he also had time for his work with the St Vincent de Paul Society.

'Let's go,' he said and Patrick followed him.

The open space of the quad was emptying rapidly as the bell for ten o'clock began to toll. A few professors in flowing gowns with long sleeves, like Professor Lambert's, strolled along the gravelled paths, while undergraduates in their shorter gowns, with lapels instead of sleeves, rushed through doors.

'In here.' Together they plunged into another stone corridor and the professor opened one of the doors and Patrick followed him to find that he was on a stage at the bottom of a hall tiered into rows above them like an ancient Roman amphi-theatre. The benches at the very top were packed, the boards before them piled high with notebooks and textbooks, but the front few rows were comparatively empty. A sudden silence fell when the professor came in and all rose to their feet until he signalled to them to sit. There was a mutter of conversation – everyone eyeing Patrick with interest.

'There they are, Sergeant; that's who you are looking for, every single one of those layabouts in the back row. Take them all off to the gaol. The university will be all the better without them.' The professor's voice boomed through the hall and there was a roar of laughter. He was obviously a character in the eyes of his students and Patrick rather liked him when he said gravely, once the merriment had died down, 'But seriously, gentlemen, a very tragic event has taken place. The sister of a Mr Fitzsimon in the second year – most of you will know him, Mr Gerald Fitzsimon, his sister, Miss Angelina Fitzsimon, was missing after the Merchants' Ball on Monday night and very sadly has been found dead.' He looked around. There was complete silence. 'Now I remember Mr Spiller danced with her at my request, but if any others were there also, and either saw the young lady, talked with her, or danced with her, then the sergeant here would like to have a word about how she seemed . . .'

Several had been there, but the only one that had remembered Angelina was the young Mr Spiller so Patrick took him out into the corridor.

'Odd, isn't it, Mr Spiller, that you are the only one who remembers dancing with Miss Fitzsimon, or even seeing her,' he said once they were out in the corridor. Young Spiller was a good-looking lad with a clean-shaven face and well-oiled jet-black hair.

'Not really, Sergeant,' said the boy. 'Most of our crowd like to get a few drinks in them before they start dancing. The parents and old people dance in the early stages – they don't start serving that big dinner until about nine o'clock and that's when the hall clears a bit. In fact most of our crowd don't go down until we're away with the slates,' he said with naive pride. 'I was on the way up to the bar myself when Professor Lambert nabbed me so I had to finish the dance for him.'

'Can you remember what Miss Fitzsimon talked about?'

The boy thought for a moment. 'I can't, you know. Shy sort of girl, I think. Don't suppose I did too much talking myself. One thing at a time, that's what I say. When you drink, drink; when you dance, dance.'

'But do you think that she seemed distressed, worried, anything like that?' persisted Patrick.

'Can't say that I do. Sorry, Sergeant, but I got very drunk afterwards so the whole night is a bit of a blur. Just remember Lamb, I mean Professor Lambert, landing me with this girl in a silver dress and then skipping up to the bar himself.'

'And did you see Gerald Fitzsimon; you would know him, wouldn't you? Was he there?'

'In the bar, I think, can't honestly say that I remember.'

'But you do know him, don't you?' persisted Patrick and then, not leaving a pause, he said quickly, 'Someone told me that you were at one of his ether parties, is that right?'

Spiller made a slight face and then shrugged his shoulders. 'Just the once. Didn't like it much. Prefer the good old porter.'

So Gerald Fitzsimon was the one holding ether parties, thought Patrick with satisfaction. Dr Scher knew that, also, he guessed. Motive, means and opportunity; Gerald Fitzsimon had them all. How much was Mrs Woodford's fortune worth, he wondered, and decided that he would drop into the Mr Sarsfield's office on the South Mall and get that piece of information out of him.

'Well, thank you, Mr Spiller, I hope I haven't made you miss too much of your lecture,' said Patrick and the boy gave a grin.

'Actually, we usually just write limericks during this lecture – he teaches us medical ethics and no one takes much notice – different, of course, when we're doing things about lungs, tuberculosis and so on. But he's a decent fellow and gives everyone a jolly good mark at the end of the year – so the second years say, anyway.'

It all fits, thought Patrick as he walked out into the deserted quad. No one much noticed her because these students didn't go down to dance until they had got pretty drunk and by that time she had disappeared. In fact, it seemed as though it were the older men and their wives were there at the beginning, waiting for the dinner to be served.

And the prospective bridegroom, if he were to be believed, only danced with the girl once.

And what about Eugene Roche, lecturer in English, Patrick asked himself as he made his way back to the porter's office.

'Any chance of a word with Mr Eugene Roche?' he asked and added apologetically, 'Sorry to keep bothering you.'

'No bother at all, no bother at all, just having a look at the timetable. No, he's not teaching. Wonder is he in the Common Room? No, I'll tell you where he'll be, probably playing chess in the restaurant. He's a great chess player. Let me take you to his room and you can sit there in peace for a minute. He's not there, because I've just been in there to make up the fire.'

A good-looking young man, thought Patrick, left alone in the cosy room and studying the portrait over the fireplace. It was a large picture of Eugene Roche in hood and gown and holding a scroll in his hand. They didn't get paid too well, these lecturers, he had heard that. They did a bit of teaching and bit of research and all in all it probably was a nice life. He had some beautifully bound books, too, not arranged in matched sets as in Joseph Fitzsimon's house in Blackrock, but tumbled around, some askew, some lying on top of other books, some open and face down on the desk. This was the room of a man who read a lot. He wondered whether Angelina Fitzsimon had been very much in love with him. Her father had seemed to hint at that. He was looking through one of the books when the man came into the room and he put it down hurriedly, fishing out his badge and introducing himself.

'I just wanted to talk to you about Miss Angelina Fitzsimon,' he said quietly.

'Yes.' There was a question in his voice and he looked apprehensive. 'I heard that she had died,' he said. 'I was out of town for the last few days, but I heard something about it this morning.'

'She was murdered,' said Patrick, purposefully brutal.

'What!' The man moved quickly, went to the window, flung it open and took in deep and audible swallows of the foggy air. Patrick waited for a moment and then went over and touched him on the shoulder.

'Could I get you a glass of water, sir, or something stronger?'

'No, thanks.' The young man spoke in a muffled voice but after a moment he turned around. His face was ashy pale and he wiped it with a handkerchief. He closed the window down again and went to sit by the fire.

'I'm sorry,' he said after a minute. 'That was a shock. I had heard of the death, but I thought that it was a heart attack, or something. Do sit down, won't you. I thought that it was just an accident. I've been away for a couple of days – I had no idea.'

Patrick sat down and looked across at him.

'You were in love with her, were you, sir?' he asked.

'No,' said the young man. 'No, what put that into your head.' His voice did not sound startled, though. However, that might be because the aftermath of the shock had deadened all further feelings.

'The young lady's father thought that there was some sort of understanding between you, sir.'

'No, no, he, well, I don't like to say too much, but he isn't a very nice man, Sergeant, he wasn't very nice to poor Angelina. But I assure you, Sergeant, there was no hint of a love affair between me and Angelina.' Not Miss Fitzsimon, noted Patrick, but Angelina. Still, perhaps Eugene Roche was that sort of informal person. He waited. Let the man talk. He was the type that would spill out everything.

'I was just sorry for the poor girl; that was all. I used to tell her that she should try to get away from him.'

'And what was her response to that?'

'Said she couldn't: not until she was twenty-one.'

'Perhaps you could tell me all about your rela . . . about how met Miss Fitzsimon and what sort of terms you were on.'

'I met her at a tennis party and we discussed literature. She was really well read and she would have loved to take a university degree. We discussed it and I told her that she would be welcome to attend a few classes and to see for herself. She told me that her father was very against the idea but that she could suit herself in a few months' time, when she reached the age of twenty-one.'

'And that was all?' Patrick looked penetratingly at the young man and saw his cheeks redden.

'Well, more or less all,' he said and then, after a minute, 'Well, I suppose that I was a bit in love with her. She was a sweet girl – a little flirtation; that was all.'

'But no engagement; there was no promise of marriage

between you?' Patrick decided not to mention the pregnancy – since the man had been out of town he would not know about that, perhaps, had not heard about the inquest. He would have to gather some more evidence and see whether this young man should be on his list of suspects.

'Certainly not. As a matter of fact—' said Eugene Roche, flushing slightly. He stopped and then resumed quickly: 'I forget what I was going to say.'

'You knew her brother, didn't you, Gerald Fitzsimon, went to parties that he gave, those parties where you were all experimenting with ether.'

Eugene Roche looked a little taken aback and then laughed with a hint of nervousness. 'You know everything, Sergeant. I can assure you that I had nothing to do with the theft from the Mercy Hospital. It was all just a bit of fun, as far as I was concerned. I wouldn't have condoned robbery. I only went once or twice. Got tired of it. You don't suspect me of doing anything to Angelina, do you?'

'No, no,' said Patrick soothingly. And yet, he thought, this man jumped very quickly to the conclusion that ether had something to do with Angelina's death. Was it exceptionally quick wits, or did he know something about this death?

He rose to his feet. 'One last question, sir. Did you attend the Merchants' Ball?'

'Never miss it – best food and best drink in the town.'

'And did you dance with Miss Fitzsimon?'

'No, I didn't, actually.' He looked puzzled. 'I did expect to see her there, but when I looked around for her I didn't notice her. Of course, there were loads of girls there that I wanted to dance with, or that I felt I should dance with, so it's possible that I just overlooked her.'

'I see,' said Patrick. He wasn't quite sure that he believed this. If Angelina Fitzsimon was pregnant, the most likely thing was that the baby was of Eugene Roche's creating. They were friendly, met often, had interests in common. She was a beautiful girl and he was a fine young man. It seemed to make sense.

But why should he strangle the girl and throw her body into the river? An idea popped into Patrick's mind. What if the young lecturer were engaged to someone else . . .?

'And may I ask if your fiancée was present?' He put the question in a matter-of-fact fashion and the young man looked startled for a moment and then shrugged his shoulders resignedly.

'How did you find that out? It's supposed to be a secret. Well, you know the Lavitts – I'm no way good enough for their daughter, don't earn enough for one thing, youngest son in my family, you know. Still, I'm hoping for the best. I need to settle down, do a bit of work, get my doctorate, bump off Professor Clancy and take his position as head of the English Department and then I might be in with a chance. Only joking, Sergeant.'

'And is there anything else that you can tell me about Miss Angelina Fitzsimon?' Patrick didn't approve of that sort of joking – dangerous talk, he thought.

Roche sobered instantly. 'Nothing, Sergeant, nothing, except that she was a very unhappy girl.'

He had sounded genuine that time, thought Patrick as he walked back towards the barracks.

But, of course, that did not exclude the possibility that he had killed her.

There was no doubt that Angelina was having a hard time with a mother in the asylum and a father who was unsympathetic to everything that his daughter wanted to with her life and who was trying to force her into a marriage that may well have been quite distasteful to her, as well as – and he was sure that Angelina, from what he had heard of her, was clever enough to have realized what was going on – trying to rob her of the fortune which her grandmother had intended to be hers.

I wonder what the Reverend Mother will make of this, was his thought as he settled down to write up meticulous notes of his three interviews during the day.

EIGHTEEN

St Thomas Aquinas:
Deceptio est corruptio scientiae.
(Deception corrupts science.)

'I'm going to ask Dr Scher to tea this afternoon, Sister Bernadette; he's been very good and helpful to me and I would like to thank him.' No point in mentioning that she had asked Sergeant Patrick Cashman to call in at the same time. There would be plenty of sweet things for both – Sister Bernadette would make sure about that. The Reverend Mother turned back to her work in designing a new annex to her school where the girls would be taught practical skills and would be able to sell the products of their labour to the well-off of the city. Perhaps, she thought, she might be able to involve Mrs O'Leary as a consultant. The ladies of Cork would always need new hats.

'I think it is important to establish the truth about the fundamentals of this case,' she said firmly to Dr Scher and Patrick when both had eaten a sufficient amount of cake. While they had been eating she had read Patrick's summaries of his interviews and had nodded approval to him. In the presence of Dr Scher she would say nothing, but allowed them to discuss the situation while she listened in a slightly abstracted fashion.

They had begun to go around on the well-trodden path of motive, means and opportunity when she interrupted them. They looked at her, slightly startled, and she nodded. 'It's almost certain that the body of the girl, the body that I found which had been washed into the chapel gateway, was murdered, but there is another question. And this,' she said dogmatically, 'is a very important question.' She paused, looking keenly at both before saying simply: 'Who was this girl?'

She had to bite back an unsuitable smile at their puzzled

expressions. After a minute Patrick said hesitantly: 'She was Angelina Fitzsimon.'

'How do you know?' She asked the question as if she was examining him on his catechism and he responded like a well-drilled pupil in the sure knowledge that he held the correct answer.

'Because her father identified her.'

'But what if he made a mistake?'

Neither man answered so she continued. 'Mr Fitzsimon's daughter did not come home from the Imperial Hotel on the night of the Merchants' Ball. He came to the barracks to report a missing person on the following morning. He was faced with the body of a girl, bloated from the river water, possessing the same distinctive colour of hair and of eyes and wearing,' she said with emphasis, 'the dress that she had bought for the occasion. Didn't you say, Patrick, that Mr Fitzsimon said something about how much it cost and that it was from Dowden's – almost as though he had looked at the gown more than at the girl – perhaps we were all guilty of that, were we not?' She didn't wait for a reply, but went on smoothly, 'But, of course, the actual scientific evidence, the evidence provided by a well-qualified and experienced man like Dr Scher, that evidence was overlooked and disregarded, even by the doctor himself.'

Patrick looked at Dr Scher, who looked with pursed lips at the Reverend Mother. The doctor was beginning to understand, she thought, but Patrick was still puzzled. He was a boy who dealt in facts.

'St Thomas Aquinas,' she said, 'warns us that a lack of truth can corrupt science. The man of science, Dr Scher, found from the fact that the collarbone had not yet knitted together that this girl, the murder victim, was only seventeen, and yet Angelina Fitzsimon, by her father's and all other evidence, was within three months of her twenty-first birthday. That was the first point. The second was that the murdered girl appeared to have suffered from malnutrition judging by her teeth and by the bones in her legs. I myself noticed that her wrist was very thin. One would not have expected that a girl of that class, probably carefully fed and looked after by a trained nanny, could possibly have suffered from malnutrition. And

there is another point.' She looked at the two attentive faces
and smiled at the wondering expressions. It was, of course,
very much against her vows of humility to triumph over them,
but her conscience had become more elastic with old age.

'The tea-planter, Mr McCarthy said that she felt different,
isn't that right?' she continued. 'And he was a connoisseur in
girls, according to himself,' she added demurely. 'And then,
of course,' she went on, 'the contents of the stomach were
strange – nothing in it but porridge – an odd and unusual food
for a young lady's afternoon tea or supper, but the mainstay
of the poor. Taking everything together, then I do not believe
that this girl that we have just seen buried was Angelina
Fitzsimon, but was, in fact, a different girl, a girl who had a
poor background.' She sat back and looked at them calmly.

'But, but, it wasn't just the dress, was it?' stammered Patrick.
'She must, they must have looked alike. It seems impossible.
The father did, definitely, identify her.'

'They were, I would say, probably extremely alike, certainly
in colouring,' said the Reverend Mother, 'sisters – half-sisters,'
she amended conscientiously. 'They shared the same father.'
Her mind went to Mrs O'Leary, the hat-maker, and her
comments on Joseph Fitzsimon. A thought of Lucy and her
granddaughters invaded her for a moment, but she pushed it
aside. Her duty now was to two young girls: to Angelina
Fitzsimon, whose whereabouts were a mystery, and who might
be in danger, and to the dead girl, who should, she thought
fiercely, be avenged and her killer placed where he could do
no more harm.

'Who was she, then?' It was Dr Scher who asked the question, but it was to Patrick that she turned with the answer.

'She was Mary O'Sullivan from Sawmill Lane,' she said
quietly. 'You remember Mrs O'Sullivan of Sawmill Lane?
There are lots of her children here at the school, one of the
younger sisters, Nellie O'Sullivan, has just left us – but none
of them looked particularly like Mary – in fact there is little
resemblance between any of them, which may point to a
different father in each case. Mr O'Sullivan,' she said calmly,
'went off to England quite a number of years ago. I haven't
seen Mary O'Sullivan for a few years, but I was haunted by

the feeling that I knew this dead girl – that I had seen that colouring before on a girl – it's unusual in Cork, those very bright Mediterranean-blue eyes, almost the colour of those glassy-alleys that the children play with – *marbles*,' added seeing Dr Scher's puzzled face and remembering that as a small child he had played on the streets of Manchester, 'and the chestnut-coloured hair,' she continued: 'we have lots of red-heads here in Cork, but they are light red, or fox-red, not that shade of almost brown, like a horse chestnut just out of its shell. That,' she said, 'is quite unusual here in Cork. And then when I heard about Joseph Fitzpatrick's reputation of being seen around Sawmill Lane,' she put in that circumlocution in order to avoid shocking Patrick by her knowledge of prostitutes and she saw his eyes widen before she went on thoughtfully, 'I thought that was the solution. I had known Joseph Fitzsimon's father, you see, and he had that colouring.' Eileen, too, she remembered, had probably recognized the colouring, but was distracted by the expensive dress.

'So where is Angelina Fitzsimon now? What's happening to her?' asked Patrick.

'Did she run away from home because she was pregnant?' asked Dr Scher.

The Reverend Mother sighed impatiently. 'There is no reason to suppose that Angelina was pregnant,' she pointed out. 'Mary O'Sullivan was, but that's a different matter.'

'How did they meet?' Patrick, she was glad to see, had gone to the crux of the matter. She turned her attention to him.

'I think it was probably through the St Vincent de Paul Society,' she said seriously. 'Angelina Fitzsimon, according to Professor Lambert, helped with sorting clothes. I wouldn't be surprised if she visited homes, also, although the professor was very careful, very cagey about confirming this as he felt that her father would have disapproved.'

'And Mary O'Sullivan wanted to emigrate because she was pregnant, because she wanted to get away from the life that her mother has led.'

Reverend Mother was conscious of a feeling of warmth, almost, though it seemed fanciful, of a feeling of self-worth. Patrick was going straight to the heart of the problem. He had

justified her faith in him. They looked at each other – the nun
in her seventies and the young man in his early twenties. Each
knew that the other would strain to the utmost to solve this
murder.

'And what about Angelina?' he asked. 'What was her
motive?'

'She had a lot of pressures on her, this Angelina,' said the
Reverend Mother. 'There was the pressure from her father to
marry . . .'

'So that the brother could inherit; and the father could be
free of paying his debts, maintaining him in an expensive and
idle way of life,' reminded Dr Scher.

'And the refusal to allow her to go to university – she needed
to get away from her father perhaps in order to begin to establish a new life for herself.'

'It all seems a bit trivial, though,' objected Dr Scher. 'Why
didn't she just sit quiet and wait until June? She could do
what she wanted then. She couldn't be forced into a marriage
that she didn't want, not in these days. Why do something so
dramatic as to disappear? I just don't understand that – what
could the father do to her? Granted she couldn't know that
the poor girl would be murdered, but . . .'

'You forget,' said the Reverend Mother, 'that her father was
instrumental in getting her mother shut up in the lunatic asylum,
something that probably meant that he now controls Anne
Woodford's – Anne Fitzsimon's fortune. Perhaps Angelina
feared that this might happen to her – perhaps it may have
been threatened.'

'She had only another few months to go,' said Patrick slowly.
'From the sixth of March to the eleventh of June – not long;
if she could just keep out of the way until she was twenty-one
. . . Perhaps she saw an opportunity and took it; what do you
think, Reverend Mother?'

'And the other girl, this unfortunate Mary O'Sullivan, she
was desperate – expecting a child – seeing no future for herself
or her baby – down the quays, an early death through disease
or violence, and the poor child neglected or abused,' said Dr
Scher in the sorrowful accents of one who had seen many
terrible sights.

'The resemblance must have struck them, certainly must have struck Angelina, when they met first at the St Vincent de Paul shop, or even perhaps at Mrs O'Sullivan's house, room, rather; it must have set Angelina's mind working,' said the Reverend Mother.

'So where has Angelina gone now?' asked Dr Scher. 'You're not hiding her, concealed beneath a habit, wimple and veil?' He directed his question mischievously at the Reverend Mother and she looked back at him coldly and did not bother to reply. But his words did make her think.

'She only has a few months to wait out,' mused Patrick. 'You'll remember that she took a cheque for fifty pounds. She spent five pounds on the first-class ticket and cabin to Liverpool and gave ten pounds to the girl, to Mary O'Sullivan. That leaves her with thirty-five pounds.'

'Wonder why she did that; why she bothered with a first-class ticket and a first-class cabin,' put in Dr Scher. 'I don't suppose this poor girl, Mary O'Sullivan, wanted that grandeur. She probably would have preferred to have the money.'

'You must remember,' said the Reverend Mother briefly, 'this was to benefit Angelina as well as Mary O'Sullivan. In hunting terms, she laid a false trail – a trail to Liverpool. By the time that they found out about her purchase it would have been days, even weeks of enquiries. And, of course, those pursuing her would then have sought for her in Liverpool and not found her.'

'Whereas she had stayed in Cork, perhaps, and still possessed thirty-five pounds with which to maintain herself,' said Patrick. His upbringing gave him an appreciation of that sum of money, but Dr Scher put a different interpretation on it.

'Pocket money for a girl like that,' he said scornfully. 'You'll find that she has holed up with some relation or another. So why not just go straight to that relation and never mind all the changing of identities.'

'Her nearest relative,' said the Reverend Mother 'is, of course, her mother. And she is incarcerated within those stately walls of the lunatic asylum. And Angelina's mother is, of course, Anne Woodford, a considerable heiress in her own right, whose affairs are now arranged by a solicitor and by her husband. I'm not sure . . .' she said slowly, scanning through her mind the complicated web of family relationships, and thinking about her conversation with Lucy, '. . . I'm not sure that I know of any near relative who would be in position to take charge of the girl and protect her from her father.'

There was a dead silence after she said that. Neither man, she thought, was able to get to grips with the thought that one of their brother men, Joseph Fitzsimon, had deliberately locked his wife up within the confines of a lunatic asylum so that he could get his hands on her considerable fortune. She, herself, found difficulty in thinking about it, but her life for over fifty years had accustomed her to dealing with difficult and unwelcome occurrences and she tried to face this as courageously as she could. The important thing now was to save the girl, Angelina, a worthwhile girl who had risen above her background and now badly needed help.

'Angelina gave herself a few days' start by this switching of identities; no doubt she relied on being sighted, I mean Mary O'Sullivan being sighted, wearing her ball gown and wrap, going down to Lapps Quay towards the shipping office, actually going on board the ship. She would have been a memorable figure, boarding a midnight ferry in those clothes. If there were a hunt for her during the following days someone was sure to remember this strange occurrence – the men in the ticket office for the shipping company – do remember, Patrick, that she gave her true name there when she bought the ticket for Mary – these men would remember and report if there had been enquiries after her. The bank would report that the cheque had been cashed. And, of course, the father and the brother would be certain that it was Angelina herself who had taken the ferry and would assume that she had a friend in Liverpool. In fact,' said the Reverend Mother, looking back into the past, 'I think that there was some sort of cousin, one of the Newenhams, who moved with his wife to Liverpool when I was young. Angelina might have relied on a certain amount of time being spent on hunting down any relation, or even school friend in Liverpool or in its vicinity.'

'Clever girl,' said Dr Scher appreciatively.

'But, of course,' said Patrick thoughtfully, 'there is now another problem.' The Reverend Mother noted how he looked from one to the other, at the two pairs of elderly eyes, each on either side of the fireplace and how he bent his neatly clipped black-haired head and studied his well-kept hands while thinking. Now he raised his head and looked directly into her eyes. 'Perhaps this is more of a police problem, more of a matter for the civic guards, but it must be solved. We have to decide who was the intended victim of this murderer – was it Angelina, or was it Mary O'Sullivan?' He sat back and blushed slightly as the Reverend Mother gave him an approving nod. He really was going to be very good at his job, she thought smugly, and allowed Dr Scher to release a string of questions and surmises.

At that stage the Reverend Mother rang for fresh tea. The troops need feeding was her thought. Sister Bernadette beamed at sight of the empty cake tray and when she came back she brought with her some hot scones, dripping with butter and decorated with pats of blackberry jam from the pantry.

'I suppose you send some child labour out to pick the blackberries,' teased Dr Scher, but she refused to be deflected. This matter was too serious. As soon as Sister Bernadette had gone, she began to put her thoughts into words.

'If Angelina was the intended victim, and the man who thought that he had killed Angelina Fitzsimon finds out that she is still alive, then she is in terrible danger,' she said soberly and knew that this was a matter with which she had to concern herself. Her mind went back to Lucy's words. 'Could it have been her father, himself?'

'I still think it was the brother,' said Patrick. 'He had everything to gain.'

'*Motive* – he inherits the grandmother's fortune; *opportunity* – he was present at the Merchants' Ball; and the *means* – he could supply the ether to make her feel weak and dizzy, a brother handing a sister a drink would go unnoticed. And he could easily get her to leave the dance hall, saying that her father had summoned her – something like that. Even if we remember that it was Mary O'Sullivan, not Angelina, wouldn't she respond to his tone of authority, to his obvious certainty

that she would do as he wanted.' Dr Scher looked around.
'Wouldn't she, Patrick?' he asked.

'It would seem strange, though, wouldn't it, that the brother
would not recognize the sister, would not know that this was
a different girl if he actually talked to her. I know we have
decided that the father might have made a mistake, but that
was a bit different. The girl was dead by then. Bodies look
subtly different after death, especially ones that have been in
the water – there is a certain bloating, a swelling – and I've
noticed that often relations don't even want to look properly
at the face. They can't bear to do so sometimes. And if Gerald
actually danced with his sister, although he denies this, or even
if he just handed her a drink with the ether in it, then you
would expect him to realize that something was wrong – that
it was not the same girl.' Patrick frowned over the problem.
'The trouble is,' he said eventually, 'up to now we have been
investigating the murder of Angelina Fitzsimon – all the work
that we've done has been looking at suspects who might have
a reason for murdering her, but now I don't know what I am
investigating.'

'I would just carry on the way you are going,' said the
Reverend Mother encouragingly. 'Who have you been
talking to?'

'I've had interviews here with the lecturer, Eugene Roche,
and with a young chap, Spiller, who was the only one of the
students at the university who remembered dancing with her
– neither of them were much help. Spiller danced with her,
but Roche did not remember seeing her. It turns out that he
is engaged to one of the Lavitt family.' Patrick cocked an
eye at the Revered Mother and saw her nod thoughtfully. 'I've
discounted Spiller,' he said,' but I've kept Roche on my list.
Perhaps if he made Angelina pregnant then the Lavitt heiress
would probably give him the push. But then, of course, he
could marry Angelina and from a worldly point of view, that
would be as good a match.' He stopped and looked exasperated. 'Of course, Angelina wasn't pregnant; it was Mary
O'Sullivan. So that takes his motive away, doesn't it? Unless
he, like Mr McCarthy, guessed that she was pregnant, put the
question to her and for some mad reason . . .'

Patrick paused and looked across at the Reverend Mother. 'What does your instinct tell you?' she asked bracingly.

'It tells me that this is all nonsense,' he said unexpectedly. 'And it tells me that this girl, Angelina Fitzsimon, as she was described by Dr Lambert, would not take either young Spiller or Eugene Roche too seriously.' He looked across at her and saw her nod and felt pleased – pleased with himself and with his diagnosis.

'It's very hard to find many people who remembered Angelina – Angelina or Mary O'Sullivan, that night,' he continued. 'I do think she may have been killed early in the evening.'

'What you need is some sort of chart,' said Dr Scher dogmatically. 'Have a big list of all the motives, of all the links, everything and then put big arrows across where any names meet . . . or something like that. I remember going to some medical lecture where the chappie did something like that about diseases of the blood. Very clever fellow. I fell asleep unfortunately, but it all looked very clever to me.'

The Reverend Mother allowed them to chat on while she went through Patrick's notes. He was certainly very thorough, she thought approvingly. His English was concise, succinct but the whole interview could be visualized by the reader. Her mind imagined the scene, the two scenes with two men, one a lecturer, one only a student, but both, she got the impression, quite young and fairly carefree. She agreed with him that it did not look as if either of them, as he had described them in his notes, could be the murderer of that poor girl on the night of the Merchants' Ball.

The Reverend Mother put the notes away thoughtfully. Dr Scher and Patrick seemed to have abandoned the idea of the chart with the arrows and were discussing Gerald Fitzsimon.

'Which is the greater force in human nature, fear or greed?' she asked them in the tones of one who knows the answer to the question that she has set.

'Fear,' said the doctor without hesitation.

'I wouldn't agree with that exactly,' said Patrick. His tone was polite but assured. 'In my experience, I've found that a man will kill for a pound note if he is desperate for food.'

'Perhaps,' said the Reverend Mother, 'the two can be the
same. Perhaps man will kill from fear – fear of starvation is
one fear, but there are other fears and their importance differs
from person to person. What is essential for a human being
is survival, survival of the body and survival of the spirit.
Perhaps the motivation that drives a man to commit murder
depends on the man himself, depends on what is necessary to
him, what he feels is essential to the survival of body or spirit.
Sometimes that may be something quite nebulous, neither
food, nor safety.'

An idea had come to her but she wanted to think about it
before she committed herself to an opinion. She let a pause
develop and then glanced at the clock. Patrick took the hint
and got to his feet and Dr Scher followed him looking at his
watch and exclaiming that he would be late for his lecture at
the university – throwing pearls in front of hung-over, brain-
less swine, as he expressed it. She rang the bell for Sister
Bernadette, but when the nun arrived, Patrick politely took the
door handle and waited for the sister to go through, laughing
and joking eagerly to Dr Scher. And then he quickly closed
the door on the two in the hallway and said apologetically:
'There is something that I must tell you. The superintendent
wants another search of the convent, Reverend Mother. Eileen
was definitely seen entering the grounds. I'm sorry it will have
to—'

'You must do your duty, Patrick,' said the Reverend Mother
serenely, though her heart skipped a beat at the thought of
what her cupboard held. 'I have to go out on urgent business
just now, but if you'd like to come back with your men in half
an hour or so, that would be the time, after school, when it
would be the most convenient to search the place without
disturbing and upsetting the children.'

NINETEEN

St Thomas Aquinas:
Bonum communae praeminet bono singulari unius personae.
(The good of the community has to have preference
over the good of single persons.)

When Patrick had gone the Reverend Mother went immediately into her bedroom, took up a soft leather bag and stuffed into it Eileen's breeches and coat – the blood by now had turned into a hard black patch, and would, she reckoned, be there for the life of the garment. Still Eileen might not mind that, might wear it like a decoration, she thought, and her lips twitched slightly. She did not approve of guns or of shooting, but courage, resolution and a feeling of wanting to better the lives of your fellow citizens were something that she understood and applauded. Thomas Aquinas, she thought, felt the good of the community was more important than the individual's and hoped that would absolve Eileen from the sins of the present. In any case, Eileen, she thought, would go on doing what she felt that she had to do, and there was little that she could say which would deflect her from her chosen route. The girl would be pleased to have her rather dashing uniform returned to her.

But then the Reverend Mother wondered what to do with the gun. Dr Scher definitely did not want it and it would not be fair on him to bring it to the house on South Terrace and she could not dump a dangerous thing like that for a child to find. She could leave it in her cupboard among her linen. It would, she thought, be a brave civic guard who would dare to disturb a Reverend Mother's clothing. However, one never knew. Eventually, she ruthlessly sliced a swathe of pages from the centre of the old Victorian Bible on her shelf, placed the gun within it, bound the book with a faded ribbon and put it into a hinged Bible box. She doubted that the search of her private quarters would be thorough, but it was just as well to be certain. Then she rang the bell, gave her instructions to Sister Mary Immaculate about facilitating the search of the convent and its grounds by the civic guards, endured the passionate exclamations and queries about what the world was coming to and then put on her cloak, picked up the leather bag, declared that she was already late for a meeting and bustled out of the convent, walking swiftly through the puddle-filled lanes until she reached the South Terrace.

The door was opened to her by Eileen, wearing, rather incongruously, a calf-length dress, far too large for her, belonging perhaps to Dr Scher's housekeeper, a grandmotherly cardigan and a pair of down-at-heel slippers. She was touchingly pleased to see the Reverend Mother and led the way to the kitchen, where, she explained, she had been left in charge of the doctor's supper as it was the housekeeper's afternoon off and the maid had popped out to buy herself some hairpins.

A few pots were bubbling feebly on the black range, but Eileen seemed to be more engaged in putting a high shine on her well-moulded leather boots and the scrubbed deal kitchen table was littered with buffing sponges, chamois leathers, tins of polish and a bar of saddle soap.

'Nice, aren't they?' asked Eileen, holding the boots up for admiration.

'Lovely,' agreed the Reverend Mother, conscious that there was a scrap of envy in her voice. She did rather envy those boots, not just as comfortable and practical footwear, but as a symbol of everything in life that had passed her by. All was changing for women, she thought. Short skirts were convenient for girls to run in and indeed, she thought, rather pretty; the first women doctors had already qualified from University College and one of her own past pupils had authoritative articles published in the *Cork Examiner*. The Reverend Mother thought back to her own life when she was Eileen's age and when the possession of a dress made from chartreuse-coloured satin, draped over a whalebone crinoline, was the summit of her desires.

Eileen, she knew, was leading a dangerous existence as

a prominent member of the Cork Republican Party, on the wrong side of the law – at the moment – though any moment the situation could be reversed, the treaty with England which meant that Ireland forfeited the most prosperous six counties of the country, almost the whole of Ulster, might be repudiated, the Republicans of de Valera might gain ascendency over the Free-Staters of Michael Collins; and Eileen, like Countess Markievicz, whose uniform she copied, might end up a member of parliament. She smiled slightly at the idea, hoped that if it were true that Eileen would stand up for the rights of the poor and the powerless. The Bishop of Cork, she knew, would not agree with Thomas Aquinas that the good of the community must take preference over the good of the individual but then, thought the Reverend Mother, the Bishop of Cork was not a very intelligent or thoughtful man.

'How's the arm?' she asked. The girl looked well, she thought. The colour had come back into her face and she seemed to be able to move her left arm without any noticeable wince of pain.

'Great,' said Eileen enthusiastically. 'Dr Scher put some silver on it – silver salts, he called it and there's no infection – it's as clean as a whistle. We could do with some stuff like that, I was telling him,' she went on casually, but with an eye on her former teacher.

'And what did Dr Scher say to that?' enquired the Reverend Mother calmly.

Eileen giggled. 'He told me just to take some because he'd prefer to give it away than to have a visit from the boys. But whatever I do, and he made me promise this, I must make sure that they don't take his silver in the cabinet – have you seen his silver, in that little room leading off his study, Reverend Mother? He's been telling me all about it, showing me a teapot that ladies would have used in the time of Jane Austen. He's got cream jugs and trays, and they've all got special marks on them, *hallmarks* – he's been explaining them all to me. One of them is very old and it's got a little ship coming down a passageway through two castles – a tiny little picture, stamped on the silver bottom of a teapot. They're all Cork-made silver, but this one is the oldest of them all. You should get him to show it all to you, Reverend Mother.'

The Reverend Mother had seen Dr Scher's silver on many occasions – he was a notable collector and had a small cabinet leading off his study filled with baize-covered shelves and kept spotless and dust-free by his incessant presence and his gentle handling and replacement of his beloved articles. She had had to endure many of his learned lectures on it, so she hastened to cause a distraction by opening her leather bag and took out the tweed coat and well-cut breeches. Eileen's face lit up.

'Thank you, Reverend Mother,' she said with shining eyes.

'Well, keep these clothes hidden or Dr Scher won't sleep well at night.' The Reverend Mother frowned thoughtfully. 'You never thought about taking the veil, Eileen, did you?' she asked.

'Jesus! Reverend Mother.' Eileen stared at her in consternation. 'That wouldn't be me at all!'

'No, I don't suppose so.' There was an idea at the back of her mind, but she left it there for the moment. 'What's it like being a Republican?' she asked curiously. And then feeling that she was being irresponsible, she said hastily, 'You're living outside the law, Eileen, and that must be a terrible worry for your poor mother.'

Eileen looked scornful. 'Have you ever been in to my mam's kitchen, Reverend Mother?' She didn't allow the question to be answered, but rushed on – 'Well, it's got the walls absolutely covered in pictures of Patrick Pearse, McDonagh and John Connolly and all of those 1916 lads. They're all heroes to my mam. She's even got framed speeches up on the walls.' She quoted softly: '"If you strike us down now, we shall rise again and renew the fight. You cannot conquer Ireland; you cannot extinguish the Irish passion for freedom; if our deed has not been sufficient to win freedom, then our children will win it with a better deed."' Her eyes were shining and slightly moist with emotion.

I'm old, thought the Reverend Mother, that's what's wrong with me. I'm old and I'm practical. I don't want the lives of idealistic youngsters to be thrown away. She was willing to fight injustice and inequality with words, to fight with reason, with logic, with deceit and with flattery if necessary, but she was not willing to take human life for a possible gain.

'We have such fun, you know, Reverend Mother,' said Eileen unexpectedly. 'There's a great crowd, in our place, lots of them were university students, but they gave up everything to set their country free. Liam Lynch has us all organized into divisions. Our division swears by the ideas of Liam Mellows – he was a socialist and the Free-Staters executed him,' she said passionately and the Reverend Mother's heart sank at the note of hatred in the seventeen-year-old girl's voice. However, in a moment, Eileen was smiling again as she thought of the fun and comradeship in those remote encampments in the empty countryside.

'We all know what to do and we trust each other with our lives. We have great discussions about things – about distribution of wealth and suchlike. But you should hear us, sometimes, Reverend Mother. We're like a pack of kids in sixth class. We have great *craic*. One of the lads has a banjo and a couple of us have tin whistles and we have a bit of fun with dancing jigs and reels up there in the mountain with no one to hear us.' She stopped and her tone changed to a slightly apologetic note. 'I wouldn't have ever made a nun, Reverend Mother.'

'I know that, Eileen, I was thinking of something else, actually. I was thinking of how I dressed you up in the habit and then you just looked exactly like one of the sisters.'

'A disguise, you mean?' Eileen had immediately grasped the point, but then she giggled again. 'I don't think I could ride pillion on a motorbike, or in the back of a Crossley Tender in all that rig-out.'

'No, I don't suppose so,' said the Reverend Mother and she saw Eileen look at her curiously.

'You're thinking of someone else, not of me, aren't you?' she said with all the quickness that had made her the most rewarding pupil that the Reverend Mother had ever taught.

'That's right, I'm thinking of someone else.'

'Someone in danger?'

'I think,' said the Reverend Mother, 'that she might be in deadly danger.' Her mind went to the man who had given the

ether to Mary O'Sullivan, was on the point of strangling her
when he had spotted the drain cover in the cellar under the
Imperial Hotel and who had sent her to a certain and terrible
death down there in the flooded sewers. If this man realized
that he had murdered the wrong girl, then Angelina Fitzsimon
was a living threat to his life and to his liberty. She looked
thoughtfully at the intelligent face in front of her. A girl who
not only had brains, but who had learned to keep a secret,
learned to hold the lives of her friends within her hands.

'And you want to hide her? Are hiding her already?' Eileen
was certainly quick.

The Reverend Mother shook her head. 'I don't know where
she is,' she admitted.

Eileen leaned back on her chair, tilting it dangerously, and
put her be-slippered feet on to the edge of the range.

'They'll burn,' pointed out the Reverend Mother, sniffing
the slight smell of scorch that rose about the aroma of steamed
pudding. She was about to tell Eileen not to tilt her chair, but
stopped herself. Their relationship was not now that of teacher
and pupil, but more of fellow conspirators, she thought with
a qualm of conscience.

'It's all right – not as if they're my boots,' said Eileen
absent-mindedly and then a minute later, in a different tone
of voice, 'Do you remember the time when I was in your
chapel and you were pouring that communion wine down me,
and then later on, in your study, you asked me whether that
girl reminded me of anyone?'

She didn't wait for an answer, but continued, 'And I thought,
later on, when my wits were coming back to me, that you
wouldn't ask me that for nothing.' She smiled a little and
looked across at the nun. 'You always used to do that,' she
said with a certain note of affection in her voice which
surprised the Reverend Mother. 'You used to prompt us to
find something out for ourselves by asking a question, by
acting dumb. It was one of your little tricks. Well, you're
right, of course. Yes, she did remind me of someone. It was
Mary O'Sullivan, wasn't it? I remember her eyes – eyes like
a doll's I used to think. I remember when we were little kids,
in second class, I'd say; well, some of us were *doing Pana*,

going down Patrick Street – it was Christmas time and we saw this doll in the window of Dowden's and I said to Mary: "That doll has eyes like you." She was ever so pleased.'

The Reverend Mother was conscious of a pang. The display in Dowden's shop window would probably be the nearest that Eileen and her eight-year-old friends would ever have got to a doll. She remembered a doll of her youth that had come from Dowden's – a lady doll with a magnificent wardrobe of clothes. She had never liked it much.

'Funny, when I was young I always wanted blue eyes,' said Eileen in a nonchalant fashion that seemed to indicate that now, at the age of seventeen, she was quite satisfied with her own grey eyes. The tone in which she made the remark was slightly absent-minded, though, and after a short silence, in which she shifted her steaming feet to the bar of the range, she said thoughtfully: 'So was the dead body Mary O'Sullivan's?' And then, when the Reverend Mother didn't answer, she said with professional breeziness: 'Anything that we discuss will be private. I promise not to give the story to the newspapers until you give me the word.' Her eyes were sparkling with interest – no doubt she would make a great story of it all eventually. It was somewhat sad that she could contemplate the death of one of her former classmates so easily, but many had already died from tuberculosis or other diseases or disappeared without trace.

Eileen had always been a trustworthy girl and the Reverend Mother decided to follow her instincts.

'It must be kept secret because it's important that the man who murdered the girl, whoever she was, is caught before he does the same thing again,' she said and Eileen nodded emphatically.

'The story will be none the worse for the keeping,' she said and then, quite quickly, 'so, if the murdered girl is Mary O'Sullivan, where's the other girl, where's Angelina Fitzsimon?' There was another silence. The Reverend Mother kept her eyes fixed on the stove and waited. And the response came with lightening quickness.

'You have her hidden at the convent; she's wearing a veil and all the rest of the rig-out.'

'Not my convent,' said the Reverend Mother. 'She wasn't one of my girls, Eileen.'

As soon as she got back to the convent, the Reverend Mother lifted the phone. 'Montenotte two, three,' she said into it, grimaced slightly as the woman at the exchange recognized her voice and she had to endure several minutes' conversation before being put through. However, a moment later Lucy answered the phone.

'Your granddaughters all went to the Ursuline Convent in Blackrock, Lucy, didn't they?'

There was a silence at the other end of the phone. Lucy, thought the Reverend Mother with amusement, would be trying to work out what her cousin really wanted. She put her question and got a cautious answer.

'Difficult woman – French, you know. I don't know why the Ursuline Convent in Blackrock has to go to France to choose a mother superior.'

'You don't care for her?'

'I wouldn't say that – most of the parents find her difficult to deal with. Even you would find it hard to bring that one around your thumb.'

The Reverend Mother smiled to herself in the darkness of the back hallway and then asked the important question.

'What's she like with the girls, with her pupils?'

Lucy's voice became more enthusiastic. 'Oh, as to that you couldn't fault her. She's very good with them and they respect her advice immensely – would listen to her more than to their mothers and fathers, according to Susan. She takes a great interest in them, even when they've left school. Why do you want to know, anyway? She wouldn't take one of your girls, you know. She's very much of the aristocrat – she would have no interest in one of them, no matter how clever they are, or how much you think that they would benefit from a boarding-school education.'

'Well, we'll see,' said the Reverend Mother vaguely.

'About that matter we were discussing the other day,' said Lucy, her voice changing subtly. She seemed to choosing her words carefully – no doubt, there were some listening ears.

'It was likely that the story we were talking about is entitled "The Lawyer, the Doctor and the Man who Needed Money" – an unholy trinity, don't you think?'

'I see,' said the Reverend Mother. 'Thank you, Lucy. Sounds like a good title for a crime novel.'

So, if she understood Lucy's words correctly, there definitely was a conspiracy to get control of the former Anne Woodford's money – her lawyer and her doctor had gone into alliance with her husband. No doubt Rupert had picked up the story at that gossips' marketplace, the golf club, and had entrusted it to his wife under a veil of secrecy.

TWENTY

St Thomas Aquinas:
Idea est regula cognoscendi et operandi.
(An idea is the rule of knowledge and of action.)

The Reverend Mother sat very upright in the back of the taxi on the way to the Ursuline Convent in Blackrock and listened indifferently to the driver's prediction of what the high tide of midnight would bring to the city. She had more important matters on her mind than worrying about floods, she thought, but allowed him to continue while she pondered over the idea that had suddenly come to her.

'A few missing streets in the morning,' he said gloomily. 'That's what I'd guess, Reverend Mother. We'll find the South Mall a river and the Grand Parade will be no better. As for Patrick Street, well, that's already gone under water. You're all right there on St Mary's of the Isle, aren't you? And of course, anyone outside the city and on the hill – well, it's just a day off work for a lot of them, isn't it. Though I have heard tell that Ford's factory is going to dock the pay of those that don't arrive at work at eight o'clock in the morning, did you hear that, Reverend Mother? But of course not everyone is like Ford's – Americans they are. Still perhaps you can't blame them. All very well for them that can stay at home nice and warm and dry, but people like myself have to be out and about. Flooded my engine the last time, it did. Filthy water, too. Had to have a day at the garage where they took everything out and dried it. Cuts into the profits, that sort of thing, Reverend Mother.'

The Reverend Mother made a suitable and automatic rejoinder to all those predictions of gloom and doom and thought her own thoughts. She was going over her reasoning, sure that she was right but determined to check the evidence. And remembering the young reporter from the *Cork Examiner* on the day of the funeral and his assiduous work in noting names, she thought that she probably was correct.

He had written her down as representing the community at St Mary's of the Isle, but that was not all. There was a long line of names in the paper the following day representing all of the great and good of Cork: civic guards; the Lord Mayor; the town council; the breweries – all three of them, Murphy, Beamish and Crawford; wool merchants; butter market group; importers of tea; corn merchants; the professor of medicine representing the university (a compliment to Gerald, or to his father who paid the fees); Professor Lambert representing the Society of St Vincent de Paul; Canon O'Connor representing the injured Bishop of Cork and so on.

But there had been one notable absence.

Angelina Fitzsimon, the girl who had been buried, who had been born and brought up in Blackrock, had been a pupil at the Ursuline Convent in that village – at least during her teen years – the photographs in the lobby of her father's house testified to that.

And yet there had been not a single representative of the Ursuline nuns present at the funeral. The Reverend Mother was sure of that. She had been the only nun present.

And she could think of only one reason to account for it.

The Reverend Mother of the Ursuline Convent was a relatively young woman, she thought, in her forties – of French origin, though she spoke English with the slightly sing-song intonation of the people of Cork city. Reverend Mother Aquinas had met her on a few occasions and formed the impression of a woman of very strong faith, rather partaking of the Jansenist movement, with its fanaticism and its rigidity: a woman to whom truth would have been of the utmost importance, a woman who would not have told a lie, or allowed herself to seem to condone a lie. And although a woman who, according to Lucy, was devoted to her pupils' interests, in the circumstances, Mother Isabelle would not, could not, have attended that funeral – an act which, to her, would seem to have sanctioned an untruth.

The Reverend Mother mused upon this as the taxi passed Ballintemple, went on down to Blackrock, turning up the road towards the castle and then swinging around and driving through the ornate gates to traverse the avenue that led up to the Ursuline Convent where the nuns boarded and educated the young ladies of Cork city and those from its county. She herself had been at school here more than fifty years ago and she felt that she had received a good education for the era.

The convent nuns were at supper when she arrived. Refusing the seclusion of a chilly parlour, Reverend Mother Aquinas opted to wait near to the front door. She strode up and down the long corridor and examined the photographs, neatly labelled and arranged in calendar years, and hanging in groups on the walls.

Angelina Fitzsimon featured prominently in most of the photographs of three years previously. Starring in a Gilbert and Sullivan operetta; holding a silver cup presented for excellence in mathematics; lined up in the centre of the lacrosse team as their captain; and looking businesslike in goggles, standing behind a row of Bunsen burners in the new science laboratory for the school. Yes, Angelina's years at the Ursuline Convent in Blackrock had been happy and successful. Reverend Mother began to hope that her hunch, based on Eileen's impulsive action of seeking refuge from her former school and headmistress, was going to prove true. She began to plan her strategy. The woman, Reverend Mother Isabelle, she guessed from what she knew of her, would not lie, so the way forward should probably be a direct one.

Mother Isabelle was no easy opponent, though. She professed herself overwhelmed with pleasure to receive the Reverend Mother from St Mary's of the Isle, insisted on sending for refreshments and taking her in to sit by the fire. When the question about whether she had seen or had any knowledge of the whereabouts of a missing girl was put to her, she became very wary. She took refuge in a whole series of vague statements, emphasizing her respect for the law and her strict adherence to its dictates and talking so fluently and at such length that it was difficult to edge in another question. When pressed a little too hard she took refuge in her supposed lack of English and pretended not to understand so the Reverend Mother, who had profited from that year spent in Bordeaux with her cousins when she was seventeen, immediately switched into fluent French and put the question again.

'I was surprised not to see you at the funeral,' she said, and approved the challenging note in her voice.

Mother Isabelle sat a little straighter at that and there was a spark of anger in the fine eyes. 'I don't understand you, Mother,' she said stiffly.

'I remarked on the fact that you did not attend the burial service for Angelina Fitzsimon,' said the Reverend Mother affably. 'At least that was what the Canon of Blackrock called it. But you and I know differently,' she added. 'Perhaps I should give you a few facts before inviting your confidence in me,' she continued after the silence between them had stretched beyond normality. 'As far as I am concerned, Miss Angelina Fitzsimon has a perfect right to live here if she found her father's house to be unpleasant, or even threatening. I can speculate about her reasons for disappearing. There might have been things said, efforts to force her into a marriage that was not to her taste, threats to interpret her natural distress and anger as a sign that she was going insane – and she had her mother's fate of being incarcerated in an asylum before her,' she finished in a low voice. She was not sure whether Mother Isabelle knew about Angelina's visits to the lunatic asylum, but she guessed that she probably did. Her face had changed when she mentioned the asylum and her bloodless lips had tightened.

'What is it you want from me?'

'Two things: two things only. I want to know that Angelina is safe with you and, if possible, to speak with her.' She said the words firmly. Mother Isabelle was not a woman for weaknesses, or one who would respond to pleading. She had to earn her respect.

'But first let me tell you what I think happened,' she continued. 'Angelina Fitzsimon, in the course of her charitable work for the St Vincent de Paul Society, came across a girl who was, to all intents and purposes, almost her double.' She eyed Mother Isabelle and saw the spark of interest in the woman's eyes.

'So much so . . .' continued the Reverend Mother and then paused delicately. Mother Isabelle was nodding.

'Just what I thought myself,' she murmured obscurely. 'Could almost have been twins apparently – it does happen sometimes, that the sire's prepotency . . .'

'Just so,' said the Reverend Mother briskly. The French, she thought admiringly, no matter how genteel, how religious, do seem to know the facts of life.

'Angelina had reasons to hide from her family for a few months, until she reached the age of twenty-one and had control over her own life and over her fortune,' she said bluntly and was rewarded by another nod.

'And you were fond enough of her to help her in this. Perhaps,' she said, feeling her way, 'perhaps, indeed, you were the one who suggested it.'

The statement seemed to melt the resistance. Madame Isabelle threw out her hands in a very theatrical movement.

'I said to her, "*Ma chérie*," I said to her, "why not make a little *retraite* – take the veil for a few months, no one will know, here you will be a postulant sent from another convent, sent for your health to be near to the sea. None of the sisters will question this."'

It was well thought of. The Reverend Mother had to admit that. A postulant took the veil for a maximum of six months – after that they either left the convent or made preliminary vows and became a novice – and the excuse about being near to the sea was a good one, not that, she imagined, any of Mother Isabelle's nuns would dare question their superior on any point.

'It was very cleverly arranged,' she said with sincerity. And then, 'Could I speak with her, Mother Isabelle? I mean her no harm, but there is some information that she can give. You understand, this other child, the girl who was buried in her place, her name was Mary O'Sullivan; well, she was one of my pupils and . . .'

'I will fetch her myself,' said Mother Isabelle graciously.

It was the nun's robes, she thought as the woman entered, closed the door behind her and almost instantly turned the key in the lock. The uniform made sure that they all looked the same. Angelina was probably almost forty years younger than Mother Isabelle, but for a moment she had thought it was the same woman. And then she raised her eyes and even in the dimness of the one meagre gas lamp the Reverend Mother could see that they were of a rich blue, the colour of bluebells.

With one swift movement she removed veil and wimple, both together, took out a couple of pins and tumbled her chestnut hair around her shoulders. And there was now no doubt that the two girls were almost identical in appearance, but not, she thought, close up, and not to someone who knew Angelina well. The eyes might be the same colour, but their direct gaze, their intelligence was not shared with the girl's half-sister, if her former teacher's memory of Mary O'Sullivan was correct.

'Mother Isabelle thinks that I can trust you.' Her voice was not as exaggeratedly well bred as some of her class – just pleasant and low. The blue eyes were full of steadfast courage. She went across and poked the smouldering fire with an air of assurance, remarking that she hated being cold.

'You joined the St Vincent de Paul Society. Professor Lambert told me that.'

'That's right; they do good work.' Her voice seemed to be quite at ease now, but she still looked into the fire.

'You took some food parcels to the families?'

'Occasionally. Professor Lambert wasn't keen that I should do so. I think he was afraid that my father would make a fuss. I was supposed to work at the shop, to sort clothes, put them in bundles for various ages. But I did get out sometimes. It was quite an eye-opener.' She gave an unsteady laugh. 'You will think me very ridiculous, Reverend Mother, but before I started that work, I was unaware of prostitution. I didn't know that men paid women to . . . to have sex with them,' she said firmly, but the Reverend Mother could hear from the note of strain in her voice, how much it cost her to say the words. She honoured the girl for her straightforwardness.

'And sometimes these girls are very young, very hungry and very cold,' she added softly and left a silence after her words.

The Reverend Mother, though concerned to show the girl

that she was not shocked by her outspokenness, guessed that she would have a limited time before Mother Isabelle tapped on the locked door and so she pressed on. 'And you met a girl who looked just like you,' she prompted.

'Yes, I met Mary.'

'And when was that?'

'It must have been about six months ago, probably September. I know there was terrible flooding – Professor Lambert had left a message for me not to go down Sawmill Lane or anywhere like that because the water had come into the houses and there was typhoid there, but there was a food parcel to be delivered so I went.'

'And did you go on seeing Mary O'Sullivan?'

'No, I didn't see her for months after that, not until a few weeks ago.' The girl's voice had become hesitant. 'It's difficult to explain,' she said. 'The first time that I met her I didn't really notice the resemblance so strongly, though I did notice her eyes, but then the second time, in the shop, as a matter of fact, I had just come in, had brought in a bundle of clothes and she was crying and one of the other women there told me that she was in trouble. I tried to cheer her up, took out a dress, out from my bag, it was one of mine, one that I had always liked, the colour matched my eyes. I held it up against her . . .' Angelina hesitated for a moment. 'There was a bathroom upstairs where we sometimes allowed the women to wash their children, wash themselves, so I took her up and I washed her hair. It was almost like having a doll again, but she loved it. She sat on a chair while I towelled it and combed it with a fine comb and when it dried and was clean – it just looked so like my hair. I was astonished. There was a small mirror there and I let her look at herself. And then she put on the dress and she did look so like me that we both laughed. We stood there, peering at ourselves in the mirror and laughing. I didn't think anything of it then, but later that night I began to wonder.'

Reverend Mother said nothing. The next bit had to come from Angelina herself.

'I wondered,' she said with some difficulty, 'whether we might actually be . . . whether my father . . . you know that my mother is in the asylum, so . . .'

'I think your father had a name for seeking out prostitutes in these areas, in Cove Street, Douglas Street, Sawmill Lane, even well before your mother was taken off to the asylum,' said the Reverend Mother in a straightforward fashion and felt a little sorry when she saw her wince. However, Angelina deserved the truth and she could not prevaricate in the face of the girl's courage and her honesty.

She recovered quickly though, and said almost immediately: 'So that's where Mary O'Sullivan comes from; I suppose that I had an instinct that she was my sister – she has a mother, lots of sisters and brothers – no father, I think, and I've seen some of her younger sisters and they did not have the same hair or eyes as Mary.'

'She was a pupil of mine, once,' said the Reverend Mother.

'*Once* . . .' There was a minute's silence before Angelina said sadly, 'So it was poor Mary who was killed, wasn't it?'

'If she is the girl to whom you gave a ferry ticket, ten pounds, a bag full of clothes – well, yes, she is dead,' said the Reverend Mother and bowed her head when Angelina said instantly:

'And the police are trying to find out who wanted to kill her – kill me, I suppose?' She did not sound too distressed or too surprised either. A girl of high courage, thought the Reverend Mother.

'That's right,' she said. 'They don't suppose that the death of Mary O'Sullivan from Sawmill Lane would benefit anyone.' She thought about Angelina's brother, Gerald, and the fortune to inherit and wondered whether the girl's mind was travelling along the same lines as was Patrick's. Perhaps speculation about her father might be a step too far even for a girl of such courage.

'Poor Mary,' said Angelina pityingly, 'you know, she was as excited about the dance as she was about going to England and trying to find her sister in Liverpool. We had been practising the waltz in the back room of the shop; she was very good at it. And she had been practising what she called a "posh" accent.'

'So her resemblance to you gave you the idea.'

She nodded. 'It's difficult to explain to you why I wanted to disappear.'

'I think that I can guess most of it,' said Reverend Mother in a matter-of-fact voice. 'I know about your mother, met Dr Munroe from the asylum, and I know about Mr McCarthy, the tea-planter, so I think I can guess that you were having problems,' she added.

'I see.'

'What was the purpose of her going to the ball that night?' asked the Reverend Mother.

'I had to lead suspicion away from the convent, away from Mother Isabelle; she was willing to shelter me, but if my father found out he could compel her, by law, to hand me back – much better to have been seen at the Merchants' Ball and then when enquiries were made it would be found that I, or at least my double, had travelled on the boat to England. I bought the ticket openly in my own name – just the day before in case anything got out about it. They were welcome to search Liverpool for me. They would not be searching in the places that Mary or her sister would be living. I coached her in the part to play, told her to pretend to have a sore throat, to whisper, and if anything bothered her, just to go and hide in one of the cloakrooms.'

The Reverend Mother nodded, but then there was a tap on the door and a voice said softly: 'It is I.'

'That's Mother Isabelle,' said Angelina.

It would be – anybody else, thought the Reverend Mother resignedly, would say: 'It's just me.'

She went to the door instantly, unlocked it and admitted the nun, then relocked it. Mother Isabelle gave her a hard look, but made no comment.

'One more question, Angelina,' she said coming back to stand close beside the girl. 'Was there any possibility that your father knew of your friendship with Mary O'Sullivan – had he ever seen her with you?'

'I don't think so,' she said doubtfully. 'I only met Mary in the shop. He never went there.'

'Or your brother?'

She shook her head again, and then said shortly, 'Gerald would not concern himself with anything like the St Vincent de Paul charity.'

'And did anyone except Mother Isabelle know of the plan that you and Mary made?'

Angelina shook her head decisively. 'Not from me. And I warned Mary. Not even her mother or her sisters, or anyone in the shop, not even Professor Lambert himself was to know of our plan.'

'I must go,' said the Reverend Mother rising to her feet, 'but before I do, I must warn you that you may be in danger. The police are fairly sure that you were the intended victim.'

Angelina picked up the wimple and veil and reassembled it with practised fingers. 'This is my safeguard,' she said.

The Reverend Mother felt sorry to see the glowing chestnut hair once more smothered by the veil, but even more sorry to see the bleak look that had come over the girl's face. Did she, like the police, suspect her brother of the killing of the girl who had taken her place at the Merchants' Ball?

Angelina did not say goodbye, but slipped silently away, her eyes on the ground like a model postulant nun. The Reverend Mother stared after her regretfully for a moment, but there was no more to be done here just now. The killer had to be uncovered and Angelina had to be made safe before she could resume her place in the world.

'I'll get someone to telephone for your taxi, Reverend Mother,' said Mother Isabelle.

She accompanied her visitor to the door, waved away the lay-sister, took the massive bunch of keys into her own hand and then strolled beside her down the avenue towards the gate. When they reached it, the taxi had just arrived. Both nuns stopped and looked at each other.

'You will look after her carefully, won't you?' asked the Reverend Mother.

'You really do think that she is in danger, do you?'

'If it comes out who is buried in the Fitzsimon tomb down at Blackrock – well, yes, she could be; no,' she corrected herself, 'not *could be*, *will be*. Even without that, the murderer may suspect something. May have noticed at the time that he killed the wrong girl. I have known both girls. The resemblance was strong, but they were not identical. Angelina may have been the intended victim, but at the last moment the murderer may have realized that a mistake was made.' The Reverend Mother didn't bother asking Mother Isabelle to keep silent. Like all nuns, she would be a safe repository for secrets.

'I see you think as I do,' said Mother Isabelle, speaking now in French, but nevertheless giving a quick look around, before saying softly in a low voice whose resonance was lost within the folds of her veil, 'I suspect her brother; he's a bad lot. I've heard plenty about him.'

The Reverend Mother bowed her head in response. She could not comment on this and she knew that she was not expected to.

'No one will have access to her without my permission,' said Mother Isabelle firmly and dangled in her face the massive ring of keys by the biggest one of them all before exchanging the ritual kiss – an approach, mid-air, of cheeks sheltered from human contact within the starch of the wimples. Then she waited until the Reverend Mother was in the back seat of the taxi before raising her hand in farewell and turning to go back up the avenue.

'The police barracks, first, if you please,' said the Reverend Mother as soon as she had disappeared.

'You don't mind if I drive quickly,' said the taxi driver as he handed her a rug. 'You chose a bad day for your visit, Reverend Mother. I'm afraid that it's flooding badly in the city; we'll have a job to get past the quays.'

TWENTY-ONE

St Thomas Aquinas:
Sed secundum ius naturale omnia sunt communia, cui quidem communitati contrariatur possessionum proprietas.
(But according to the natural law all things are common property, and the possession of property is contrary to this community of goods.)

The taxi driver was right. As soon as they arrived in the city, the car slowed down to a crawl as the wheels sloshed through the water. After a few minutes of this the engine spluttered and died. The driver muttered something and got out, flinging up the bonnet.

'I'll walk, it's not far,' said the Reverend Mother as she joined him. She produced her purse and paid him quickly before he could argue, and set off down Albert Quay, making more progress on foot than the car had done. She kept to the middle of the pavement, well away from the waves that were rising above the quayside and avoiding the water that came bubbling up from the drains and the sewers and was now rapidly spreading across the roadway. There was, she thought, an odd atmosphere about the place. It was going-home time so that it was natural for streams of people to be moving along – the professional class and their children who went to city schools, or worked in banks and offices, were all making for Albert Quay station, bound for Blackrock or the seaside villages of Carrigaline and Crosshaven; the others were going to their houses on Anglesea Road or Copley Street. But there was a strange unease abroad. People walked fast, looked nervously over their shoulder, wasted little time in greetings and continually surveyed the rooftops of the houses. It wasn't the flooding – Cork people were used to flooding, and this flood, despite the heavy rain that fell, would probably not reach its height until after midnight.

And what was even stranger was that people seemed to be pouring out of the public houses and the bars that lined Albert Quay. Even to someone like the Reverend Mother who did not have much knowledge of the ways of these inns and taverns, it did seem a bit early in the evening for drinking to cease. She suspected that there might be going to be a raid; the news of that would spread soon and there was an air of apprehension about the people.

The River Lee split into two just at the beginning of Albert Quay. The Custom House stood there, facing down-harbour; the north channel and the south channel went on either side of it and then proceeded on their separate ways. The Reverend Mother had thought of crossing the street at that spot, but the roadway was just a river, with more water welling up from the drains every minute, so she went on down Albert Quay's pavement, keeping beside the south channel. The pavement also was very wet; her shoes, stockings and the lower five or six inches of her black habit were all soaked, but she ploughed bravely on among the crowd. And it was the crowd that worried her. Where were they all going? They seemed to be hurrying along, few of them talking or laughing or indulging in the usual Cork backchat. Some were women, some were men, but most of them were urging on companions, holding the slower or the weaker of the two by the hand. One man even touched her on the arm as she faltered for a moment and said hastily, 'Come along, Sister, get yourself home quickly.'

And at that moment the shooting started. It seemed to originate from Albert Quay railway station. She could hear the guns exploding and the cries ringing out. An armoured car tore down Albert Quay, sending a shower of water over the pedestrians on the pavement.

'Bloody Republicans,' said someone behind her and a moment later she heard the words, 'Murdering bastards, those Free-Staters.'

'There's a raid at the station,' shouted one man across the road to a man close behind her.

'Don't worry; once they take the cash box from the ticket office they'll be off.' The man at her back sounded bored and irritable – used to these raids, no doubt. The Republicans kept themselves in funds like this, though they were, on the whole, scrupulous about stealing only from the rich, or government concerns. It was definitely a raid. There was a sporadic sound of firing from the railway station and then the roaring of machine guns.

Realizing then that she was about to be caught in the cross-fire between the two warring factions, the Reverend Mother hurried on, swept along by the crowd trying to get away from Albert Quay station as fast as it possibly could. Everyone wanted to get indoors and away from this almost nightly exchange of bullets which seemed to happen in one or another part of the city. A second vehicle came sloshing down the street and a spat of fire from a sub-machine gun, aimed by a daring lad perched on top of a garden wall, skimmed over the Reverend Mother's head. Her heart beat fast, and although she slightly despised herself for it, she breathed a prayer of appeal that she might not be shot tonight. She had so many things to see to, she added to the end of her prayer. She remembered that Sister Bernadette was a great authority on which saint to pray to at a moment of emergency or need: St Agatha against fire damage, St Agnes against a threat to purity (rape, no doubt), St Denis against headaches (St Denis had his head chopped off so was presumably immune from that problem) and then there was St Michael for strength. It was only when a second shot hit the pavement in front of her that she remembered that St Jude was the patron saint of lost causes. He did seem rather appropriate at the moment, what with the river on one side with its rising flood waters and the battle to gain control of Albert Quay station raging on the other side and over their heads.

By the time that the Reverend Mother had reached Parnell Bridge she had begun to get worried. The river was battering the arches and a barrier had been placed across it, shutting it to traffic. There were ominous creaks and groans coming from the stonework as a few heavy coal barges that had been swept loose from their moorings and snatched up by flood waters crashed against the arches. In the distance she could see that South Mall Street had disappeared and that a flowing sheet of water spread down between the offices and warehouses, lapping at the steps that led up to the front doors. The Grand Parade and Patrick Street would be just as bad, and the lanes that had been built on the western marsh, beyond the North Main Street and the South Main Street, would now be all under water. It would be impossible for her to get to the barracks.

She tried to ease her fears by telling herself that if the city was flooded then the murderer was unlikely to try to do anything tonight. Angelina was, almost undoubtedly, clever and resourceful, and was well guarded by Mother Isabelle. Nevertheless, it was important to catch this man before he did any more harm. Just as a dog that has killed one sheep will go on to kill, again and again, so, in the same way, she reckoned, a man who has killed once will kill again, especially if there is any threat to his safety.

It was at the moment that the bell from the Church of the Holy Trinity on Morrison's Island sounded for the seven o'clock benediction service that she saw a familiar figure and she immediately forgot how soaking wet, cold and slightly frightened that she was. It was definitely Nellie O'Sullivan.

Nellie, wearing a pair of staggeringly high-heeled shoes and a very short skirt, was walking arm-in-arm with another girl. The Reverend Mother, hampered by her dragging skirts and by her three score and ten years, envied them their youth, their companionship and above all the shortness of their very fashionable skirts. They were giggling together – she was near enough to hear the sound of their voices and though the shots overhead – something they had been accustomed to from their childhood – evoked screams, their cries seemed to be as much of excitement as of terror.

And behind them came a man wearing a large sack that had been slit down one side in order to form a hood and cape – a common form of dress for the dock workers, but somehow there was something familiar about this figure. Angelina had warned Mary to say nothing to any of her family about the swapping of identities, but Mary may not have obeyed. And it would, she thought, have been like Mary to confide the fact of her pregnancy to her younger sister. Whether or not; there was a great likelihood that the man who killed Mary would fear that she had done so.

'Nellie,' she called and the girl, by some miracle, heard her and swung back for an instant. Her eyes widened.

'Reverend Mother!' The words came out as a gasp and the next second the heaving crowd had swept on and around the elderly nun, carrying the two young girls away with it.

Had she done enough? Had she done too much? Had her presence, her intervention alerted a desperate man to the danger that he was in if she had managed to get hold of Mary O'Sullivan's sister?

The thought, she knew, would torment her all night, until she could be sure that the girl was safe, and other girls, also, but now she dare not think of it. She drove her way through the crowd, desperately elbowing people aside, trampling on feet that got in her way,

The crowds between them shifted and changed as people quickened or slowed their footsteps. There was, however, one constant figure. It was the man, wearing the hooded piece of sacking. He walked behind the two girls. He never got nearer to them, and never dropped back, or went to the other side of the pavement. He followed them doggedly, a dock worker perhaps – certainly the heavy sack he wore over his head and shoulders and the over-large tweed cap beneath it seemed to indicate this. And yet, in her heart, she felt that this was no dock worker; she felt that she knew his name and that she knew his face, now hidden. The Reverend Mother struggled on, trying to catch up with the girls. Her presence would immediately act as a deterrent; she was certain of that. She spoke his language and she knew what would frighten him. Her eyes went to the river and she prayed that it might swallow up this evil man before another girl lost her life. If only she could catch up with him, could confront him with his crime.

But her legs were like lumps of lead and she had started to shiver violently. There was no energy left in her. She was old and useless, no spring left to give her an extra burst of speed when it was so badly needed. She tried to call out, to say Nellie's name, but her breath sobbed in her lungs and the word was distorted and lost in the cries and shouts of warning and the flat bang of a bullet and the explosion of the sub-machine guns. More armoured cars were coming now, built high off the ground and with powerful engines they sped across the shaking bridge, firing wildly and indiscriminately while the people on the pavements shrieked and screamed.

The man was nearer to the two girls now. He was edging past them, moving them towards the quayside, just as a dog moves a herd of cattle. The Reverend Mother panted heavily, trying to catch up with them, bitterly despising herself for her age, her infirmities, and for her failure to keep herself as fit and as young as others around her. All her life she had believed in mind over matter, but now her faith deserted her.

The situation along the docks was extremely dangerous. In one long, continuous line the armoured cars from the army barracks on the top of the hill tore down the roadway sending up clouds of spray. The rebels on the walls discharged their sub-machine guns; the river in full spate thundered against the swaying bridge and sent long curling envelopes of water across the pavement, arousing shrieks and screams from the struggling pedestrians. The city police, the unarmed civic guard, with their distinctive uniforms covered with yellow oilskins, made an appearance shouting at the people to get under cover. The enormous twenty-foot-high steel gates of an empty warehouse on the quayside ground open with a rusty squeal which momentarily drowned the noise of the river, and the screaming pedestrians were channelled by the guards into the warehouse depths. For a moment the Reverend Mother lost sight of the two girls. They were young and energetic and had pulled ahead of her. They had vanished: and so had the deadly figure, in the guise of a dock worker, who had haunted their footsteps.

Pray God, she thought, they are in the care of the civic guard. She tried to see whether Patrick was amongst those oil-skinned figures, but her face ran with rain and the water from the river. Her body trembled and her eyes were dim with exhaustion. There seemed to be a momentary lull in the screaming, a cessation of the crossfire, perhaps even in the violence of the storm. It almost seemed that the wind was holding its breath; that it was holding back the surging waters.

Another minute and the river fought back. With almost deadly accuracy it flung a barrage of water at the people on the pavement. The Reverend Mother felt it hit her, and reeled beneath the force of its blow. She staggered, straightened herself and then shrieked aloud.

There was a gas lamp beside the quayside warehouse that still, miraculously, burned with a blue light amidst the tumultuous spray from the river. Beneath it she could see three figures. The man with the hooded sack over his shoulder had caught up with the two girls. They had turned aside from the river's onslaught, their hands and arms raised to shield their heads from the deadly blow of the water. He had seized his opportunity. He had slanted his steps, had moved his body to divert them from the crowd that were now making for the safe haven within the empty and solidly built warehouse, raised several feet above the level of the pavement. Blinded, sick and giddy from the blows of the water the girls had staggered, the one had let go of the other and in that moment the assassin had acted.

Perhaps it was only the Reverend Mother whose eyes had been fixed upon Nellie, with her short skirt and her long legs, staggering along, screaming with a mixture of excitement and panic – perhaps she was the only one who saw what had had happened, but the man in the docker's garb had succeeded in inserting a wedge between the two girls. The linked arms were driven apart for an instant, but an instant was going to be enough.

For a moment the Reverend Mother could not see what was happening. The water from the river blinded her. She turned sharply, raising her arm up to shield her face. And at that moment she felt her feet go from under her and an acute and terrible pain running down through her from her shoulder. She struggled desperately and then a man bent over her, helping her to her feet. She tried to thank him, but felt sick and giddy and he kept his hand on her arm.

'I've broken my other arm,' she gasped and wished that he would let go of her.

'I'll fetch a civic guard,' he said, still keeping a tight grip on her. He steered her towards the wall and left her there, leaning against it, unable to risk trying to sit on it and cradling one arm within the other.

And then a familiar figure, in breeches and tweed coat with a beret pulled well down over the head, running lightly through the flood water, caught her eye.

'Eileen,' gasped the Reverend Mother. 'Eileen! Look! Look at Nellie O'Sullivan. That man is following her!'

Eileen did not hesitate for one second. Her hand shot out, the pistol held high, pointing upwards, the noise of the shot sounded clearly above the roar of the water as she fired without hesitation into the air above the heads of the crowd. 'Nellie O'Sullivan, mind yerself!' she screamed and her young clear voice was startlingly loud.

And in a moment the man was gone. He had melted into the crowd. By the light of the gas lamp the Reverend Mother could make out the two faces of the girls who turned back towards herself and Eileen.

'Get inside there with the guards, ye pair of eejits.' It was extraordinary how the Eileen's voice rose so high above the thunder of the water and the frightened screams of the soaking-wet pedestrians. Nellie and her friend dived towards a civic guard in oilskins and a protective arm swept them into the warehouse. With that admonition to her young neighbours, Eileen tucked her arm under the Reverend Mother's.

'They'll be all right now, but you're going to go down with pneumonia,' she scolded in a motherly fashion. 'I bet that habit of yours is soaked through. Let's see if I can get you a lift home.'

'Eileen,' said the Reverend Mother, 'I think that I have broken my arm. What am I going to do?' She despised herself for her weakness, but there seemed to be a deadly faintness coming over her. She felt sick and giddy and black spots danced in front of her eyes. Eileen's figure seemed to shift slightly and then to become blurred.

But then a shrill blast from Eileen's whistle penetrated through the mist of her faintness. The Reverend Mother took in a long breath of wet, wind-filled air and bowed her head to below chest-level, waiting until the blood came back and throbbed against her eardrums. Dimly, she realized that a lorry had drawn up beside her, the smell of petrol strong in her nostrils. She heard Eileen saying something like, 'No sign of the St Luke's crowd yet.' And then a man's arm was around her, Eileen was saying something about a broken bone.

'Let's get her into the Crossley; the army are coming down from Luke's Cross, I've just seen them.'

'Go! You go quickly. Eileen, leave me, you must go!' Her own voice sounded strange in her ears and she did not know whether she had spoken aloud, or just in her mind. She was less faint now, though; she could see the man, young, she thought, wearing a gabardine raincoat and a soft hat well pulled down, its brim dripping.

'Be careful, Eamonn; she's probably as old as the hills.' Oddly enough, that sentence made her feel better, in fact, it almost made her chuckle. It was, she had discovered long ago, the lot of teachers to overhear candid opinions about themselves. Eamonn was the medical student, she thought, and hoped in a dazed way that he would not try to operate on her with a penknife, relying on his year at the university pre-med course.

Her next conscious thought came when she was sitting in the front seat of the lorry, sandwiched in between Eileen and the driver – Eamonn, apparently, who was competently revving up his engine and shouting comments over his shoulder. With a cautious glance she could see that the back of the lorry was stuffed with figures whose faces were almost covered by soft hats and that the space was bristling with guns held menacingly pointed to the sky.

'Nellie,' she said once, and Eileen immediately said, 'Don't worry. She's safe.'

As her vision cleared the Reverend Mother could see by the gas lamps that the majority of people by now had been ushered into the warehouse by the oilskin-clad civic guard and she no longer feared for Nellie. Had she recognized that man? She didn't know. Perhaps he had just been an innocent dock worker struggling through the flood, but perhaps not. He had melted away very quickly after that shot from Eileen's pistol.

'We're taking you to the Mercy Hospital,' said Eileen. And then, teasingly, 'You'll be able to tell the Bishop that you were rushed to hospital by a Crossley Tender.'

Despite her pain and her sick feeling, the Reverend Mother found her lips stretching into a responsive smile. The Crossley

Tender was a lorry-like vehicle, used originally by the Black and Tans, but so many of them had been hijacked by the Republicans that they were now completely associated with the rebels. It would, she thought; make a good story over the genteel cucumber sandwiches and fruitcake gathering that the Bishop held for the clergy of the city every summer.

The next minute another huge Crossley Tender overtook them, racing through the flood water, sending up showers of spray, but with its large wheels managing to keep going until it reached them and paused momentarily, with its engine roaring loudly. There was a toot-toot from its horn and then it sped on ahead, swinging around to the left.

'The Mallow crowd – useless *shower* they are, too. Can't shoot,' shouted Eamonn with contempt in his voice.

'What do you expect from that pack of buffers?' demanded Eileen with the city girl's contempt for the country cousins. She had turned her head towards the young men in the back and was engaged in a spirited reconstruction of the raid on Albert Quay railway station. Somebody had been at university with the leader of the Mallow brigade and was giving a humorous account about how the fellow had blown up the science laboratory on their first morning there.

'How'ya doing?' It took a few minutes for the Reverend Mother to realize that the question was being asked in her ear, but she was saved the necessity of answering by Eamonn saying curtly: 'Fractured humerus, shock, too, I'd say.'

And then she drifted off to the noise of what seemed like a lorry-load of medical students arguing over her case in the back of the Crossley Tender.

TWENTY-TWO

St Thomas Aquinas:
Vetustatem novitas umbram fugat veritas noctem lux.
(Old flees from the new, shadows from the truth, night from light.)

When the Reverend Mother came fully back to consciousness she realized that she was in the Mercy Hospital. She knew the place very well. It was staffed by a different branch of the order, but she had overall jurisdiction over both the teaching nuns and the nursing nuns.

She was lying in the best room of the hospital, one that even had its own closet opening off the bedroom; she had, she remembered, once visited the Bishop himself in this very place. Then it had been overcrowded with visitors, with bunches of flowers and gifts of fruit and dozens of cards, balancing precariously on windowsill and mantelpiece, but now it was empty and quiet.

Her arm, she realized, touching it first gingerly and then with more confidence, was now in plaster and from the faint smell of chloroform that hung around her, she guessed that she had already undergone an operation. She turned her eyes to the window, seeing that it was still raining, but that the day was advanced and then her eyes moved back to the door as she saw the knob turn cautiously and silently.

A figure in a white coat came in softly, a man; no, it was a woman; a woman with neatly shingled hair, wearing a white coat above the trousers, and a stethoscope hanging from the neck. It took a moment for the Reverend Mother to realize who it was and then she said nothing for a moment, waiting to make sure that the door behind her visitor was closed securely.

'How are you feeling?' Eileen approached the bedside in a businesslike manner. 'Pity they had to put you in here; it would be easier to slide away if you were in a ward, but I suppose that they would want you to have the best room in the place.'

'Where did you get the coat? If you don't mind me asking,' added the Reverend Mother, reminding herself that Eileen was no longer a pupil.

Eileen giggled softly. 'Pinched a pile of them from a laundry basket last night,' she said, her voice, lower than a whisper. 'I brought them out to the lorry. Eamonn and Mick put them on and they went back in and brought a stretcher out and carried you into casualty. And I walked behind them. They just dumped you there beside the desk and strolled off. The lads went back to our place, but I thought I'd hang around and make sure that you were all right. They're going to pick me up at nine o'clock tonight. How are you, Reverend Mother?'

'I'm fine,' said the Reverend Mother, endeavouring to make her voice sound resolute and strong. 'Now, Eileen, I do think that you should go and hide somewhere until they come. I wouldn't want anyone to recognize you.' There were, she reminded herself, still posters up asking for sightings of Eileen O'Donovan, a girl with long black hair and grey eyes, aged seventeen years. The newly cut short hair, though, she thought, did alter the girl's appearance and the white coat made her almost invisible in this large and busy hospital.

'See you in a while.' Eileen's quick ear caught a sound and she had melted away as the noise of trolley wheels and the loud remarks of some nurses had come to the Reverend Mother.

Later in the evening after she had seen the consultant, had endeavoured to swallow some chicken broth, Sister Mary Immaculate arrived, full, as usual, of exclamations and of questions, which she ignored by the easy method of just closing her eyes and sighing gently, but she snapped them open when the nun said: 'I have a note here for you, Reverend Mother, somewhere, in some pocket. Send by the Mother Superior of the Ursuline Convent, Sister Bernadette told me. Apparently the good Mother telephoned for you about lunchtime and was told of your accident. So she sent a note up by a boy all the way from Blackrock. Not important, I'm sure, or I would have brought it earlier – just her prayers for an early recovery, I suppose.'

She searched her pockets and eventually produced the crumpled envelope, addressed to 'Reverend Mother Aquinas' in a fine French hand. The Reverend Mother turned it over, cynically noticing signs of a small tear on the flap of the envelope. Sister Mary Immaculate would not have been able to hold her curiosity at bay.

The letter, however, might not have rewarded her greatly. It was a flowery effusion, written in French, bewailing the accident, rejoicing in the news that her arm had been attended to and that she was recovering in the arms of her sister nuns. Only the last paragraph revealed the reason for the telephone call and then the letter sent by hand.

Sœur Marie Goretti, she learned, had left the convent, quite unexpectedly and without a word at lunchtime today. A letter had been brought and she had been seen running down the avenue towards a waiting car with a man in it. Mother Isabelle finished with a few pious sentences and signed herself in English as 'Yours in the bosom of Christ'. The Reverend Mother put down the letter and stared, unseeingly, at the wall ahead. She was no expert on obscure saints, but she had a notion that this Marie Goretti had been a virgin martyr, who had been killed while resisting the sexual advances of a young man.

A touch fanciful, perhaps, to equate Angelina with this unfortunate girl, but it was probably the best that Mother Isabelle could do on the spur of the moment.

She put down the letter and turned her head towards the window. It was, by now, completely dark and a glance at her watch showed her that it was already seven o'clock in the evening – almost exactly twenty-four hours after her fall yesterday. She had been drifting in and out of sleep throughout the day, but now she was wide awake.

As soon as Sister Mary Immaculate had left, she went through it step by step: Angelina, according to Mother Isabelle, had 'departed' – not been snatched, had left of her own free will, had been seen alone running down the long avenue to the gate. She had got into a car there and no more was seen of her. So it was a man, and a man with a car. The Reverend Mother thought through the possibilities. A man that Angelina knew, a man that she trusted, a man who had brought a message so urgent that it had made her immediately leave the convent.

And where did he take her?

The thought of the flooded river came to her, of the drains, the sewers and the manholes. Did Angelina Fitzsimon end up in one of those this morning, after all?

The Reverend Mother moved impatiently. If she were right, then this man could not afford to have another enquiry into the death of yet another blue-eyed, chestnut-haired girl. No, this death was to be a statistic, a death from natural causes.

'Eileen,' she said softly, 'Eileen, are you there?'

The door to the closet opened and Eileen emerged. In her white coat and with her stethoscope around her neck she looked every inch the young professional.

'I thought I'd wait for a while to make sure that *she* was definitely gone,' she said nonchalantly. '*She* was always a great one to go out of the room and then to tip-toe back in again just to catch us talking about boys.'

The Reverend Mother ignored this slur upon her assistant.

'Eileen,' she said, 'do you remember that you talked of doing an article about the lunatic asylum one day?' She saw the girl's eyes widen in surprise and rushed on: 'I think that Angelina Fitzsimon, the girl who looked like Mary O'Sullivan, I think that she may have been taken there, taken against her will and I think that she could be in deadly danger.' If she is still alive, she thought, but then tried to buoy herself up with the conviction that this would be a murder intended to look like natural death – death that would occur at night. 'I wondered whether there was any possibility – I would not want you to run any risks,' she tailed off, but remembering these tough young men in the back of the Crossley Tender, with their rifles in hand, she thought it was unlikely that the over-worked medical staff in the asylum could stand up to them. 'You said something about them coming back tonight at nine o'clock,' she tailed off, feeling guiltily that she should not be suggesting a thing like that.

'Let's hope that Eamonn and Mick have remembered their white coats,' said Eileen and then she gave a sudden grin. 'Well, if I'm caught I can always say that you made me do it, Reverend Mother.'

'Save Angelina and you can say what you like,' said the Reverend Mother recklessly. She watched while Eileen peeped up and down the corridor and then sauntered out with her stethoscope swinging jauntily.

Would the Bishop of Cork designate this irresponsible sending out of a lorry-load of armed men, and women, members of a proscribed and excommunicated organization, by the Reverend Mother of St Mary's of the Isle Convent, to be a 'reserved' sin, to be pardoned by the Pope alone and only if one knelt in contrition at his knees in the Vatican City in Rome?

But she found that she did not greatly care as long as Angelina was rescued. It was time, she thought, for old age to hand over the quest to youth.

TWENTY-THREE

Countess Markievicz, 1921:
'But while Ireland is not free I remain a rebel,
unconverted and unconvertible.'

The Eglinton Asylum was such a huge place that there was something about it that made one deeply uneasy, thought Eileen, as the Crossley Tender sped along the flooded Western Road. Even through the dark and the rain, the vast gloomy, ugly structure, its roof studded with the long line of over a dozen triangular facades jutting up at regular intervals, menaced the city beneath. Almost every window in the enormously long building seemed to be illuminated, and it loomed above them as they crossed the bridge. Eileen peered through the rain-striped windscreen as the Crossley Tender struggled up the almost perpendicular hill. The road was empty of almost all traffic and she was not surprised.

'Built to house five hundred patients but now, someone told me, it has a thousand patients in it,' said Eamonn knowledgeably. 'You'd want to bring that out in your article, Eileen. They started off by having separate houses and joining them with little fenced-in yards and then when it started getting over-crowded they put roofs over the yards and built some sort of accommodation beneath. It's a terrible place. Can you imagine trying to care for thousand people in that building? Time we put this country on its feet again,' he remarked. 'Only lunatics would build a place in a long line like that, making it impossible to heat.'

'Anyway, it's not good for mad people to be shut up away from others – ever read Freud?' said Liam. A furious argument started up in the back about Freud and then someone asked what was the significance of a whole lorry-load of them to be going up to the lunatic asylum in the first place – was it just the final proof that that they were all mad as hatters and this

A Shameful Murder

223

caused a huge laugh, but Eileen did not laugh or join in the conversation. She was studying the building intently. Wish I had a good camera, she was thinking, remembering the American editor that the Reverend Mother had talked about who said one picture is worth a thousand words. Still, she thought, a thousand words is not a lot and I can bring my own feelings and impressions into my article.

But first, and foremost, this poor girl had to be found.

A building one thousand feet long. Could anyone be found quickly in a building of that size – a building that was the size of dozens of ordinary large houses?

A building where every door was locked.

And then she glanced over her shoulder at the guns held by the pack of loudmouths, as she and Aoife called them, and grinned. One gun is worth a thousand words, she told herself. Nevertheless when the Crossley Tender drew up in front of the huge establishment, she felt her breath come in quick, short pants.

Once inside the driver swept the lorry around in a wide semicircle to face the open gate and he did not switch off his engine; that was their practice, always. No matter where they went in the city, they would always have to have their exit ready. Charlie slipped into the driver's seat while Eamonn and Liam got out and pulled on their white coats. *I'm in charge*, Eileen told herself. She waited effortlessly until all was silent except for the sporadic roar of the engine. The men in the back were pressing up against the partition and she turned to face them.

'I want no gunfire,' she said sternly. 'Unless I authorize a warning shot,' she hastily amended her instructions, thinking how effective that could be on occasion. 'Wait to hear my whistle. I'm looking for a young woman – I'm the only one who will know her so Eamonn goes with me, and we'll leave Liam by the desk. Liam, you whistle if you need back-up.'

'Why don't we just go in, full-strength, and out again quickly?'

Charlie always had to argue, thought Eileen.

'Because there are a thousand patients and we can't examine every single one of them. I'm not going to cause too much of a fuss. The Reverend Mother told me to find a Dr Munroe if I can and he will know the girl – used to be sweet on her, that's what I think, anyway. Let's go.'

Somewhat to her surprise, the front door stood open. There was a young nurse at the desk, but her head was lowered on to a pile of papers and she was soundly asleep. Eileen nodded silently at Liam who took up his position beside the telephone on the desk and she and Eamonn looked at one another and then tiptoed creakily past the nurse.

The fog and damp from the incessant rain and flooding seemed to have got into even this building, erected high above the marsh and the river, thought Eileen, imagining how she would describe this place. They went down a long corridor whose oil-painted walls dripped with moisture and where the tiled floor was as slippery as if a film of grease had been spread over it. Here and there on the ceilings patches of fungus sprouted and the few windows were opaque with streams of water drops sliding down their ornate patterns of stained glass.

Eamonn in his white coat marched stiffly down the corridor keeping his back stiff and his head high and Eileen strolled at his side. A couple of nurses passed them, glanced at them, but none spotted the pistol that was in each pocket, or if they did they were too tired to worry. These were war-like times and no one saw fit to ask too many questions.

'Dr Munroe?' Eamonn asked the question abruptly and the nurses looked at one another uneasily. Eventually one pointed to a door and began to sidle away towards the front desk.

'No telephoning, now, ladies,' said Liam to them. He came out of the shadows, coming forward, swinging his rifle carelessly. 'I'll keep these girls company, and the telephone,' he said with a grin, and Eileen looked at Eamonn and shrugged her shoulders.

'Let the little boy play at being a soldier,' she said.

'There's Dr Munroe,' said one of the nurses and a young man in a white coat came out of a room marked 'Doctors Only'. He looked very tired and very drained. A man pushed beyond his limits, thought Eileen and imagined how she would describe him. Every effective article needs a human face as well as facts and figures, and, Dr Munroe, she thought, would be her hero.

'The Reverend Mother at St Mary's of the Isle sent me,' she said in a low voice, and then, just to make him feel at ease, she added: 'I used to be one of her pupils.'

He shrugged his shoulders, a man used to emergencies, she thought with approval. His eyes went to her armed guard but he made no comment, just stood very still, his hands hanging loosely by his side, conspicuously non-threatening.

'I need your help to find a girl who was brought in here,' she said quietly in his ear and he nodded.

'By her will, or against it?' His eyes were still fixed on the man by the desk with the rifle.

'I'm not sure,' said the Eamonn, joining in the conversation and then, recklessly, Eileen said, 'The Reverend Mother Aquinas is afraid for her; thinks that she may have been brought in here drugged, perhaps unconscious.'

He looked puzzled and she wasn't surprised. It was a strange and a fanciful notion. She looked at him with a hint of impatience. 'I must make sure,' she said and then he nodded.

'When did she come?'

'Today, I think.'

'Up here,' said Munroe and turned a corner and then began to climb the stairs. The staircase was enclosed with iron bars from top to bottom, giving a curiously caged impression. She kept a cautious hand on the bars as she climbed. The architect who had designed this impressive building had not known about the fogs of Cork and perhaps had envisioned his building having a better heating system – the walls dripped water and the marble tiles of the steps were as slippery as the corridor had been and, she thought, must be very dangerous for the patients.

'Here's my office,' said Munroe, over his shoulder, producing an enormous key from his pocket and unlocking the door and they went in with him.

Once it was securely shut behind them, Dr Munroe lit the gas lamp and then threw a careless leg over one corner of the table and rested his hip on it. The room was icy cold, but the young doctor did not seem to notice. His eyes were on them both.

'Now,' he said. 'What's all this about?'

'We haven't time to explain everything,' said Eileen impatiently. 'We have to look for her.'

'For who?'

'For Angelina Fitzsimon.'

'I was told that she was dead.' He had started violently at the name, and then quietened himself with an obvious effort.

'They thought she was, but . . .' Eileen gave an impatient movement and a jerk of the head. The impossibility of explaining everything, the elaborate disguise of one girl, the murder – a dead girl who had been identified as Angelina Fitzsimon, but had been, in reality, poor, stupid Mary O'Sullivan . . . A death whose consequences seemed to have ended with the interment in the Fitzsimon tomb in a cemetery in Blackrock. But now? Once Angelina appeared again, then the other death would be investigated and the murderer would be located. The important thing was that Angelina, according to the Reverend Mother, was in deadly danger from a man who knew that he faced death by the noose if caught.

'You'll have to trust me, Dr Munroe,' she said imperatively and with all of the authority that she could throw into her voice. 'This is a matter of life or death – we may be too late, but I don't think so. The Reverend Mother thinks that the murderer will probably strike in the night; she says that is the time when most deaths naturally occur. All you need to know for now,' she finished, 'is that we are looking for Angelina Fitzsimon and she will be locked up somewhere – in a ward or in a private room.'

'Drugged?' Dr Munroe looked terribly tired. He ran his hand fretfully through his red curls and then looked across at Eileen, almost as though appealing for help. She edged the butt of her pistol from her pocket and stared back at him stonily.

'Yes, undoubtedly, and we intend to find her.' There was a warning note in Eamonn's voice.

'You'd know her, wouldn't you, Dr Munroe,' urged Eileen. 'The Reverend Mother told me that you had played tennis with her.' He had admitted the girl to see her mother, had gone so far as to steal a nurse's uniform for her – well, certainly he should have been able to recognize her.

'Could have the head shaved.' Dr Munroe seemed to be slightly invigorated by that energetic voice. 'Don't expect to recognize her by the chestnut hair – it's probably all gone – all shaved off – they do that to the poor things– makes life easier for the nurses. Let's go. Stick by me. We don't want any disturbances. Once you're with me, no one will take much notice. Take that lamp. They'll have the lights low at night. Keep that fellow with the rifle out of the way, for God's sake.'

They went down a different set of stairs; this time Eileen found the bars caging them in to be less intimidating. Her eyes were beginning to accustom themselves to the dim light. As well as that she was now filled with the sense of a mission. Come what may, she would rescue Angelina Fitzsimon from an almost certain death.

But then she heard something, something like a distant thunder or rumbling. For a moment she could not think what it could be and feared that the building might be collapsing with damp, but the sound swelled and grew higher and she realized that it was the sound of human voices, of sobbing or hopeless wailing, of shrill cries and half-formed words. She looked at Munroe with horror, but the doctor appeared to notice nothing, just went on down the stairs, each marble tile ringing from the sound of his swift footsteps. The noise of human voices swelled as the three walked silently, shoulder to shoulder, down the broad corridor.

'In here,' said Munroe, fitting a key to the lock and turning it with a loud click.

The room that they entered was a long one, floored with huge slabs of limestone, its brick walls whitewashed – some time ago, judging by its yellowish appearance and by the innumerable and disgusting stains that spattered the surface. At the top of the room was a tall window, divided by limestone mullions into three sections, each of the three finishing with a sharply pointed arch. The city lay down below and she could see the yellow glow of gas lamps piercing the fog at regular intervals. Down there the people of Cork would have finished their day's work at office or warehouse and would be endeavouring to get back to their homes. Up here was a place for the damned.

The two long walls of the ward were lined with small iron-framed beds, set at regular intervals, and on each bed lay a woman – some of them half-naked, others lightly covered with stained yellow blankets that looked thin and frayed. A padlocked chain was attached to both the top and the bottom of the bed and she could see that most of the inmates were chained by wrist and ankle. The stench was appalling and at their entrance the noise rose to a deafening level.

'You check that side and I'll check this. There's no nurse here for the moment so be quick.' Munroe seemed to be unaffected by the scene that struck the Eamonn motionless and dumb for the moment. He was already moving rapidly down the row, scanning the faces, even stopping to write some instruction on the slate which, with its stick of chalk, hung from string at the bottom of each bed. Eileen stayed by the door for a moment and then joined him. Eamonn strolled around, looking for all the world as though he had completed the last four years of his medical course at the university.

Eileen's mind was in a whirl. I must do something about this if I come out of this place alive, she thought. She forced herself to put the suffering out of her mind and to concentrate on the faces. Surely none of them could be Angelina. She tried to remember the face of the girl in the satin dress that she had seen that morning lying on the flood water in the laneway on St Mary's of the Isle.

By the time that she had reached the window, Munroe was already standing at the door beckoning to her impatiently. He had instantly realized that she was not here, while she had lingered, trying to discover a trace of humanity in the faces of these unfortunates.

Still, she endeavoured to be speedier as they traversed the second ward – a mirror image of the first one. It was, he knew, only a matter of time, before they were discovered. There might be a pitched battle in this terrible place. That wouldn't help the unfortunate patients.

'How many more of those wards?' she whispered to Munroe when they were in the corridor once again.

'The high-security female wards? Just another eight.'

Eight more! What had happened to the relations of all of

those people? How could they have allowed this to happen to them? She walked after Munroe trying to keep her mind away from the horrors and focused on one thing for the moment. She had to find Angelina and to take her out of this place as soon as possible, before the poor girl was driven mad.

There was a nurse dressing a sore on one of the women's arms in the next ward. She said nothing, intent on her work, but Eamonn and Eileen stuck close to Munroe and nodded their heads wisely to a few murmured comments. This ward was very quiet, no one shouting, and there was a tray of mugs on the long table by the door at the end of the room.

'They've had their laudanum for the night,' said Munroe when they were back out in the corridor again. 'It quietens them down for a while and then they start to get the horrors.'

'Dr Munroe!' The shout came from above their heads and they saw Munroe lift his head and peer up through the murky atmosphere. Rapidly she moved into the shade of yet another staircase. Eamonn, she noticed, had instantly moved into the darkness of the shadows.

'Yes, Dr O'Connor,' called back Munroe.

'Come up into my office, will you?'

'I was just doing the rounds,' objected Munroe while Eileen held her breath. There had been no telephone on Dr Munroe's desk, but there probably was one in this Dr O'Connor's office.

'I tell you, come up here, Doctor,' called Dr O'Connor imperatively. 'I want to see you. You can finish your rounds afterwards. What's the hurry?'

'I'll have to go or else he'll come down,' Munroe whispered noiselessly in Eileen's ear. 'You try number fifteen and number sixteen and then wait for me here. Keep out of anyone's way. If a nurse comes in, just write "bed sores" on a slate. They've all, all of the patients, they've all got them and the nurses hate attending to them. They'll clear off quickly if they see you write that.'

They waited until Munroe had run up the stairs and until they had heard a door above slam closed before going into the next ward. They had to find this girl soon. The murderer could not allow her to live; that was what the poor old Reverend Mother had said.

But she was not in ward fifteen – there had been one young girl that they both had looked twice at – the shaved heads made them all difficult to tell apart, but this young girl had opened eyes of the palest shade of grey and then shut them again. Not Angelina, but sweetly pretty and lost – her expression blank, her scratched arms bearing witness to her frantic efforts to free herself. Nor was she in number sixteen; there had been a nurse there who looked rather intently at both of them, but who turned away and bustled out of the ward when Eileen had frowned heavily, looking down on a patient and written 'bed sores' on the slate, tapping it authoritatively before stalking out.

There was still no sign of Dr Munroe when they emerged. Then Eamonn looked around and saw another door marked with the letter F so Eileen nodded to enter it, though the noise that was coming from it daunted her to the soul – the screams of the dammed.

But hell, she thought despairingly, when she entered, was never as bad as this. From beside her she heard Eamonn suck in a deep breath.

It was a long room with a huge window at the end of it – divided into five sections with the mullions, like steps of stairs, rising to the centre and then decreasing again on the other side and each section enclosing some ornate stained-glass picture. The room had alcoves along each side of it and the brick floor sloped down to the centre – as if it were a cattle mart.

Each of the alcoves held a stone bath and in each of the baths, pinioned by an iron bar, was a naked woman. Four nurses were hosing them down and the water seemed to flow from a hole at the bottom of the bath and down to the drain in the centre of the floor. A pile of ragged towels were on a table beside the doorway and a row of wheeled stretchers, each one covered with a rubber sheet, were ranged in front of it.

The nurses turned startled faces as they came in. Eamonn raised a hand and nodded, then seized one of the stretchers and turned smartly on his heel and wheeled it out. Eileen followed, numb with compassion and anger. No written article, no picture could ever tell this story as it should be told to the people of Cork, she was thinking as Dr Munroe came running back down the stairs.

'I know where Angelina is,' he whispered in her ear. 'Saw it in the admissions book when he went over to the window to count the pound notes for my salary. It must be her – different name, but just one person came in today – different name – Mary O'Sullivan, aged twenty. She's been put in a private room – down this corridor.' He seized the trolley from Eamonn with a whispered: 'Well done, yourself,' and wheeled it with a nonchalant air down the corridor, past several windows looking down upon the River Lee and the city beyond.

Pray God, she is still alive, thought Eileen as she followed, trying to put the last scene out of her head. At least if they could save Angelina and get out of this hell-hole she would find words that would scorch the consciences of all that allowed this terrible lack of care, this dreadful insult to human dignity.

And it was Angelina. She recognized the eyes. The girl lay on a narrow bed inside a small room which was like a cubicle. There was no sign of the nun's clothes that she had worn up to a few hours ago, no sign of any clothes at all. She was naked under the blanket, completely unconscious. Her hair had been shaved, but her eyes, those very Mediterranean-blue eyes, the blue eyes of a high-class doll, that Eileen remembered, were wide open and staring sightlessly at the ceiling. On the slate at the bottom of the bed was printed in large letters: FOUND IN STREET. BYSTANDER REPORTED THAT SHE HAS BEEN INSANE FOR YEARS. HAS HAD SEVERAL EPILEPTIC FITS ON THE JOURNEY HERE. RAVES IN BETWEEN. UNLIKELY TO SURVIVE.

Instantly Dr Munroe gathered her up in his arms and transferred the body on to the trolley, covering her, including face and head, with the blanket. He looked down on her for a moment, then went to the door and placed it slightly ajar, then returned and delved in his pocket taking out a packet of face masks. He put one on. Now only the flaming red hair and the eyes were visible. He handed the other two to Eileen and Eamonn. They obeyed him instantly, becoming doctors on an operating case without hesitation.

Then with an air of resolution Dr Munroe took a small

scalpel from the breast pocket of his white coat, pulled a white arm out from the blanket. Before anyone could stop him, he drew it across the girl's arm. Blood flowed out instantly from Angelina Fitzsimon, staining the blanket, dripping down on to the trolley.

'Now run,' said Munroe with an appreciative grin at Eileen. 'Keep up with me, Doctor, won't you? This is an emergency, you know.'

And then he was off running at breakneck speed, pushing the trolley. Eileen's leather boots thundered down the corridor in pursuit, the stethoscope swinging wildly from her neck, the white coat tails parted and flying like wings. They met several nurses, but none seemed even interested, just stood back to allow the trolley to pass. This was an institution that lived with emergencies and attempted suicides. At the sight of them, Liam jumped to his feet, pushed open the two front doors and set off running ahead of them. Eileen felt her heart lurch sideways. They were so near now.

The engine of the Crossley Tender still ran noisily, still turned and facing the gates. As Liam approached at high speed, someone shone a torch, the back was let down and then Charlie switched on the headlights. In a moment Liam and Eamonn had efficiently collapsed the stretcher, carried Angelina, still stretched upon it, into the back of the lorry. Eamonn produced a small pocket torch and Eileen climbed up after the girl, lying beside Angelina with her arm over the cold body, doing her best to warm her and to keep the wet from her. They should have picked up more blankets, she thought. This girl seemed to be halfway towards death. Eamonn reached in, felt the pulse and then shouted, 'Let's go, Charlie.'

'Go where?' Charlie was speeding down the hill towards the river.

'Same place as last night,' yelled Eamonn. 'Mercy Hospital, again. We're their best suppliers.'

TWENTY-FOUR

St Thomas Aquinas:
Et aequo animo ferre iniuriam sibi signum est perfectio, sed est
alius iniurias patienter sufferre imperfectionis et actualis peccati.
(To bear with patience wrongs done to oneself is a mark of
perfection, but to bear with patience wrongs done to someone
else is a mark of imperfection and even of actual sin.)

Sergeant Patrick Cashman was at the Mercy Hospital by
half-past nine on the following morning. He had come
into the barracks, found a lay sister from the hospital
waiting for him, and at her news, he straightaway put his hat
and coat back on again and without waiting for a word with
the superintendent left the building.

'How is she?' he asked, trying to slow his footsteps to the
woman's.

'Bad,' she said with a gloomy shake of the head, 'very bad.
Unconscious.'

Looking around he saw a taxi cruising along and hailed it
quickly with a raised umbrella.

'Get in,' he said shortly to the lay sister. 'We'll get there
more quickly. The flooding is still bad. We'll have to take a
roundabout route.'

There was a feeling of oppression, almost of fear within
him when he paid off the taxi, entered the doors of the
hospital and strode down the corridor towards the reception
desk. The Reverend Mother seemed to be an essential part
of the scenery in Cork, as old as the statue of Father Matthew
which was the focal meeting point for all at the top end of
St Patrick Street – she was as old and as solidly reliable, he
thought, remembering the flood waters lapping in a futile
way around the knees of the statue the last time that he had
seen it.

He almost held his breath as the accompanying nursing

sister tapped on the door and then threw it open. 'A visitor for you, Reverend Mother,' she said respectfully.

'Patrick!' said the voice, clipped, decisive, clear as always. The Reverend Mother was out of bed, and dressed. Only a sling made her appear different.

'Very good of you to come,' she said briskly and refused, on his behalf, the offer of a cup of tea. Patrick found himself grinning.

'The Sister told me that you were . . . "lying unconscious and very bad", that was what she said.' He was almost stammering with relief.

'Nonsense,' she said crisply. 'I've just stupidly broken my arm. As for what you were told that was one of those conversations, like parallel lines, where the two minds never meet. You were talking about me; the sister was talking about Angelina.'

He immediately became grave. 'Angelina?'

'Word came to me that she had been enticed from her place of refuge; been immediately chloroformed and then hidden, naked and with a shaved head, among the unfortunate insane people in the Eglinton Asylum. I entrusted her recovery to some reliable friends and she is now here in the hospital.' The four extraordinary pieces of information were delivered in the Reverend Mother's usual, concentrated, concise and matter-of-fact style.

Patrick gasped, but knew from the look in her eye that no questions about those reliable friends were invited.

'And how long will she remain unconscious?' he asked and got a nod of approval.

'The doctors tell me that it may go on for days. Her life is no longer in jeopardy, but it is considered, by the medical authorities, to be safer for her if she awakes naturally, without any artificial stimulants. Her life was at risk for some time last night, but with the skill of the physicians here she is now considered to be out of danger. In any case,' said the Reverend Mother, going as usual to the crux of the matter, 'I feel fairly sure that she did not know who abducted her. Remember what a murky day it was yesterday, Patrick. It did not stop raining for the whole day. A man in the darkness of the car, hat pulled down, coat collar turned up . . . a pad of chloroform placed over her mouth . . .'

'But where was she? You said a *place of refuge* . . .'

The Reverend Mother considered that for a moment, and he thought that she might say 'with a friend', but after that pause she said, 'Angelina retreated to the Ursuline Convent of Blackrock, without the knowledge of her family or her friends.'

'But the man guessed.'

'Yes.' The Reverend Mother's very green eyes were brooding over this. 'It is possible that my visit there was injudicious,' she acknowledged, 'but I fear that the first victim, Mary O'Sullivan, told the man the whole story – Angelina's as well as her own. She was always, poor little thing, a silly girl, who liked to try to make herself important.'

Patrick looked at the Reverend Mother, wondering how much she would tell him. That she knew the whole story he had little doubt. There was a gleam of the hunter in her eyes and she wore an expression that he had seen on the faces of some chess players when a possible checkmate was envisaged.

'Was Angelina the intended victim on the night of the Merchants' Ball?' He tried the question and was rewarded with a gracious nod. Thirteen years ago, he would have been given a sweet; the thought was fleeting, as now all his energies were concentrated. Like a runner, he was on the home trail and he knew what he would have to do.

'So it was Mary O'Sullivan,' he continued. 'By plan or by chance?'

Her expression became a little remote and so he quickly amended this to: 'It must have been by chance. He could not have expected to see her in that place, wearing that dress, but, once he danced with her, well, he knew both girls . . . is that right? He knew both girls, and when he was close up he realized that it wasn't Angelina, but Mary, all dressed up.'

'Go on,' she said. And she looked at him, like a teacher who has faith in a pupil's ability to find the right answer.

'Of course!' he exclaimed. 'This man was the father of Mary's baby. He had made her pregnant. She saw him, told him that she was pregnant, perhaps, told him about the swap and about the Ursuline Convent refuge for Angelina.'

'Do you remember,' said the Reverend Mother slowly. 'Do you remember, Patrick, telling me how many pregnant girls have been fished out of the river during your time as a policeman? You are a young man who has not been long in the force and yet that has been your experience. I wonder how many others he may have murdered. This was a man whose self-image may have depended on the good opinion of those around him. He, I feel, could not afford to be seen as loose living – it would spoil his image – not just in others' eyes but also in his own. His own self-esteem depended on the esteem of others.'

'A priest!' Patrick exclaimed, but she shook her head.

'Not a priest,' she said, 'but a man who had aspirations towards the dignity of being one of the Pope's Knights of Malta, because of his work among the poor of Cork.'

He was beginning to understand and looked across at her.

'We are strange creatures, we humans,' she said unexpectedly. 'I have heard myself called charitable, but only I know how much pride, how much mental satisfaction is mixed in with my so-called charity. But charity, of course, should be love; pure and simple love – the Latin is *caritas* but, although I don't know Greek, I understand that it comes originally from that language and means *unlimited loving-kindness*. This man found that charitable works not only boosted his sense of self-worth, which perhaps had been very low, but also led him into the company of unfortunates who would do anything in order to be fed, to be given sweets, food, coal, clothes and he discovered that above all he found pleasure in very young girls who so wished for pretty clothes. At first it was probably just a matter of touching, inappropriate, perhaps; but starving mothers turned a blind eye and the children themselves, were, in certain cases, too young and too innocent, and, in other cases, too greedy for what he could offer.' The Reverend Mother stopped and said, 'Not only a priest works among the poor.'

'A doctor!' exclaimed Patrick.

'I thought about that – and then I remembered the visits of the man from the St Vincent de Paul to the O'Sullivan household, the gifts of clothes for the girls – given by a man who, because of his appearance, because of that terrible disfigurement, would not have found it easy to get from girls of his own class, affection, love or sexual favours,' said the Reverend Mother bluntly.

Patrick stared at her and then his eyes widened. 'And, of course, he was at the Merchants' Ball. Terrible disfigurement. You're talking about Professor Lambert, aren't you? And he said that he had danced with Angelina. If he knew both girls, then he must have realized that it was not Angelina. He must have known instantly that it was Mary O'Sullivan. He would not have been fooled by the dress and the necklace.'

'And she probably asked him for money. Mary O'Sullivan would not have missed up on that opportunity,' put in the Reverend Mother dryly.

'He's of the Lambert family; he wouldn't have been short of money,' said Patrick decisively. 'So why didn't he give it to her?'

'For fear that something would leak out, I suggest. This man would have killed to keep his secret.'

'I suppose,' he said slowly, 'he got quite a shock when he realized who it was and then when Mary made the mistake of trying to blackmail him, he slipped her some ether. It would be easy for him, as a doctor, to get hold of ether; it would be one of the tools of his trade, he would have it in his bag, and so he put the ether into a glass of champagne – the tea-planter fellow reported that she seemed sleepy and complained of feeling sick. Professor Lambert had danced with her, had handed her over to one of his students and had gone upstairs. But later he probably slipped down again and then he came back to her, met her in a dark corner, probably got her in the lift, went down, instead of up, as you suggested, Reverend Mother. Started to strangle her – he is a powerfully built fellow in the arms, chest and shoulders – I remember noticing that – saw the manhole and decided on a cleverer course. He just popped her down, dropped her through the manhole and into the sewer.'

He stopped. 'What made him do it, Reverend Mother – a man like him, so esteemed, so praised, what made him abuse young girls?'

'I would imagine,' said the Reverend Mother primly, 'that if marriage was an impossibility, if a woman of his own class would never look at him because of his terrible disfigurement then in order to satisfy his male urges he turned to the young and the innocent and that,' she said firmly, 'I find unforgivable.'

Patrick took in a deep breath and then jumped to his feet. There was a surging energy bursting up through him. He could not wait to get back to the barracks and to pick up a warrant and a pair of handcuffs. He would have to explain matters to the superintendent first, but all was now very clear in his mind and he knew that he could convince the man.

'Thank you very much, Reverend Mother; I would never have got on to his trail if it were not for you,' he said gratefully.

'It might be a good idea,' suggested the Reverend Mother, 'to go to Nellie O'Sullivan's place of work – the pub on Albert Quay – and get a statement from her. Perhaps take her back to the barracks with you.'

'Will she be willing to do this, and to stand up in court, what do you think?'

The Reverend Mother did not answer for a moment. She appeared to be contemplating a picture in her mind's eye and when she spoke it was with her usual decisiveness.

'I think, Patrick,' she said, 'Nellie O'Sullivan would give a very good performance in front of Judge Magner and his fellow lawyers. Go now, and do what you must do,' she added.

Did she, he wondered, as he went down the corridor rapidly, feel any sense of compunction about what might seem as a betrayal of a friend – at least he supposed that Professor Lambert might be a friend – he spoke in the same way, came from the same background, and perhaps more importantly, had also chosen to work among the poor of Cork. He shook his head impatiently. It was none of his business, he thought, and he had little idea of what went on behind the mask of that pale face and those heavy-lidded, luminous green eyes framed by the snowy white wimple – a face that seemed to have remained exactly the same since he had been a young child. The Reverend Mother was probably as old as time itself and as inscrutable. Patrick turned his thoughts towards the superintendent, marshalling his arguments, lining up the facts. It would be good, he thought, if the answer could have appeared to come from his superior, if he could manage the man in the same way that the Reverend Mother had led his thoughts towards the discovery of the truth. However, he had little hope of this and he had no time for stupidity this morning. A man who had killed once would kill again and pretty little Nellie O'Sullivan, at this moment, would be running gaily down the quays going to work at the bar. The murderer must be arrested and locked up before any further harm came from him. His fate after that could be argued out in front of the judge. He would take a cab to Paddy's Bar on Albert Quay, he thought. The sooner he got there the better.

It was still early when they arrived at the barracks, but the superintendent, according to Tommy O'Mahoney, was already in his office. Patrick left Nellie with Tommy, took in a deep breath, straightened himself, tapped on the door and went in.

'Ah, Sergeant!' The superintendent seemed in an irritable mood, fussing with the papers on his desk and frowning heavily. 'I've just had the *Cork Examiner* on the telephone asking whether there was any news of an arrest in the Angelina Fitzsimon case. What's going on with it?'

Patrick took a seat without being bidden. He forced himself to sit very straight and to look the superintendent in the eye.

'You'll be able to telephone them back with the news by the end of the morning, Superintendent,' he said confidently. 'I think I've solved the case and with your consent hope to make an arrest within an hour.'

'What!'

Patrick ignored the exclamation. He would be very simple and straightforward, he decided. It was not a moment to pay tribute to the various helpers, indeed, it would seem like a fairy tale where a Reverend Mother had solved a murder and her minions from the Republican Party had rescued a girl from near-death.

'This was a case of double identity and of blackmail,' he began, speaking briskly and confidently. 'Angelina Fitzsimon is alive, she was concealed in the lunatic asylum, on the point of death; her almost identical half-sister, a girl from Sawmill

Lane, was the murder victim.' He went on explaining the switch
of girls at the Merchants' Ball, glad that shock had robbed the
superintendent of words and speaking rapidly in order that he
could get through his report before being interrupted.

'Mary O'Sullivan had been made pregnant by Professor
Lambert, who had frequently visited the house to give charitable parcels from the St Vincent de Paul Society. I guess that
she told him, at the Merchants' Ball, that she was expecting
a baby, tried to blackmail him and he panicked, gave her some
ether and then took her from the ballroom, strangled her and
dropped the body into the sewer in the basement of the Imperial
Hotel.' Patrick kept his voice neutral as he added: 'He had
been afraid that he would be unmasked in Cork society as an
immoral man.' He noted, without trepidation, that the superintendent's eyes were almost popping from his head and waited
for the storm to break.

'You can't prove any of this!' The words were spluttered,
but somehow they did not sound as outraged as he had expected.
Was it possible, he wondered suddenly, that the superintendent
might have heard some rumours about Professor Lambert in
the past? In any case, he could not afford to lose time now, so
he played his trump card.

'Angelina Fitzsimon has been rescued from her incarceration
at the asylum and the Reverend Mother of St Mary's of the Isle
is with her now,' he said mildly, though suppressing the information that Angelina was still unconscious, and then he added,
'and Nellie O'Sullivan, sister to the murdered girl, has made a
statement. You can see that she names Professor Lambert as the
cause of her sister's pregnancy. She's waiting outside in case
you wish to examine her.' He took the piece of paper from his
pocket and passed it across the desk and then waited patiently
for the warrant to be issued.

TWENTY-FIVE

St Thomas Aquinas:
Iustitia vero sit quaedam rectitudo animi, per quam homo
operatur quod debet facere in tempore quo eum.
(Justice is a certain rectitude of mind, whereby a man does what
he ought to do in the circumstances confronting him.)

'He committed suicide,' said the Reverend Mother. 'He was found dead by the policemen who came to arrest him. He had an empty glass beside him. No doubt he had discovered that Angelina had been taken away from the asylum and guessed that his deeds would be exposed.'

'That's good,' said Lucy briskly. She ate one of the grapes she had brought for the invalid and, head on one side, appraised her bouquet of hothouse flowers. 'Much the best way around things; I suppose that it will all be hushed up, now.'

'Not if I can have anything to do with it,' said the Reverend Mother firmly. Patrick had come into the hospital half an hour earlier with the news, looking angry and cheated. 'Poor man,' the superintendent had said when he heard the news, according to Patrick. There would be a closing of ranks, a silent conspiracy to shield a wealthy family from shame. She had tried to console him, thinking that Thomas Aquinas would agree with his ideas about legal justice being a necessity for society, but the murderer of poor Mary O'Sullivan might, she thought, now never be exposed. Unless, of course, powerful forces demanded that justice should be seen to be done . . .

'Well, believe me, it's best left alone,' said Lucy, vigorously giving her reasons, while the Reverend Mother mused on the abstract concept of justice and tried to think of an influential ear, into which she would drop a hint. 'Do you hear me, Dottie,' she said sharply, and then with an exasperated sigh: 'The trouble with you nuns is that you don't live in the real world.'

The Reverend Mother thought about her world, remembering her last morning before her accident when she had to break the news to six children in her school that their father had thrown himself under the wheels of a train and had sent instructions to the kitchen to make up a parcel of food for another family where the youngest child had complained of 'a belly ache' from hunger and then promised a distraught woman to contact a landlord about the terrible rat problem in one of the tenements in Cove Street. However, she bowed her head meekly and tucked her hands into her large sleeves and Lucy looked satisfied.

'How is the girl?' she asked.

'Angelina is making good progress,' said the Reverend Mother cautiously. 'Her father and brother have been to see her. One of the nursing sisters informed me of their presence and I sat by Angelina's bedside. She did not speak during their visit,' she added.

'Did you say anything to them?' Lucy sounded a little nervous.

'Just a greeting: I was saying my rosary,' said the Reverend Mother blandly.

They had been ill at ease, she had thought, watching them from beneath lowered eyelids as the black beads slipped through her fingers. Guilty-looking, both of them, she was sure of that, but was it guilt for the pressure they had put the girl under, or was there anything more than that to be read from their uneasiness? There was no doubt but that Angelina had felt threatened enough to stage a disappearance in order to escape from the threat that they posed. It was important that the girl's future should be safeguarded.

'You're not my first or even my most important visitor, Lucy,' she said mildly. 'Yesterday the Bishop of Cork, the Reverend Daniel Cohalan, came to see me. He had some interesting news. Apparently the Bon Secours Sisters of the hospital in College Road are having a new Mother Superior, someone from France, someone who is known to both of us. She is, was, Sœur Marie Madeleine from Bordeaux, now, of course, Mère Marie Madeleine. I shall be meeting her at a diocesan reception next week, by the kindness of His Lordship.'

The well-powdered, discreetly rouged face in front of her did not change and the blue eyes did not falter, nevertheless the tension in the air was almost palpable.

'And . . .' said Lucy, stony-faced. She looked across at her cousin and the Reverend Mother looked back at her resolutely. The young had to be protected. That had been her creed for over fifty years.

'Edmund and Angela,' she said, 'were very nice people, but not, you know, people of a practical frame of mind. They both thought that once the baby was born then it was theirs, almost as though,' said the Reverend Mother with an unaccustomed flight into poetry, 'it had been bred of their bone, and born of their blood. But you and I, Lucy, know better. Joseph was not, is not the true heir to the Fitzsimon estate. He is the cuckoo in the nest, the interloper, and has no legal right to the property that he now uses as his own. They left no will, though I suspect that, in any case, the property was entailed, so a will would not have helped. Joseph's birth was illegitimate and, as the law stands, this means that he could not inherit, even if Edmund and Angela were his real parents, even if they had married subsequently. The real truth of Joseph's birth is known only to three persons who are alive today.' She paused for a moment. 'However, even one is enough and I propose to make use of that one.'

Lucy broke her silence after a minute. 'You would betray me,' she said harshly. 'There's Rupert and the girls, my granddaughters . . .'

'There will be no betrayal,' said the Reverend Mother firmly, 'just a simple statement, under oath, from a nun who presided over his birth, stating that Joseph Fitzsimon was not born of Angela and Edmund Fitzsimon, but was the illegitimate son of a young girl living locally in west Bordeaux. It will be made clear that no further steps will be taken while his daughter Angelina remains safe and unthreatened.'

There was another long silence and this time it was the Reverend Mother who broke it.

'I propose that a letter be written to Joseph Fitzsimon by a French lawyer from Bordeaux, stating that an affidavit about the illegitimate birth has been placed in his care and that it will remain under lock and key while reports that Angelina is well, sent by a respected person of the community in Cork, continue to arrive. That, I think,' she said with satisfaction, 'should probably do the trick, especially, if, as I imagine, an account of my meeting with the Mother Superior of the future Bon Secours Hospital is reported in the *Cork Examiner*. No doubt there will also be a photograph . . .'

She would make sure of that, she thought. Let Joseph feel uneasy, let him wonder and speculate, let him envisage the loss of his property and be terrified by such a prospect. It would be best, she thought, planning for the future, if Angelina, once released from hospital, did not return to the house in Blackrock, but openly stayed as a visitor with her friend and former mentor, the Mother Superior of the Ursuline Convent in Blackrock. Between the two of them, Mother Isabelle and Mother Aquinas, they should be able to ensure the safety and the happiness of Angelina Fitzsimon and to get justice and proper medical treatment for her unfortunate mother.

The Bishop, she remembered, had preached his annual sermon last year to the religious orders of Cork on the theme of the three churches: *ecclesia militans*, those Christians struggling on earth; *ecclesia triumphans*, those who had obtained the happiness of Heaven; and *ecclesia penitans*, those who repented in Purgatory. To these divisions of the church she would add a fourth. Joseph Fitzsimon would find that his every move was watched over by the *ecclesia materna*.

After Lucy had gone, she relaxed in her chair, nursing her broken arm and planning her visit to Mère Marie Madeleine. Once she was discharged from here, she thought, she would get Dr Scher to order her into the Bon Secours for one of those new-fangled X-rays of her arm. No one in her convent would question a visit to a rival hospital with the money for superior facilities. And she would make sure that she and the new Reverend Mother had a long conversation together. The secret would be kept as it had been for over fifty years, but the safeguard for Angelina would be put in place.

Next, the Reverend Mother turned her mind to the other girl, to Angelina's half-sister, Mary O'Sullivan. Was it right that her violent death should pass unmarked just because her killer was a member of the leading family in the city? Patrick had done his best. It would be injurious for him to pursue the matter any further. But, who would be willing to take up this matter and pursue it?

And then the door opened and a slim figure in a white coat, borrowed stethoscope slung around the neck, a clipboard in hand, sauntered in.

'You're going to get caught one day, Eileen,' said Reverend Mother, sitting up very straight and feeling new hope running through her veins.

'I'm rather getting to like this place,' said Eileen airily. 'Perhaps when all the fighting is over, and if Connolly's vision of free education for all comes about, *free education even up to the highest university degrees*; that's what he said, well, you might see me a doctor, Reverend Mother, what do you think?'

'I think that you might make a very good doctor,' said the Reverend Mother, 'but at the moment I was thinking of your occupation as a journalist . . .'

TWENTY-SIX

Cork Examiner, 24 March, 1923:
The civic guard have thirty vacancies for a cadetship.
Successful applicants will become high ranked senior
officers in Southern Ireland's police force.

'I nabbed him on his way home,' said Dr Scher, pushing Patrick ahead of him into the Reverend Mother's parlour. 'He's looking cold and tired, isn't he?' he said over his shoulder to Sister Bernadette. 'They work him too hard at the barracks. He could do with a nice cup of tea and perhaps a slice of your cake.'

Patrick, thought the Reverend Mother, did not look well. She had not seen him for almost a week and it struck her that he might even have lost some weight.

'Come and sit by the fire, both of you,' she said hospitably. 'What a terrible evening; still, at least it is a west wind so we shouldn't get any flooding.'

Dr Scher, she noticed, had a folded newspaper, stuck into his capacious pocket of his overcoat. He allowed Sister Bernadette to take the coat, but extracted the *Cork Evening Echo* from it and held it like a baton in his hand while he bullied Patrick into relinquishing his coat and escorted him solicitously to the armchair that he normally took for himself.

'I'm just a little tired,' said Patrick, stretching out his hands to the fire. 'I've been staying up late every night, studying for the cadetship examination – not that I have a hope of promotion to inspector, no matter how hard I work, or no matter how many marks I score. If the superintendent has anything to say in the matter, and I'm sure that he will, then I'll be a sergeant for the rest of my life. I'm not in very high favour at the moment. Spoke my mind a bit too freely. Can't help feeling bitter about it, all, can't stop thinking about it. Poor girl!'

'I always find it more rewarding to focus on one aim at a time,' said the Reverend Mother crisply. 'You've done your best for Mary O'Sullivan, now keep your mind on your studies and I'm sure that you'll succeed.'

'And here's something that will cheer you up,' said Dr Scher, unfurling the newspaper with a flourish. 'Pretty good article here, written by someone who calls himself a patriot.' He cast a sly look at the Reverend Mother and then began to read aloud: '"Justice discards party, friendship, kindred, and is always, therefore, represented as blind," said Joseph Addison. "And indeed, since Roman times, she has been depicted as the statue of a blindfolded woman, holding a sword, a balance."

'That's probably as far as the editor read,' said Dr Scher, lowering the paper to look at his audience. 'And this is how it goes on: "But is justice impartial here in Cork city? Is there one law for those without friends in high places and another for those who belong to wealthy of the city? Do we hang the dock labourer who kills a man in a drunken fight and then turn a blind eye to the gentleman who murders the girl that he has impregnated?"

'Good, isn't it?' said Dr Scher. 'I had forgotten about old Joseph Addison, studied him as a boy, of course. Clever point, though, isn't it?'

The Reverend Mother smiled discreetly. She, too, had forgotten about Addison. She had dug out a copy of his essays from her own school days and had read and discussed them with Eileen, presenting her with the book as a reward. At that stage she had been hoping that the girl, beating off the competition from the well-drilled boys from the Christian Brothers' North Monastery, might gain the coveted Honan Scholarship, which would have ensured her three years of free education and living expenses at the university. However, nationalism and the rhetoric of Patrick Pearse and James Connolly had won the day. She sighed slightly and turned her attention to the present.

'What!' Patrick had sat up eagerly, colour rushing into his cheeks.

'"*Who decides to withhold information from the people of this city?*"' Dr Scher read on with emphasis. '"*Who decides that the life of one poor girl was not worth as much as the reputation of her killer who committed suicide rather than face the disgrace of being unmasked and punished for his crime?*"" Dr Scher declaimed the rolling periods sonorously while Patrick, his face lit with a wide smile, nodded his head enthusiastically.

The Reverend Mother gazed at them both with affection. They had made a good trio, she thought. Patrick, meticulous, careful and hardworking, Dr Scher with his medical knowledge and she herself, with a brain that she had feared was stagnating, had unravelled the complexities. Together they had solved the case of the body from beneath the streets and with the help of Eileen and her comrades had rescued Angelina Fitzsimon from the fate of her half-sister Mary O'Sullivan.

It had been a good team, she thought and with a slight feeling of shame, she realized that already she was missing the challenge. She had so enjoyed using her reasoning powers working on the problems of the case and she was guiltily conscious that lurking in the back of her mind was a hope that Patrick might bring her another problem in the future.

After all, she thought, as absent-mindedly she accepted a cup of tea from Dr Scher, St Thomas Aquinas himself said that reason in mankind was like having God in the world. Her patron saint would approve of her using her brain.